PINEAPPLE

A Novel

JOE TAYLOR

Sagging
Meniscus

Printed in the United States of America.
Set in Mrs. Eaves XL with LaTeX.

ISBN: 978-1-944697-27-3 (paperback)
ISBN: 978-1-944697-28-0 (ebook)
Library of Congress Control Number: 2016957284

Sagging Meniscus Press
web: http://www.saggingmeniscus.com/
email: info@saggingmeniscus.com

Acknowledgments

The following people helped a good deal on this novel: Angela Brown, Scott Ely (in memoriam), Susan Ludvigson, Pat Mayer, Kat Meads, Rich Schellhammer, Stephen Slimp, Tricia Taylor.

PINEAPPLE

Contents

Invocation

Late one night, as I rose up to piss,
my muse gave ambush, with this sweet kiss:
"Think Chaucer," sang she, "think Byron."
Lord, Lord, I do keep a-tryin',
but something always drips amiss.

Prologue: A humble treatise on comedy,
its besting crude morals derived from tears.
Composed in heartfelt rhyme, defying foul jeers,
it will disprove the Wilde Oscar's homily
about bad poems that ring out sincere;
it will, despite its rhyming anomaly,
give reason to—for Granny's sake!—go drink some beer.

The trouble with comedy, people think,
is that it's funny. It's not. To prove this
impels my high intent. A cat at nine lives' brink,
I swear to die if you derive the smallest bliss

from these sad lines that follow. I'll take large chance
and lay it bare: The time has come
to talk of many things. Of bombs that dance,
charbroiling bones in fierce atomic scum;

of cabbages, kings, tortillas, refried beans,
and creeps. Right soon and here I dare to ask,
"Why is it, yes, that briny tears distract our genes
far more than one good laugh?" Me, I'd rather bask

in deepest belly rolls or e'en one small chortle,
but oh no-no, the critics, academics,
and philosophes all skip for brine's dank portal
to cite their so-fine morals and polemics.

When filled, they mince, "Comedy? Toss that pabulum to
poor lowly dweeps." If somewhere were a muse's court
I swear I'd wing right up and sue
those critical creeps. Comedy's fuse burns short,

exploding with a cackle. Tragedy drones,
its whine unending, intently sucking
a babe like thumb. Catharsis? Empathy? Those moans
just one thing mean: self-preening and mucking.

With comedy, cerebra have to reach out—
and ring intense as Ma Bell's finest cell—
then thought gives skip and slip, a boxing bout
that fires the brain to fume unnerved, unwell.

Hey, didja see that one? Catch that? What's it mean?
Twist and slide, shake it on out, come on, Brain,
work it on out. Yes, comedy jumps: active, lean.
Tragedy smushes blooded pudding through a strain.

So doncha see? Tragedy's just too damn tame.
Face it, they both reveal one beastly thing.
Yes! Comedy and tragedy ram the selfsame
theme! *Life, please stop your abominable sting!*

Life runs amuck, a wreck, a mess;
both whirl about to point this sad state out.
Comedy sends the memo with finesse;
Tragedy uses a blackthorn stick, blunt and stout.

You don't believe me? Count the deaths in Willy:
an even eight in *Hamlet* alone,
enough to leave an audience silly.
To start out then, I'll focus on and hone

some thoughts sublime, divine, for sure correct.
Wiser and truer than Swiss John Calvin,
you'll soon be weft to stroll amongst the Elect
as I shock and move you like Galvan—

I mean, for sure this'll pop your valve on:

3

Ode to Betty Opp's Los Alamos Toes

While Robert drank his cold martinis;
While engineers built imploding devices;
While children ate pineapple and weenies;
While wives clacked out numbers nice as
you please; While Groves strutted to keep
Army demeanor and his tummy in shape;
While MPs and tanks guarded the new-made heap;
While all concerned planned on global rape;
While Betty Opp's lips did open and leap
to take in Lethe's river—I mean gin neat—
Betty Opp's toes gave curl, even in sleep.

Nothing, I think, lies so darned sweet
as ten lovely toes that curl in deep
short nap. As angel lips would kiss those feet,
dear angel eyes would gladly weep.
I think. "Dipsomania," people did bleat,
but Rabelais, a fellow all time will keep,
did give it us quite clear and neat:
"Drink up, Shriners, for soon enough you'll sleep."

Wherein, my friends, doth lie a fault? Not in those toes.
Did they skip and curl from bed to bed?
Rumors creep, but blast such rumors, who knows?
E'en *if* they trekked, *they* didn't leave scalded heads
to make a fifth, not of gin, but one million dead.

So again, I'll sing: Bless those Betty Opp toes!
Clean, pure, and pink! All ten stayed amazing!
Sweet Reader, you can watch atom bomb shows
of mushroom clouds floating and grazing
on air, burnt flesh, debris, on anything that blows

a thermal draft to drop, forever lazing,
a Geiger count that clicks off, then throws
our minds to numbidity at the razing.
What *should* you watch? Those curling toes.

Let's sing it once more, with real conviction:
Bless Betty Opp's ten curling toes!
Bless 'em wholeheartedly without restriction!
Bless 'em where'er they goes.
Just bless 'em, friend,
and laugh, and drink your gin!

Chapter One: Just wringing the blues— blue meal, blue date, blue song, blue fact, blue shoes

Reader! The dish we want? Blueberries and cream.
The dish we get? Soured goulash to burst our spleen.
Sous-sous-chefs concocting some epicure's dream,
we bake, we shake—our grease retains its sheen.

Small Paula Deens, we fumble 'twixt 'twixt and 'tween,
we blend desire with glut in charred tureens.
Methinks that Puck, who soared this world blue-green,
sang out best: "Cooks such as mortals, I've never seen!"

But stir we must, not dally in some summer's dream.
So travel west, where chow chews dry and lean,
to fair Los Alamos, whereat we bake our scene.
Behold, a war—no!—a defense *think tank, I mean:*

"Dude, she's got green eyes big as two bedrooms,
black hair, cut sharp and trim like aspens get,
and best,"—Dave cupped his hands—"two fine bazooms
like pine, uh, apples."

                    Dave's friend Hank fretted that set,

The loading dock drink machine coughed—okay, fine;
a parting semi belched—not near sublime, yet fair;
but typists dancing Inner Sanctum's line,
with pineapple-y breasts? Hank thought, *Beware!*

"Dave," he started, when a voice like a kitten's purr,
a spinning top's whir, a breeze in summer,
gave chant, "Excuse me, guys, but is one of you—er—"
No matter her finish, she started a hummer.

"—Dave?"

Whose knees knick-knocked. A forklift braced him,
else off the dock he would have done a tumble.
"Him," Hank glurred at eyes so green, hair so black, so prim.
"Him, not me." My, but her emeralds made him fumble!

"Well, Hanson wants you." Did those eyes betray
love-liking, skirt-hiking, lip-siphoning?
Our gallants roared fantasy Harleys into fray;
they revved, they faced . . . yon lady's cell went ring-ling.

" 'Scuse me." Her hips did turn—no pineapples they—
before our boys could joust. The prize? Her love, I ween.
"Oh, in Room Four." Did those hips speak? It seemed that way.
They left; our bike-less lads stayed on scene.

"Hanson," they sighed. Each sigh for sure meant hips,
To dockside working grime, Hanson rhymed with Manson.
A bowtie clutched his throat, bleached teeth made rips.
Last summer he called out our two for ransom:

a Thermos left on dock did summon Bomb Squad,
did fling eight brave brains studying gravity
toward black holes, pink dwarfs, or some place odd.
"If I could *dock* your pay," Hanson had set free

in punful snarl. "No overtime for sixteen weeks.
Damn union won't argue that." His bowtie gave bob.
Sans overtime, Dave nearly lost his Harley sleek,
while Hank did lose his girl, a college heartthrob

who hated books, reserved smooth love for gems and beer.
No overtime trimmed both, so off she slid to rock.
E'en now, just Hanson's name left Hank quite mad and queer.
He scooped a blue silk slipper—how'd *that* get on dock?

"Good thing I saw this, or he'd de-clock us again."
"Good thing it's no blue bra, or I'd—"
"Perversion! Just go and see the man. Spin
and think good glads. Three sun hours left gives time to ride."

Dave slumped away; Hank waved a Fed-Ex on in.
"Some hanky-panky?" laughed the driver.
Hank wished he *had* committed any blue sin,
but dunked the slipper into pocket, a diver.

To bathe therein? Flux out fine pearls?
Not likely. "Sixty Next-Days," the driver chimed.
"What they do's so hot?"
                                "Gravity gun that swirls."
"Woo-hoo!" The driver hopped, but Hank just signed—

full sixty times, since each required receipt.
What do the pencil-necks do in their concrete labs?
Hank handed back the Fed-Ex pad, counted and neat.
Pull protons from nostrils? Irradiate scabs?

Eggheads slumped down in chairs could never get those.
Hank waved Fed-Ex out the gate. Hey, what strange name—
what Native Am name for the figure who arose
at each man's death and ate all scabs, erased all shame?

But woe to any scab-less! Them he gobbled
as if they'd never lived. Well, had they?
What is that name? Back to the dock Hank hobbled.
I call my cycle "Bike," so there's no blessed way

I'll dredge up exotic. That last word worked:
thin dancers tumbled to kiss his mind's third eye.
(While yogis seek enlightening, Hank groped down and dirt;
count him hormonal and ex-Marine—semper thigh!)

He felt a mid-section stir; he watched a bird.
Damn, wee willie chimed, *push that bike to Albuquerq*
und Donna's, with all them tits. His pants he gave gird;
he judged himself a suave rake, not a jerk.

Speak we of Hank or willie? Alas, you'll find
as eventide arrives, but little diff it makes.
Female or male, or 'twixt quite gaily designed,
when sunset hormones moan, each body quakes.

Fine college girls swilled beer in Donna's—*That damn*
bitch, Hank thought, giving his ex, her Heineken,
her jewels, her heinie—
      The dock door did slam!
Out pranced Dave, his legs stilts, his bod a manikin.

"Got us a date," he smirked.
        "Us?" Hank's eyes slid narrow.
"She's got a roomie, name of Carla."
           "Who she?"
"Pineapple woman. She's sucking my marrow."
"More perversion. Let it be. Which for me?"

"Pineapple's mine. You got piña-colada, though,
named Carla. Bro, I did you good, so buy my beers,
enjoy a woody that will grow and glow
like secret shit in Dumpsters all 'round here."

Hank gave an eye-roll and fingered the slipper
he'd tucked so lonesome by his ham hock. "Hey, just what
did top-pop-Hanson want? One for the gipper?
Give United? Some patriotic snot?"

Dave stiffened his lank six-feet and munched his lips.
Hank gave a shove. "I'll guess. He thinks I spy for Chinks?

Requests reports on twisting of my sneaking hips?"
Dave gazed off.
                    "Pal, we barely got water for drinks

"much less oceans where loose lips ships can sink.
Hanson, schmanson." Hank tossed the sun a kiss.
"But she's a looker, bro. That far I'll go."
                                    "Ya think?
Ten ticks left. Let's scout any Thermos we missed."

Soon home they rode, their real bikes a-pop,
their glands a-whir, their boy-skin tiger taut.
By Stop-n-Go they made no stop,
such constant vision their hormones wrought!

A bath one, shower t'other, glans a-glee.
Will I, each willie warbled, find the pudenda
whose spritely hole lives just to hump and never pee?
No shoulda, no coulda—I yam a contenda!

Both spent their time thus: glop, goop, golly, garble.
Most lads, though men, remain boys, after all.
One hardly can expect them to warble
out opera. Such blues we've sung since Adam's Fall.

Will that song ever change? I say no. Make your call.

Chapter Two: *As we cycle our way plans go a-gley*

Away 'cross-town: "You got your wish, Carmen.
A date for us both—"
                    "Ay Chihuahua, *Sacré* blue!
I got a morning math test that's alarmin'!"
"Carmen! 40 squared, plus 2?"
                              "Cher! What you do?"

"Carmen, your skin's straight Mex, but your tongue's that stone
Napoleon, uh . . ."
                    "Rosetta, Lorett—"
Our gal with pineapples made her eyes go zone.
"Not my name. Kentucky, coal, horses, I forget."

"And *my* polyglot tongue keeps Mexico unlit.
10-02 answers your quest." C gave a twist
and raised a finger. "Beard?"
                              "Sorry. Moustache, thin lips."
"Muscles?"
          "Motorcycles. Loading dock grist."

"Goo-gah," Carmen sang, "no brains, big brawn."
The brainless part, my Reader dear, you might judge true:
did Dave not nomenclate young Carmen wrong?
Will Hank whisper, "Carla," to ruin romance's brew?

As wiser poets have noted, time will tell.
If only some such tuneful poet
could find a means to excise us from this hell
and shear us off this earthly popstand, just blow it!

But no, we're stuck here's my final guess,
unless some Los Alamos brainiac
invents a quick and cheap implosion vest—
but back to our gals; my thoughts turn maniac . . .

"Brawn at last! Instead of shrimp we'll munch on prawn."
C gave her hand a flap before her starved love box.
"A wiggly prawn will take my mind from math—till dawn."
"Oh roomie mine, you smite sacred chakras! You shock!"

Reflecting, Lorrie's Bluegrass head gave watch
as C's strong hands massaged brown breasts and nipples.
"Pep talk?" L asked.

     "Their prep for a studly hot crotch.
These boys will ride their two-wheel participles

"won't they?"

    "I guess. Hanson crept by, so talk dried."
"*I hope that moron's—*" Carmen snatched a red bra,
gave twist, and showed her gums' pink inner side,
to strap 34 B on. The sun yipped hurrah,

since he saw all, through constant plasma stream.
Tough as a cop, sharp as Homeland Security,
wise as Einstein, prying as a radar beam—
no, not all of that can lay claim to surety.

Still, he's not called 'Lucky Ol' Sol' without reason.
But I declare, if we gave insightful thought
we'd hang the lad for malfeasance and treason
for passively watching what horrors men have wrought.

C's bra went snap; she gave L a good-luck tap
then to their kitchen trotted. "Split a beer?" she yelled.

"Best not. I'm playing bitch, my guy's one tall lovesap,
so Diet Coke for me."

    "That's great! His balls should meld!"

resounded from the fridge. One dab here, one there,
both strolled to their balcony and demurely sat.
"For real, why play the bitch?"

      "He's far too cute. Blonde hair,
blue eyes, Teutonic, muscled—not one ounce of fat."

"Ah," C purred, "a pre-emptive strike with conviction."
She took a sip, L took a sip, Sol went a-dip.
"And mine?"

    "Cherokee eyes, strong, reads science fiction."
"Science . . . *madre dio*, his brain gears will skip."

New Mexico's bright sky inspired C to expound,
"A moustache, science fic—but Cherokee eyes?"
"Chocolate brown. Comes from the dark and bloody ground."
"Kentuck? That place you omit?" Out heaved two sighs.

"*Your* eyes are light, like burley tobacco
hung in a barn loft's draft to cure and dry.
His keep dark, like when Mom 'n' I used to go
spread walnuts under Granny's Danville sky.

"Granny's still there, cursing, jumping, alive.
Takes snuff, cans cukes, grows squash. Funny how we
both lost our moms, I guess."

      Carmen dared not rise
to Lorrie's words, for death had made a spree—

to leave no niece, no neph, no one she rarely saw—
just one glum dad she swept away, with mad straw broom.

And Momma's grave, which loomed. She worried that some flaw,
for sure paternal, paired her name with doom.

A pop! A snarl! There came a Harley roar!
Queens counting peasants, they gazed from their dais,
and queens—lest virgin—n'er let their hearts take soar.
So up till now, our gals have cleared all bias.

One wiggled toes, one her nose. Both did preen,
did look, did listen. Dave's bike stopped, to end the roar.
The other's yet made thrum: big, powerful, and lean.
As helmet doffed, a moustache C could not ignore

slipped her in zone: "Hey guy, why's yours so quiet?"
And will that moustache prick, like phasers on stun?
Chocolate eyes replied, "Kraut-made for a sand diet
in North Africa. World War II and all that fun."

Helmet in hand, he clicked his heels to make salute:
"Hank Riser and BMW, at your service."
Outdone, poor Dave gave belch—at least he didn't poot.
"Aw, stow the bitch, L, you'll make these cuties nervous,"

C whispered, lifting her ale. "Carmen Brown, *señor*.
Does your quiet BMW have a name?"
Hank shriveled, fretting to be caught before—
Wait. Carmen? If he'd love-moaned "Carla," how explain?

At Dave he hissed, "Carla? Are you simple?"
Then, with upward glance, "Bike," he mumbled.
"Can't hear you!" Carmen's grin cast a dimple.
She heard. She thought it cute the way he fumbled.

"*Bike! Bike!*" Dave shouted. "You'd think a sci-fi guy
could sure concoct some spacey, starry Lulu.

You got some beers?"
           "Ixnay, no terrestrial high
till we get gone; our go must flow true stellar blue."

"Desert Zen!" Lorrie clapped one hand, then two.
The girls, with dash, soon shaded enlightened asphalt.
"Boots, good. Where we go, no man has yet to do."
"A Trekkie," Lorrie cooed. "That Spock's beyond all fault."

"My math test, Lorrie. *Trek*'ll drill my brain."
"Agreed," said Hank, said Dave.
           "But his ears! So cute!"
A roar, a thrum, they rode for castles in Spain . . .
But plans go a-gley Bob Burns did say: down the route

a car that clumped against the only tree around
did halt them all. One teen sat and cried for Mom,
one searched for long-lost beer, a third gave out no sound,
just pumped red blood, not cheer. On that our I did glom.

"Shut *him* up, sit *him* down." She gave her blouse
a rip. "You, press your finger there." The boy stayed shocked.
She summoned Dave and gave the others rouse.
"Call 9-1-1! Dave, prop his leg on that big rock.

"We need warm cover! Go and search their car!"
From somewhere drifted a Pueblo blanket.
Hank frowned, *This boy'll scoot past that eater of scars.*
Maybe today, he fretted. *Shut your*self *up. Get—*

That Afghani kid, a sniper who'd
not dented body armor, yet my twenty-three
lead bullets left his thirteen years unglued.
Awaiting a siren's scream, Hank spit on the tree.

He heard a shout. His sarge? No, Carmen. "Come here,
talk this boy down. Panicked and wants his *amigo*."
She held the redhead who had searched for beer.
He screamed and strained, he ripped to go.

Hank ran on over. " 'Sokay, Corpman's in control."
They both wide-eyed Hank. "I mean, she's a doc,
like Bones on *Star Trek*. Look, he's ready to roll."
They looked: the pale lad panted, leg propped on rock.

"So where's your other friend?" C snatched the redhead's chin.
They looked: the one who'd cried for Mom held two longnecks
to suck, like nipples, in. "These kids make me spin,"
C whispered. "Lorrie was right. Stay home, watch *Star Treks*."

Ol' Sol—remember him?—gave his bare glance
to this sad piece of globe. He melted, like ice cream,
road tar below. "Where's that damn ambulance?"
"I'll call again," C said. "Hold him, so he won't scream."

A good American, C gave her cell a flip.
"Two rattlesnakes!?" she exclaimed to electron air.
Her brown eyes did dip. This was one bad trip.
"The first ambulance hit mating snakes. Logic? Where?"

she asked the others. Their three gasps meant, "What?"
Ol' Sol sent down no sniff. "That second should hurry,"
L said to Dave, who quivered like Sol's best sunspot,
his finger pressed dike-tight, though itching to scurry.

"Keep focus, kid," L said. "We'll soon watch Kirk and Spock
nibble a Tribble, travel ten times warp."
"What are—" Dave white-eyed. L gave him a knock.
"Just blood," she chided. "Don't pass out, don't go dork."

Like cowboys and injuns, robbers and cops
The second ambulance pulled up with a skid,
Jack Spratt's wife dropped a gurney with two plops,
Jack lugged himself and box toward the wrong kid.

"*Mamma mia!*" C shouted in lousy Wop,
giving the redhead a yank by boy-whiskers,
the which she loved to pluck. (A lust she couldn't stop.)
She, Hank, and red-hair pointed, three fateful sisters,

to gushing blood. Jack Spratt gave veer. The lonely boy,
beer nipple still in mouth, saw ambulance bright lights:
"Let's hide! Here come the cops!"
                                        Ah, youth and all its joy.
Without dementia and it, how bare our delights!

Two cops arrived, the ambulance scatted
Calling a wrecker, arresting the kids,
a Native Am cop turned to Lorrie and chatted,
"These three are sons of big research who-so-dids.

"We've hauled them in before." A shout from the cop car:
"The kid's okay. You saved his life is what
the ambulance guy relayed. You're gonna star:
McGuire and Devins are his mom and pop."

"Hell, I work loading dock and know who they are."
"No bragging, big boy." C gave Hank a knuckle-pop.
Wrank, went the winch; longnecks slid from the car.
Needing a laugh they did, as if never to stop.

"Um, got a heap of blood on yas," said the cop.

Chapter Three: That blue date met fate,
so where under that wry sun lay fun?

Yes, Reader dear, I too heaped worries
when the wreck appeared. I'd hoped for an excursion,
some beers, tamales, hot sexual flurries—
Hank would have allayed our Dave's perversion.

But since we're in Los Alamos, I'll say this once:
Wise Heisenberg alleged uncertainty.
And he stays not the only one, oh no! A bunch
have swum that river, climbed that caried tree.

Vanna White, her alphabet, her Wheel of Fortune
reign there most gloried. But lesser luminaries
abound: Boethius, Epictetus, cast that rune.
Aurelius, Zeno of Greece, all chewed those berries.

It's worth our while to stop and tarry.
A. Einstein didn't buy that uncertainty rot:
God flinging dice loomed much too scary.
God? You mean brainy Einstein bought that old crock?

Afraid so, Reader, but you row straight with me.
I'll fret you not with angels, devils, beings
who shift, twist mist, or derive one from three.
Create a rock so heavy it can't lift? Who flings

such jetsam? But uncertainty? Well gee, you know,
when socks all fit—no matter how threadbare they be—
you must, by nature's harsh decree, insert each toe
and trot. But smile: no one trots for eternity.

Observing the observant cop's observation
our quartet trekked right back to the girls' condo

and showered, vying for water conservation.
Who took tepid last, a place no one's fond o'?

Who? Witness that Hank and Dave sat in bathrobes pink
whilst clothes tumbled dry and Bones wriggled his nose
since Spock, Kirk, and Scottie were downing drink
on Xylophone. Don't recall this episode?

One thing I won't abide is doubt. Go on, get out,
or trust those girls were having their giggles
at nervous guys whose you-guess-whats arose, boars' snouts,
from terrycloth pink robes. TV gave niggles

to Lorrie, who now and then espied Spock's ears
as she and Carmen strutted, loosely clothed,
in feet quite bare, to serve tortillas and beers.
Nothing more! Though the occasion, ahem, arose

beneath those darn pink robes. You've been that age!
What Ferris wheels it sends. Up, down, and
around again. Hormones rage and no blessed sage
can save us. Each lad took turn showing rand-

y. Dave non-hormonally downed a beer,
hard after downing his tamale member.
Hank, also, managed at least to steer
his into something cool as Miss November.

"Hey Lorrie," Dave asked, on standing to fetch a beer.
"How'd you know what to do with the bleeding kid?"
"She was an EMT, not far from here."
"C, how'd you—I never said—don't think I did . . ."

"You talk asleep."
                          "Do not."
                                        "How would you know?"

"Point made," Dave said. "You care for another?"
He tipped his bottle—in peace, not to throw.
But Reader, be assured: if Dave had his druther

his own tamale would topsy-turvy Lorrie
whilst she burbled and wiggled her left, her right—
Miss Manners, could you please censor this story?
Hank's busy rubbing C's—can't see what in this light—

so he's ill-fit for that moral role. Perversion
exacts a toll. This we hear from politicians,
their slogans, their words, though conversion
doth oft' occur twixt sentence and deed. Magicians

all must they be, for no public ever sees.
—Well bless 'em, and preachers too. We common lot
in trailers, apartments, and rooms forego such ease.
And bless us, for sometimes I fear our lives a blot

on plain good taste. Hey, if wise ol' Three-In-One
(of whom sober writers write) truly designed
with intelligent intent, why needs send a son
to save our wretch'd race? To chaos stay I resigned.

My moral? To rescue this gnarled world
keep virgin, turn homo, bestial, or Shaker.
Imagine this happy lightsome globe, hurled
through space sans two-legged troublemakers.

Thus sex, while often sought, should be maligned.
Peruse your neighbor if you can't conceive me.
That ape underwent intelligent design?
Still, *Just say no's* a sham, believe me:

I've tried, I've tried. As well to mix rainbows
in golden goblets, catch a falling star,
remain awake while watching telethon shows,
or drive America's best fuel-efficient car.

So. Did our four expend in pre-connubial bliss?
No, for blood lay on their minds. And no matter
what Hollywood insists, blood leads not to kiss,
but to a fear that things quite dear soon will scatter,

which our boys did after the second *Star Trek*,
to separate homes, on separate cycles.
(I hope you rhymed with "pickles," but what the heck.)
Not all was lost: L proffered plans to buy crystals

in Taos. And C knew a wise old native gent
who'd have precious gems to purge precious blood
so recently spilled, dried, rinsed, and spent.
Beside their bikes Dave whispered, "Big Chief Elmer Fudd."

Neither gal heard, else topsy-turvy would have thud.

Chapter Four: Work on Friday
celebrities mighty, scarlet dropped untidy

On Friday morn, dour Hanson strolled to give a huff
and walk the requisite 25 steps away
(Count 'em, he did!) before he lit a puff
and glowered at our boys as if they'd gone astray.

"My dad says once he married a hot Mex,"
Dave offered while he pushed a worn bored broom.
"Carmen said so too. Surprised he knows about sex."
"How would she know?"
      " 'Bout sex?"
        " 'Bout Hanson Goon."

Hank shrugged. As a marine, he had ignored women;
now he adored them as mysteries beyond light,
warp drives, black holes, Planet 9, or sweet lemon:
lush creatures even sci-fi couldn't blight.

His shrug, as shrugs will do, gave wither. The dock door
thrust out three pencil-necks and one hot mama.
Hot Mom tugged Lorrie with blandishments galore:
"You saved their boy. He would have died from trauma!"

A jig came from McGuire, earth's sole Irish math prof;
his wife Devins popped elemental particles
of joy with words she gave: "You three are bof.
You bet we won't forget." Hot Mom shed articles

of clothing while Devins, McGuire, and a third
pencil-neck twirled around the three in joy.
"Our boys, our boys, our boys, mark down our word:
we won't forget." Dour Hanson neither, though alloyed

remained his joy. I'm the onlyiest saw his face.
I've seen more pleasant, I'll tell ya,
in a men's room mirror or other vulgar place.
Hey, don't think I'm tryin' to sell ya

a 4 × 6 or video of *me* dancin'.
I'm just sayin' what I'm just sayin',
in good American parlance, no prancin':
Dour Hanson's snarl would set atheists to prayin'.

Caesar wanted his enemies fat. I concur.
Hanson chiseled himself in the government gym
until his butt moved thin, like it had a burr.
This fuss around our lads and Lorrie slapped at him:

competition always rattled his yin, his yang.
He claimed platoons of pals went under sod
and told it gory how their bells got rang,
while stolidly onward he bravely trod.

He tells he nearly saved them, but alas
them Gooks crept paddy-sneaky and cruel.
He mentions bloody rice and sharp jade grass
while fingering a deep red jewel

intended once for Hank's ex and sex.
How did this creep arrive at this mental state?
I earlier promised no supernatural X,
a time machine won't better rate,

so visit a P. O., and study its mug shots,
some thought them give. But let me point out this:
just 40 years back a homo would rot
beside moist garden slugs in eternal unbliss

before he got security's clearance.
The chance for blackmail or sexual coercion
was deemed too great. A peep in Hanson's pants?
Six rounds of ampicillin from dick-submersion.

He stays a man too grand for rubber raincoats.
He's oily and slick, why, rain slips off his skin!
But pal, bacteria and viruses swim moats.
Each night's new skank could do him in again.

They come sans end. Twelve or more—math's not my forte—
ex-galfriends have threatened restraining orders
until allayed. Just what made them allay?
Enough hard cash to stay within our borders . . .

Now this brings up a secret I have to tell:
Carmen H. Brown's a spy. It's not a joke.
She is, and what's more, she's Hanson's spawn as well,
though that dark fact doth make her croak.

She keeps both facts hush-hush. Her mom too showed restraint
but mashed on Hanson's marriage button, and it worked:
newborncita Carmen took legal gringo taint
when birthed by Mom way down in Albuquerq.

Down there, our Catholic Mrs. Hanson changed her name,
and annulment was declared.
                                        Annulment? But—
I know. All faiths stash miracles in their game.
Just take my word: Mrs. Brown—C's mom—lived no slut.

Nor virgin, sure enough. Back to her daughter:
CIA, FBI, Homeland Security—
who hired her, and why? Good question. I oughter
reply. Some group wanted some surety

about a rumor, about a Mex drug cartel.
The grand Potomac River and heaven know
we really *must* keep pot illegal to sell,
else how could such fine nice folks go earn their dough?

But rumor came: one was branching out, hedging bets.
Not cigarettes, but government secrets
would run its newest game. And brown Carmen made set
to infiltrate and jump its wetback bones, you bet.

Who hired her then? . . .

                          To answer that I went to sniff
her condo when she and L stepped out last night.
I opened drawers, gave an optic whiff.
Bras, hose, panties, perfume dealt my hands a fright.

Pastel pink here, robin's egg blue there,
black lace enough to form rivers and streams—
oh such a map! I dreaded thinking where
such spumes would send my moistmost dreams.

My fingers shook, my big nose quivered.
My eyes did strain, but yet they—I must make note—
forsook that dainty fluff. My strength delivered!
No guppy sloshing dank, hormonal motes,

I drily persevered. I'm no Dave.
At last my penlight's light lit on a tiny book,
wherein within, a stub did lay. Still I no rave
laid on the female stuff—though a guy's gotta look.

I read that check's tan stub: 9-1-1 bucks, 1 cent.
I've cashed better, I've cashed lesser. Came a second,
an add-on for that ju-co math course, whose intent
was to give our Carmen cover, I reckoned.

Although my nose had hardened, my search stayed pure,
I moved my penlight's light to scan each check's maker,
but scarlet lace fast bent my eyes unsure.
I leaned and thought, *Concentrate for heaven's sake or—*

A key in the door! Off the balcony I jumped!
A writer caught snooping would have to gel
his pages; his hard drive would needs be dumped!
On ground, my memory murked. That, Reader, played unswell.

A mental wobble, doing my best to stand up,
I breathed in deep to remember. *You, axon!*
Do your work. You, neuron, stop hopping like a pup!
We've landed safe. It's time to tug some facts on.

Well, hmm. Both checks were drawn on U.S. Govern-mint.
Treasury then? Recall Amurchan spellin',
whose status indicates—money not well spent.
Alas, to whom our C her soul was sellin',

like clouds gave shift and slipped when blinds above gave clack.
My frightened legs and arms like tires did spin.
An item from my hand fell frail. . . alack . . .
a scarlet fluff. Just what on earth could it have been? . . .

Oh dear! I've left our boys and L out there on dock.
Hanson has crushed and stripped his cigarette,
pretending he fought in 'Nam. Right. And his left sock
don't stink, though he'll wear it a week with no regret.

The three smart pencil-necks and Oo-la-la have left.
We should go too. On dock, Dave and L and Hank
stare out at Hanson, who stares back, bereft
and angry. All of them come up with one sad blank.

My thought? Just as I jumped down free last night,
let us scoot off without one single angry word.
This globe already sheds enough mass plight.
Let Sol shine on: so full, so bright, so undeterred.

No sense in ending this chapt. with a turd.

Chapter Five: Hanson goes out with half a dozen friends, which means he drinks a six-pack at Todd's Deep End

Hanson carries his nose, which makes two hunks,
to Todd's, a beer-burrito dive
where Mexican girls fish for white male lunks
to buy their nighttime patriotic drives.

Once seated, he fieldstrips his cigarette.
"Da Trang," he tells the age nineteen—at best—
brown Mexican lass two stools to his left.
The barkeep, Todd, thinks, *Just give it a rest.*

"One Heineken," H orders. Was what he shared
with Hank's young ex. In fact, when Hank's overtime left,
those two the diddle did, though she showed some flair:
jewels and beer could not snag her in Hanson's weft.

Now Hanson rubs some bar grease in his hair.
The truth? It works the other way around,
since Hanson and Manson share wild black up there.
Their minds too, often similar depths will sound.

Less snorted angel dust, more legal steroids
keep Hanson un-prison-bound. Say, do you think
poor Charlie will ever get his own asteroid
with Victoria's Secret? Handsome in pink.

Not Hanson. His signature color, black,
is what he sports when he's in Todd's.
That signature, like the Inquisition's rack,
gets señoritas' attention, raises his odds.

Who'm I to criticize whatever works?
Ms. Magazine can proselytize till doomsday

but patient Griseldas will yet love jerks,
which only shows that goons are here to stay.

Dad Hanson heads this one for home of course.
He's yet to rinse the olive oil
from last night's night. He shows not one remorse
but thinks he's macho, sowing good strong soil.

Look! Two more beers and she's with him, enboothed.
The barkeep Todd gets eye-rolling exercise
at that. Todd fought in 'Nam and did not lose a tooth—
though PTSD sometimes makes him fly

to outer space, but not where Hank's aliens might like.
Those two swap stories of away back when:
Todd speaks of monkeys, fungus, and Ho Chi Minh's hike
(best known as that long trail without an end),

Hank speaks of Afghani rocks, camel dung and wind.
But neither speaks of bullets, blood, or roars or screams.
They could, for both lost more than one good friend.
Such thoughts, men say, are best dropped deep in dreams.

The blab, that's how Todd knows that Hanson's a fraud.
And how about Da Trang, how 'bout Ching Chang?
Still, Hanson yaps, expecting young gals to applaud.
Lots do, though Todd awaits at least one head-clang:

Bounce bottles off his empty skull;
tie bras around his red and stretchy neck;
paint lipstick on his blowhard hull;
take your stiletto heels and grind him to a speck.

Each time sap Hanson scores some Mexican chick
Todd flips a five to Mary of the Mountain's

jar of tips. That mission's done well by Hanson's prick.
When not infected, it can flow like fountains.

This night, as Hanson and señorita leave,
Todd tosses five more in, and gives his head a shake,
with maddened sense of glee. (It's either laugh or grieve,)
When Hank walks in, Todd says, "One more for the snake."

Hank hands over a five. "Hell, I'll match ya.
Those mountain virgin nuns do righteous work."
"Indeed they do, my friend. Here, I betcha
did never think to get a gift from that damn jerk."

Todd shoves a Heineken over with a jab.
"Señorita couldn't drink all the beers he bought."
"But you kept adding them onto his tab."
"Correct. Tonight, Da Trang was where he fought."

Hank sips the beer. "How he keeps clearance is
beyond my brain."
                              "Someone splits up his buns in two?"
Two chuckles come. Then later, standing to whiz,
Hank thinks *Blue slipper, blue slipper, blue.*

He'd placed it on a book by Philip K. Dick.
One thing he knew: something flowed slippery
about a slipper blue with no cute chick
to slip it on and prance about all frippery.

He walks back out, gives Todd a nod.
"Home early. Gonna buy a crystal in Taos."
"Just tourists, old hippies there, nearly under sod.
Want that case fiver back? Taos ain't Laos.

"You'll need rolls of 20's and Franklins to boot.
I'll guess: you got a date. Describe her.
This old man needs fantasy for his root."
Hank snorts. "I'll bring her in—if I inscribe her."

"At least you got a quill, my friend. Someone I know?"
"Carmen Brown."
                    Todd gives a start. "That young gal
gets around." Seeing Hank's look Todd says, "No,
not that. She's bright and pretty, not a playpal.

"Just seen her do a heap of listening
for a sweet Santa Fe ju-co co-ed.
But my-my, her pretty skin glows glistening.
Imagine her trilling r's while giving me head."

"Dirty old man," Hank says.
                    "Dirt's all I got.
So enjoy rose buds and use your widget."
"You're saying time's short, we're all gonna rot?"
"Short? To quote my friend Tom, 'Time's a midget.' "

Hank laughs, then hoists a single digit.

Chapter Six: Did the fairer sex diddle while Hanson, Hank, and Todd piddled?

But first, where's that nice perverted boy Dave?
On a carport oiling the chain to his Harley.
He's pulling pleasure from it, but no rave:
his oats aren't all perverted: some are barley.

He lives with Dad, who counsels over beer:
"Buy a BMW like Hank suggests—"
"Na-nope! This Harley roar keeps chicks 'round here."
Dave probes a link to think how Lorrie's finger rests—

I won't say where, for we must leave son and dad
and hop to Lorrie and Carmen's sublet condo.
Some off-key music's been played in their pad,
composed as double anti-rondo:

"Hey Lorrie, stop your tai-chi and get in here!"
"Just one more—"
                    "*Pequita hermana*
this ain't no joke. Something scary queer
has happened in my dresser and our sauna."

L's feet make pad; C tucks those checks into her jeans.
Sweet Lorrie and she have roomed just one month:
this day's unripe to bare her spy job it seems,
though truth will out in time is her strong hunch.

But what's before presses down lots harder:
entwined among her panties and bras
lie Hershey's Kisses snitched from perversion's larder.
And they don't shout the last of weird huzzahs,

for in the sauna, scrawled in ketchup not soap,
ooze these seductive words, "Virgin no more."
Seductive? Such must have been what the scribbling dope
had hoped. Then how explain that next word, "Whore"?

Those Hershey's kisses lie placid and sweet—
a fact for sure. In finer situations,
geez, they'd seem lovey, precious and neat.
But here? Like gore from John's Patmos *Revelations*.

What brand of perp would perp—oh such a thing?
Hey, whoa! Hold back your mind's slimy parasites;
It's not my bell these gals should seek to ring.
Though I admit to taking small delights

in thumbing Carmen's red-laced undies
while probing out the source of her paychecks,
I ascertain: my name is not Ted Bundy
nor claim I kin to any social wrecks.

May the Lord and Savior descend as my witness—
Agh! How weak our warbles! Did I not promise no
supernal beings, no rainbow slickness?
Let us agree to diss that celestial show.

Though snoop I did and Hershey's kisses I like,
ketchup's a dirty veggie: I abhor it:
a culinary abomination, butt-wipe.
Might we agree? It was not me. I deplore it.

If ever this comes to court can my lawyer
your deposition take? You stood there, remember,
as you watched me—I'm pulling no Tom Sawyer;
but please do keep your memory limber.

Say . . . did YOU perp this comestible mess,
whilst I unriddled Carmen's paychecks?
Such, of course, would not comprise my guess . . .
"Carmen!" Lorrie screams on seeing ketchup flecks.

The girls quick hug one another, then back to back
twirl 'round and stand unclean, uncertain. Carmen walks
and slips her hand under her bed's cozy sack,
to remove—good goddamn!—a pistol. Lorrie balks,

and hey, it ain't just she! C owns a gun?
That ups the ante for when we were searching
her checks. Yes, *we*! You lolled there having your fun.
If Carmen'd found us, we'd both gone a-lurching.

And if she'd shot, we'd both gone a-churching,
supernal or not. This detecting stuff sure ain't
that spiff. I'd rather take a birching
from some slim señorita—but that's Dave's taint,

not yours or mine. Let's watch the girls and see
if what will come will come: "Let's call the cops,"
L says, eyeing the gun, trying not to pee.
C flips her cell—these days it never stops.

"I've got some friends," she turns to L to say.
In fifty-four seconds—I'll not exaggerate—
four creeps with ties so white and shirts silk fay
fine-comb the condo without abate.

Their gadgets whir and tick, their lasers beam and snake.
Their fingerprint dust snows, like coke in Mexico.
L counts the holsters and guns, but stops at eight.
Two each? These four could knock over eight Texacos.

With Carmen's extra they could make a run,
start armies, even all-meat cafeterias.
Lorrie searches, but Carmen now holds no gun.
"Where is it'?" L asks.

                "Didn't want to weary yas."

C tugs the freezer door: inside, like a whip
scourging two packs of frozen blueberries,
is perched la *pistola*. With fingers to one lip
C lisps, "My anti-ox to belay creep worries."

But L just shakes her head with sad demur.
"Damn, Lorrie," Carmen hisses, "you toughed that kid's blood;
some guns and high-tech snoops you can endure."
"These guys, your friends?"

                "They look like they're my studs?"

The four are sniffing, bouncing about,
their polyester slacks make slack, their brown
and shiny Penny Loafers with mint pennies sprout,
their faces smile in whiplash, upside and down.

Over bric-a-brac their puppy fingers scurry,
at each outside noise their brows give wriggle.
One stubs his Penny Loafer in his hurry
to magnify a piece of blue lint's faint squiggle.

Well, with those bulging pistols, Lorrie thinks. . . .
But she keeps mum. *Mayhap my moving West
was not the fancy cowgirl dream?* She blinks.
Could KY horseshit and coal mines truly sing best?

Could even boneheaded hillbilly Ralph,
who saw himself so Romeo and hep,

beat out 1 pervert, 9 guns, and 4 strutting alph-
as? For that matter, coming down with strep

beats cowering here, twitching away from them.
Oh Carmen, I need some 'splainin'; no Lucy act
will turn me Desi spewing Cuban haws and hems.
"When they leave, I want cold taco facts,"

L whispers, pointing a finger at Carmen who
whines, "*Pequito her—*"

                          "No more Tex-Mex crap.
Carmen, let's be girlfriends true blue true;
if these four guys aren't your hot love saps—"

Just then, 1 perhaps sap hoists up 1 blue shoe.
Carmen exclaims, "Stop! That's for my wedding,
once I locate a mate. Say, handsome, do you—"
The techie dead-drops the shoe. Always dreading

sly silky Eves long since his dear mumsie
darkly hinted that her cookies, brownies, and cakes—
which so delight his tongue and tumsie—
would bake to dust if *her* love he did forsake

to take—heartbreak!—some lithe little bride,
he doth avoid forward-toward women. Shy ones
too! But his short companion, standing beside,
keeps constant lookout for hot uncrossed buns,

so fat fingers he slides through thickly-mazed
Jacuzzi goo. "Real men don't need no lab
except what natural tools they tote." He splays
and gives two licks. "Not blood. Ketchup. A dab."

My! Lorrie's KY sister would have been impressed!
She's just turned ten and watches angry cartoons.
But the three techs, L, and C gag, distressed:
exchanging blood is not preferred in Junes—

or any month, in case you're wondering.
But this real man—I wish his name were Ned—
keeps snorting, blustering and blundering:
"Not Heinz, it didn't lose no race. Instead,

this ketchup clearly won." He indicates a scrawl
the others have yet to see: *I lick your snatch.*
"Look at that drippy 'y,' he drools in drawl.
"And that 'o' has slipped, oozy, about to hatch."

"You look," L says.
                    "Hey, Ted," one workmate gives urge,
Ted!? I nearly got my wish! With laser click
Ted straightens, shamed. Has his so-weird been purged?
Of course it's not. He gives the ketchup a flick

to spin a gob near Carmen's little toe.
She's yet to take karate enough to bash
his weirdball head, so she has to let that go.
"Thanks for your help. Don't mean to be rash—"

The three not-Teds cough an apologetic hint,
grab Ted, and head in geometric surge
toward the door, their snooping heaved and spent.
Fruitless! The tallest, though, gives pause to urge:

"This may connect: Hanson's son flunked out.
Majoring in bumfuck, he's moved from Albuqurq
to some trailer west of here. He ain't no Boy Scout.
Whaddya expect from Hanson? Murk begetteth murk."

C's face gives fall. Too bad she can't hire S Plath
to off her daddy. Blood would work out swell
to ease her ever-building poppa-wrath.
"Go sniffers up! I smell patchouli smell!"

This, Ted and his white communion tie both exclaim.
With that, all four males glop off, noses twitching air,
pistols cocked, shoulders squared, and faces aflame:
perverse perps not found here, searching elsewhere seems fair.

As their shirttails flap, L exclaims. "Those four might be
more creep than the creep who scoured our Jacuzzi
and ran his nose all through your undies. Gee.
But then no one could top him, a Primo Doozie.

"Still, where'd they get those ties? Those manners?"
"Their ties from a first communion ceremony;
Their manners from a boat of rotting bananners
be-plagued with spiders, rats, and melting spumoni.

"Was an Italian line run by the Mafia—"
"Stop right there, Carmen. No Tex-Mex,
no Wop, no Spic, no Yugoblafia.
Who are they? How can you know such dreck?"

"I . . ." Carmen mumbles, "met them in math.
Dumber than lizards, they needed my help
and promised to turn the turn: if ever my path
once stumbled, I should just give a high yelp."

"In math? All four?"
                              "They're government guys.
You know those schmucks hang out like vultures."
"That one named Ted did blink with bulging lizard eyes,
not to mention his taste for plasma cultures.

"But why . . . advice to you—not me—of Hanson?"
Now how, my fine-tuned Reader, might you ask,
can C sidetrack I's mental transom
from taking bad ties and licking manners to task?

Can she prevent the spyful truth from coming out?
Will her paychecks remain anonymous, though cashed?
Can she avoid a besties' pinkie-truth bout
with lying silence? Can friendship remain un-dashed?

Might she trick through hypnosis learned in online class?
Use dark CIA techniques for casting mind waves?
Take charge like the Holy Ghost flitting at High Mass?
Recall her teen mind expansion at all-night Raves?

Or mayhap like a snake-handling X-ian,
I strain. Will she assert female intuition?
Hey, she won't even need that sexy one:
C's people smarts will simply come to fruition.

Ah-ha. So one *can* learn sans online tuition!

Chapter Seven: The wonders of Taos,
which as Todd warned,
costs loads more than Laos

The tough boys steered, the prim girls rode.
All four, on passing tiny, gnarled brown trees
thought, *Why didn't the kids crash into those?*
The youngest, then, wouldn't be having to wheeze

in and out on a ventilator. (Four cracked ribs
were found, three for him and one for t'other.
The boy sucking longnecks without his bib
did rebound sans scratch, though shouting for his mother.)

Ah well, they snuggle now with lesson learned . . .
Oh Reader, even I don't believe that trash;
no matter how badly teens get burned
they cannot learn: what happened lies dead and passed.

Is this why coaches teach our high school history?
No Washington, Susan Anthony, or Abe—
those fellas lay down a spiffier mystery:
connect X's and O's for a winning game play.

Where I'm from, these good old boys hold rule.
And where you're from? I 'spect 'tis same.
Sportballers ride Caddies, brains squat on stools.
Reader, we have only -------- to blame.

Fill in that blank with something true and you'll
—well, you'll get ignored, shot, or hung.
For now, America seems beholden to drool . . .
I give! No more. Rant done. Let's return to fun:

The four pulled up to The Coyote's Cup,
since Dave did sorely need double caffeines
because Lorrie'd squeezed his beans all up.
Was comic watching him straighten his jeans

to strut into The Sup. (Is what the locals
named it 'cause you needs a pound of jack
to send just one small sup past your vocals.
To drain a cup, tote dough in, in a Croker sack.)

Dazed Dave lunged back out with a green plastic thimble.
"Nine-fifty-eight for this." He spent a broken groan.
"Oh dear," L said, as Dave's hands gave tremble,
for he envisioned his paycheck fileted to bone.

"Oh dear," L repeated. "It's time I tell
what happened yesterday." Carmen jumped
off Bike to yelp, but, "No, C, this runs swell.
Saving that kid got me a raise, one queenly bump.

"Week after next I'll work the egghead zone:
Executive Primo Secretary Deluxe.
Hey, already my tummy has a jones
for lobster, filet, a waiter with a tux."

This was news to both Carmen and the boys.
Was news to her since our gals had spent last night
Securing their condo against the creep sans joy,
and Lorrie's mode had stayed in fight-or-flight.

So what happy tidings she'd strolled home with
went deep into cold storage until now, today.
"Lorrie, why didn't you tell me this wondrous bliss?"
L's eyes twitched, more she didn't have to say.

C gave wobble at her goof, heaving, for they'd
agreed to not discuss the pawing break-in
till they got clear how today's boyland laid.
A gal could never be certain what was shakin'

with hormones and men. It bore taking ease,
relaying news of sleaze. Besides, our Carmen
still pondered that last techie's tease
'bout Hanson's son, who sat to west—not farmin',

that much lay certain. *My half-frigging-brother,*
she thought. *As if that poor sweet girl's murder*
stank not enough.
               Whoa! Murder? How? Smothered?
Gut shot? Bludgeoned with Roswell space girders?

Reader, like Lorrie, I hoped a tasteful spot to
indulge in such bald facts. But here it pops
mis-tuned and -timed. Remember that blue shoe?
The one our hero on his dresser did plop?

Important as a truckload of gold.
Until now, spy Carmen's found just one clue:
a slipper, silken blue, on a 16-year-old
dust dead in an arroyo. So what's that to do

with costly Taos designer coffee?
My point exact! Hey, Carmen's who
brought murder up; her mind's like sticky toffee.
It's not my verse or rhyme deserving rue.

Insist I must: Yo, Carmen, damn it, stop!
What if I send a honeybee to sting on her?
Boy Dave can't hog all that S&M slop!
A sting should hurt enough to fling on her

untimely wayward thoughts, drop them down some deep drain.
Zip, zip, let it flit! Fly little bee, fly.
"Ay yi yai!" Carmen yelled in sudden pain.
She twisted round, wondering how, where, and why.

On spotting the culprit, Hank gave it a pop
and squeeze between prehensile finger and thumb.
"It's a honeybee—"
    "No, it's not!
'Sa ground yellow jacket, worst bee under the sun.

"They swarmed in Danville on my Granny's farm."
Lorrie gave search: "They always sting in bunch."
Hank reached for the bee, having stopped its harm,
but it had vanished. Didn't you hold a hunch,

wise Reader, that case might be?
     "Chihuahua bullshit,
it hurts," Carmen cried.
     "I know a sure bee cure,"
Dave said. "We make a knife cut then piss it."
Told you, told you. The boy's a pervert pure.

C moaned, "Please save me from macho bikers."
"No, Carmen. Dave is right. Let's buy ammonia.
That drugstore back there, by those hippie hikers.
We won't let Dave or his knife hone ya."

"No knife?"
  "I promise."
    "Me, too."
     "And *you?*"
Dave raised his palm, callused but clean,

honest, confused, but showing love's line true.
Back they rode, to the store. No hippies were seen.

"Twenty bucks for ammonia!"
                              The clerk raised his palms,
No loves lines showed, just grease enough from profit
to make NYSE seem beggars of alms.
Dave blurted, "Man, this place sure can sock it

to plebs." Outside, they poured the juice.
C winced, but kept her thoughts and mouth both tight.
You gotta go tough when things go loose.
(A fine ideal worth keeping in sight.)

C now needed coffee. "But not from that bee shop."
Ye Mountain Hummingbird Café soon beckoned.
Its prices gave them white-eye too. "*My* pop,"
L said. "To celebrate my raise, I reckon."

"For here or go?" a blonde barista asked.
"Five-buck booth fee. Gives Internet access."
L flared her nose. "To go. We'll forsake the byte bask."
"Six-buck green earth fee. Plus tourist taxes."

"What if we just stick four sequential mouths
in under the espresso spigot and guzzle?"
The blonde barista shrugged. "The owner's out;
his wife in back don't like no trouble."

Lorrie nodded. "To go will work. Black and plain."
C walked right up. Ammonia'd blurred her ears,
so she looked at the blonde like she had a brain.
"Used to be a Native Am named Don Walker here,

"polished jewels, crystals and rocks.
My friends and I would like to find him. Do you—"
"Don't live here. Can't afford one pair of socks
the local fifty and ten sells. *That* old guy's who

"you need to ask." The blonde pointed to a
man passing. "It's him!" Carmen gave shout
and rushed on out.
                           "Hey, you still need to pay!"
L turned at the barista's cry. "Don't you pout,"

she urged. "Your dimples will harden to wimples."
And, Brainless, you need soft. L fretted bad karma
with that thought, and I concur: Don't pop pimples
on others, be they jerks or charmers.

Outside on a fake cedar sidewalk—
how'd they make it? I don't care or know—
the Native Am nodded and began his glide-talk.
He didn't say "How," didn't say "Wampum," oh no.

Didn't even say, "I'll fight no more forever."
He sang, "I talked with your mom last night."
"Don Walker, *mi madre es—*"
                           "Death is never."
He looked up at the sky and spat hard to his right,

he looked down at the fake wood sidewalk
and giggled like few over twelve are permitted,
since laughter with accruing years begins to balk:
from it, adults get muzzled as if committed.

"She ran with coyotes, so I joined."
C's lip trembled, as if she were dim-witted.

"She looked so fresh, so tough, so newly coined."
Don searched the sky. A bird—or soul—flitted.

"She said you'd come, she left a warning."
—Reader, I know I promised no supernal,
but this old coot's just Injun-adorning.
He's off his rocker. His eyes glare infernal,

not to mention milky, wandering, crossed, and gray.
See him shift and scratch his red-man rump?
With all his momma talk, who's he trying to sway?
But our Carmen, she won't get easily trumped.

Hey wait, she *was* raised Mexican Catholic.
You whiffed their stink-o incense? Seen their statues weep?
So a social study here, no fantasy shtick;
no shiny glop to make true believers leap.

We'll soon, I hope, rock on our way.
                              "Come see my shop,"
Don Walker intrigued, with humming mystical style.
"Can we walk?" Hank asked. "My butt's gonna drop
from riding."
              "Not 'less you wanna walk a mile."

"You mean your shop's not here in town?"
"Grandson, I can't afford this place, no human way.
It's made for grabby creatures, not hand-me-downs.
I got my rocker, despite what some writers say."

His milky eyes rolled as if searching megabytes
from some smoke-signal or cloud-based computer.
Could this old fart have *my* fine lines in sight?
A contrary character, there's nothing ruder.

Look! He shape-shifts those nasty milky eyes;
I yoga-breathe behind my desk. His teeth, yellow,
crack smiles as big as New Mexico skies.
Much more mumbo-jumbo I swear I'll bellow.

I'm a nice guy, nice as the next fellow,
but if a character wizened and minor
insinuates my judgment's loose like Jell-o,
I'll make him sad he peeped from Mom's vaginer.

I'll make him wish he lived in a garbage liner.
I'll leave him looking like he has a shiner.
I'll coat him with coal dust like some poor miner.
My head aches. It's sending flashes down my spine or

I'd keep on. A writer's revenge. Nothing's finer.

Chapter Eight: Don Walker's shop, some literary slop

New Mexico's dry enough, believe me.
Avoiding cracked skin requires a pint of lotion.
But this old injun's shop parched downright skeevie;
it spooled rock dust enough to clog an ocean.

For someone who nightly strolled an astral plain
his little shop dumped out one shoddy picture.
You know just what would turn it cleaner? Rain.
His roof should leak though sixteen fissures.

And dust's not all. Soon as the coot went in
he popped some mystery to gum. Drugs? Peyote?
It weren't Altoids, mint breath, or Sen-Sen.
And him spewing nature walks with a coyote!

I don't mean to point a finger, but some peeps
just start contrary, to twist harder with age.
And you know injuns drink till they fall in heaps.
This old redskin will soon hack some druggy rage.

He ain't no sage. Just take my word for it.
Whose else can you correctly take from where
you sit? Least I'm honest and call bullshit shit.
I didn't stroll last night and meet a dancing bear

conversing with your mom, be she alive or dead.
Said bear didn't chuff an erudite warning like,
"Buy J Taylor's books, they'll improve your head.
If not, your brain—ka-poof!—will take a hike."

Enough about one old fart Indian:
You get the picture. I've had it with him.

There are others too, but they wouldn't blend in.
Still, wouldn't it be dandy to list 'em?

There's some Popes, KY's last five governors,
S. Palin, all of Wall Street and their kin,
the miffed religious right (there's no one stubboner).
But not Joe Stearns! Lord how I miss him . . .

"Step right on in, you four. Don't mind the dust;
Some visitor just left's been stirring it up.
A goddamned writer. You know, it's unjust
what we wise folk put up with from such pups."

Pup? Damn, I'll have you—
                         "But so much for him.
It's good to see you, little shapely *frijole*."
Don Walker gave G a love flip under her chin
and turned to Hank.
                         "Her mother was pure and holy,

"but as pretty and frisky a-bed
As any lover this old Indian ever had."
"Don Walker!"
                         "*Frijole*, truth should be said.
Your mom made my wigwam warm and glad."

Don Walker reached behind his left ear—
had to be that one, for t'other was mostly nub,
a drunken cowpoke bit it after five beers—
and pulled out a bloodstone to give it a rub.

"This charm's for you both, it's given, not lent.
It'll steer you from danger." He studied them all:
"So you need to cleanse the bloody accident.
Start out with quartz. Check over in that last stall.

"Quartz works to purge, renews lost focus."
Don Walker glanced at a dusty windowpane
and saw me about to call his hocus pocus.
"Beat it, licorice twist! You label *me* insane?

"Flit back to your never world and let us five be!"
He picked up a large geode; the speckled turd
meant to throw it. He did, and hit high C:
it bust the pane into a pecking bird

that cut, not to mention the geode went thunk
against my case preserving some superb word troves.
Ow, damn! Will I scar to a rogue, or to a lunk?
Forget this all-star injun! I'll write about Groves.

A fat white guy holds more appeal, methinks.
A strong military man, always clean and pure!
His medals could have book royalties make clinks.
A yearlong NYTimes bestseller for sure.

Still, a scar? My face gives pubic trouble as is—
I mean *public* trouble! This skinny goat
has crept beneath my skin; I'm in a tiz . . .
Don Walker, he turned at the four to gloat.

"Beg pardon. Thought I saw a meddling ghost.
Geodes always shove 'em off in a blast.
A writer or ghost, each one's a milquetoast.
One deals with who-knows, the other with the past.

"Of the two . . . well enough literary slop.
Sweet Carmen, my almost daughter, we need to talk.
And you, her handsome moustache friend, don't hop
off. This concerns you like lime concerns chalk."

Don Walker steered the two toward a display case
while Dave and Lorrie searched for quartz in back.
"Three times, your dead mom's told me face-to-face
how you must take care on this new work track

you've made. And just last night as she left me
she held up a hank of clothing that shone green.
'Beware!' she shrilled. You know her voice weft screes.
'Don Walker, please warn my little Carmen bean.'

"She kept on flapping that shred of green.
Was small, could have been a sock or slipper,
could have been a glove or hat. Just saw it was green.
'Beware!' Then poof! Like someone had snipped her.

"Scared me so bad I drank half the mescal
she left bedside before her body died.
You know that stuff and me aren't pals.
Like most Indians I get pie-eyed and fried,

"so my distance, I keep. Your momma, though,
she'd knock it down, then dance and sing,
a flamenco star putting on a show.
Did you know I bought her a wedding ring?"

C reached for Don Walker's gnarled hand.
"She never said."

        "Was just before she learned
about . . . Frijole, let's let all that stand.
I promised her last night while we ran in ferns

"that I'd long-hike to Los Alamos
to cleanse the green whatsit and your new job."
Here C blushed. Spying ain't easy. It's almost
as hard as laughing when you cry or sob.

And just as deceit-filled.
                            "But here you show, smack.
Saves wear on my feet and sells gemstones too."
Don Walker glanced toward his shop's back
where Dave stood perusing the tip of Lorrie's shoe,

and then her knee, and then her hip,
and then her breasts, and then her chin,
to perch upon her nose.
                            "That boy's gone flip.
What in sandstorm hell's the matter with him?"

"In love," C sighed. Hank let out a cackle.
"Be careful, Grandson," Don Walker warned.
"When that bug bites, you'll get a face full of spackle.
I should've spotted that look. I've been horned."

"Did you really ask Mom to marry?"
"Do sidewinders hide under rocks in June?
I loved her. Love when you're old's not scary;
It's like breathing easy to watch the moon."

Don Walker grabbed Carmen by the hand.
"You gotta promise: don't commit to folly.
Your momma warned some danger shifts like sand.
Really wish I could be more jolly."

From back in the shop slipped out a coo
as L gave hoist to chunks of cut pink quartz.
"That's the ticket, gal! Pick the one for you!
Go pink to straighten your mind and banish warts."

Lorrie giggled, so Dave giggled too.
"You sure he ain't touched?"
                            "Love, Don Walker.

Cupid has him quivered all through and through."
"And I always thought Dave more a stalker,"

Hank mused.
            Carmen bristled, thinking of her room.
"Just what's that comment bent around to mean?"
"He's shy. Ladies slush his tongue to 'shroom."
"Ask me," Don said, "the neither needs words, just steam."

Lorrie and Dave came up to pay for the crystal.
"Ninety-seven, ninety-nine, not counting tax."
Their mouths dropped; Don Walker pointed like a pistol.
"A joke. This ain't Taos. I'll take twenty greenbacks."

Once more, Lorrie insisted she pay,
"Else, what's the point in getting a raise?"
"Granddaughter, you I like. May sunlight light your way."
They settled up the bill, exchanged high praise.

Handing over the quartz, Don Walker sneezed.
"Damn writer's still around. You four take care.
Why's he so chicken-peck nosy? I'd be most pleased
to hear him answer that. He want to bare

"your lives? Mine? Think he's researching
a fat dumb book on skinny working slobs?
Why else would he sneak out here, come lurching
around? He doesn't breathe and live; he robs."

"You know," Hank mused, "might not be a writer.
Might be an alien whose spaceship is maimed,
here sniffing your crystals for a tighter
inter-stellar trip."

            "He reads sci-fi," Dave explained.

"Half this whole state runs loony," Don Walker said.
"Don, I try my best to pull him from stars
to gutter." Carmen made a smooch, which turned Hank red.
"Um, I know that spaceships move faster than cars,

"still I wonder: however can one get 'maimed'?"
Who asked that? I didn't catch the action,
and Reader, I really can't be blamed:
a snake had crawled to coil in compaction

while over me a lone buzzard gave hover,
to see if I could still make traction.
But Hank gave answer, being a sci-fi lover:
"In far-off futures, in writers' redactions,

"starships can think, and lots thrust out female."
"Ah so. And do they couple through a portal
with engines and atoms?"
                              "Laugh and rail,
but sci-fi writers hold visions beyond mortal.

"So spaceships *can* have feelings and *can* get maimed."
The three made stare at Hank as if he'd spewed some soured
wastewater. Me, I was glad, not ashamed:
defending writers should make Hank empowered

to run for office, at least commissioner
of artifacts, tall tales, geodes, and rocks.
But I managed just one two-step, wishin' or
hopin' that snake wouldn't strike through my socks.

"Hey, didju catch that movement in the window?"
the hoary injun asked. "Saw a real nice ring,
a cameo, spin like in a carnie sideshow.
Can writers afford such elegant bling?"

The injun's eyes widened; his hand gave reach
for a dusty drawer then stopped. "No, my
last cameo went six years back to a peach
of a squaw, was not nabbed by any writer guy.

"Those writers," Don Walker scoffed. "What's their point?
If not blowing a joint, they suck drink down in bars."
"Not sci-fi writers," Hank defended. "They're anoint-
ed."

    "Yeah, with jugs of hooch from planet Mars."

Bars? Good thought. Where's the key to my not-maimed car?

Chapter Nine: A prose plea for respecting writers, especially the one you now read

There's a philosophy writer named Ralls, though I think he might now be dead. He taught at some place far off, just where slipped my head. Anyway, he had this idea we all should be born blind. That way justice could be dished up equally for humankind. His thought sloped something like that. A little drastic, but who knows? 'S'not a bad idea, as far as ideas go. Let's show it respect. That's my point really, that we writers work hard at crafting our thoughts and words. We don't just hang 'round bars slopping down tequila sunrises, beer, and boiled eggs resembling pink moose turds.

Listen here: no one disses sportball stars when they hop about chasing spheroids with their tremendous muscles, steroids, and semi-hard-ons. No one makes fun of actors when they moon into camera lenses to pretend they're weepy when all they really want is to bite down a cheeseburger with onion rings and other fried glutens. No one makes fun of politicians when they pretend they mean what they say when they're really tabulating votes and any graft that comes their way. No one mocks rock stars when they beat up pianos or guitars and inhale so much coke that a horse would choke. And no one ever makes fun of preachers, priests, rabbis, or imams when they claim they just held chat with the almighty Big One and are authorized to repeat his galactic joke.

So. Has God ever materialized amidst a sermon to say, "Reverend, you got this all wrong"? Let's hope not. Have a guitar's strings ever grabbed a rock star's fingers to say, "You just muffed four chords in one damned song"? Hell, those fellas miss notes right and left; their amps spout so loud we stay bereft. Politicians? If they go outré they just hire some ghostwriter for a memoir, or contract to host a reality show. And who ever heard of a camera punching an actor, admonishing, "Keep your mind on the script, don't ad lib"? No one. *Camera obscura, tabula rasa*, and all that Latin crap riffs, "Keep off your mitts." And those sport balls? They don't suddenly take it in their bellies to deflate mid-bounce or –air like wilting flowers, and say, "Man, what grand B.O.! Take three showers!"

So. Your beloved friends—we writers!—reside in the selfsame vein. Though we be but entertainers, we so hope to shield poor human souls! How? By embellishing, disguising, sugar-frosting, or just plain lying concerning this globe's woes.

Listen up! (My dear and faithful Reader, this complaint aims not for you.) Listen up, you wayward, dratted characters in this beleaguered, blasted, blessed, beatitudinous novel! Back off! Show respect! Act as if you inhabit more than rhyming quatrains spewing dreck, or you. just. might. wind. up. in. some snake-infested hovel!

Chapter Ten: Starship Enterprise, a pink crystal, a bad surprise (and worse epistle), moonlighting jobs for just a whistle

"I mean it," Lorrie growled. "A cleansing rite.
You heard Don Walker. We're all in danger."
Dave held a finger up: "Okay, let's not fight.
Agreed. We'll keep death a distant stranger."

On tiptoes, Lorrie lent his mouth a kiss;
Hank snored and sent la Carmen a wink:
"I'll join, if we can watch cute Tribbles spread their bliss."
"Damn, Hank, *Star Trek* and you make good luck sink."

"But . . . '*frijole*,' that old guy did not say *we*—"
Hank shut his mouth to open the fridge,
pull out two beers, and pop their churchlike gates with key.
"He said *you* tread upon a shaky bridge."

Hank handed Carmen her beer with a nod.
Returning a blush, she started, "*Star Trek's*—"
"No, no, *frijole*. Onward let us trod.
Your Don Walker, spirit guide, would not gush drek,

and nor should ye. You *are* the one in danger."
"Hank speaks what's right. I hate to side with guys,
still that *is* what—"
                        "*¡Basta!* But pals, show no anger."
C crossed *her* heart but searched *their* eyes.

Now Reader, you watch how smart our gal is.
You think she will admit to working as a spy
pursuing murder and all that jazzy biz?
Ho ha! You ain't seen her jump and reach for sky.

"Someone broke into this condo to leave
a very filthy—" she stopped to stare
at their far wall, unable to believe
the tiny, blood-red valentine hanging there.

"Oh no," Lorrie said. "Oh no." 'Twas worth
repeating, for the blood-red looked to be real
as it hung lop-most-side, angled in its berth.
"Your cunt's a gash that never ever will heal,"

is what the loving valentine read.
Let's hope no grade school tyke ever hurls—
or catches—such a sad message in red.
The longer, though, I moan and this mad world whirls

the more I figure population growth
spawns special evil, all on its own:
not just one apple rots our barrel's hope,
but gazillion dandelion seeds sprout, freshly sown.

It's like, since Hank just brought it up,
Star Trek's episode, "The Trouble with Tribbles."
Those many-hued tribbles wheezed cuter than pups;
they'd loose a convict's mouth in honey dribbles;

they'd blurp and coo to leave humans simple.
But Roddenberry was a philosophe deluxe:
I wish that Harvard had granted him a wimple
to sport about, and maybe a swallowtail tux.

That man revealed how even a good thing
can turn to mush. If only the Catholic Church
would bless the Pill and let all women sing,
this world might just not grind its present lurch.

Why add one more poor hungry chirping mouth
to crowd the nest? Has no one read Malthus?
Cannot one sage stand tall, proclaiming out,
"Please, friends, let's stop!" Can't someone halt us?

ISIS screeches its Armageddon,
Conspicuous spending cuddles with starvation,
Ebola and AIDS send mass infection,
the angry poor swell every nation.

If only I could send a swarm of bees to sting—
the entire Vatican? But verisimilitude
once more rears its ring-a-ling-ding,
and I bow down to Truth so boorish crude . . .

Hank, in anger rank, strode for the door
to give the white cardboard one great rip.
It was a pizza box top, now on the floor,
where chunks of pepperoni had turned flip.

It's just too bad our angry lank knight
could not put on a super-hero hood,
don laser guns to project full moon's light,
and lead us from this dark, dank wood.

Instead he touched a pepperoni, cold, fat, true.
"It's happened once before," C stated.
"You think that this came from that then too?"
Lorrie asked.
                    "Wishes are overrated,"

was Carmen's reply. And she was right,
for remember the four gents she called
that night? Remember the one who ignored his sight
for nose to smell patchouli? He'd've mauled

both sign and wall this pepperoni to sniff.
Despite his so white tie, he adores some pizza
with lust invoking carnal spume's wanton riff.
That's why weird Ted always keeps a

spare tie or three, for his dietary needs.
What crescendos more than pizza? A female.
Believing his white ties make women go "Geez!"
he always sports one. In truth, they just make gals bail.

And so, if that weird fella didn't smell it
then Reader dear, it just weren't there.
(I use KY dialect to show the hell it
would've took-en for him not to be aware

of such a potent item in sub subplot.)
So it's true: this pizza box valentine glows new.
Hank gave a kick like it was hot,
but Carmen bade him stop: "It might hold clues."

Called in once more, the four white ties returned.
The Ted did give this pepperoni manly sniff:
"It's from Jill's Home Pizza, or I'll be durned."
Communion be-tied, he durst not a harsher riff.

"Anchovy and pepperoni," relayed this one
with sharpened nose, our Ted. He bent to lick.
The others swayed, their stomachs tight on stun,
for those toppings vied with the valentine in sick.

"Hey Hank, remember that greasy creep
used to come in Todd's? Thought he was hot at pool,
but he forever scratched, his ten we'd keep?
That G-word always left his mouth a-drool."

"Was his name Hanson?" Lorrie spat.
They looked to her. "I've heard him spew that—"
She pointed at the floor-gore where it sat,
red.

    "Like father, like son, and son is back,"

noted the one—let's call him Techno Two—
who'd warned Carmen about Hanson's son—
let's call him Blue, since that's what he's used to.
Blue: a *hidalgo* making *señoritas* run.

For this he became persona non grata
on the lovely campus of UNM.
So now he's moved back in with Poppa
(what he called Dad Hanson: most stuck with, "Oh hell him!")

"Not him . . . what was his name?" Dave scratched his nose,
which caught poor Ted's attention. He could only
hope he'd just met a sniffing comrade of the pose-
y. Communion ties be durned, it got lonely

when working as the only one who sniffed.
But his plans for Future Pals of the Nose
(FPN), like a dust devil, slipped adrift
since Hank, not itchy Dave, to the occasion rose:

"He called himself 'Putter.' Remember he'd joke
about the size of his—" Hank looked to L & C—
" 'iron that never broke.' "

                    "Chihuahua, I need a smoke.
Not weed, a big black *puro* would give me ease.

"You gents have one? Doesn't have to be Cuban."
The six men studied Carmen as if she'd wilted.

"What I mean, guys, is that a cigar'd be groovin'!"
She reached for her purse. It nearly tilted

being more heavy than what girlies should carry,
for she'd installed her Walther p-38k
with nine nice rounds, in case the creep should tarry.
A tough job, but blasting his balls would work okay.

She pushed pistol aside and pulled out a stogie.
Here, let me focus Trixie's red opera glasses.
T's my gal. She left and called me an old fogey
for text in two chapters next, which gave her gasses.

You see, I knew I'd need these glasses
to spy what Carmen was smoking here and now.
So I wrote two chapts. ahead—my, how time passes!
Let me focus, see it clear, and—wow!

A Henry Clay. How in blue hell can C afford
expense account, I bet. These spies all have 'ems.
We know the cigar stinks more mighty than the sword:
cognac, stogies, sex, fast cars and gems

comprise what glues a dealer's warped attention.
Hey, could the govern-mint who writes C's checks
be spot on, on this new cartel intention
of dealing top secret science, not cocaine flecks?

Time will explain—forgoing dearth of rhyme,
that is. For that would leave us a book of prose,
which never gets composed with a sense of tim(e)-
ing. Prose just offers the dainty nose a rose;

good poems whack with bulbs of garlic!
So Reader, light up and pour a glass.

Cognac for me, thanks. Let's relax and parley
whilst Carmen crams her condo with cigar gas.

"Putter, huh?" She blew a cloudy exhale.
"Yeah, but he hasn't been around this year."
"Blue's back, though." Hank gave his nose a flail.
Dating a girlie who smoked cigars was queer,

he thought, just momentarily.
        "Who's Blue?" asked L.
"Hanson's son," one more than six people replied.
"I'm the only one who didn't know? Swell."
"It's not like you win a damned pink door prize."

"Amen to that," our Carmen said. "Here, take a puff."
She passed the cigar to Hank. He took a hit.
"Smooth," he gasped out in tiny coughs. "Not rough."
"Don't Bogart, don't inhale. Then you pass it.

"We live in Native Am Country, right?
Hey Lorrie, consider this our cleansing ritual,
and bring that pink quartz over here in light.
Cigars won't cause cancer if they're not habitual."

As Lorrie did what Carmen directed,
She took great care to not exhale her smoke with "Om."
Last time, Carmen laughed till L felt rejected.
She'd have fared better to recite some sappy poem.

She scooted the pink quartz onto the table.
Everyone leaned and gazed and took a toke.
"If pink crystals and cigar smoke are able
to chase off creeps, I'll turn rock hound and smoke

Havanas. Vote poor Cuba into statehood."
Hank again inhaled the Henry Clay to please—
he didn't know it from a chunk of burning wood—
then said, "I could get addicted to these."

That was the general consensus, but
the guys would need to take their guns and rob
to buy those Henry Clays. Or give up
a delectable, or get a second job

by teaching breathing, Om, insight, and yoga.
New Mexico though, is where teachers of New Age
stroll ready-made, tote lizards, wear a toga.
The market's tough: crystals and chakras stay the rage.

So moonlighting Om to buy Henry Clays
won't cut the ketchup. Then robbing banks?
Hey no, these good guys are set in their ways,
though nosy Ted will sometimes stray confused, thanks.

Still, some second job, if they must needs smoke such rank.

Chapter Eleven: At Todd's, some info and then . . .

It's been a week since that second Valentine
was found. L's raise has come, but C's in a tiz.
Our guys have clung protective—ivy vines.
The gals, so far, stay fine with boys all in their biz.

It's Saturday. L and Dave are bluegrassin'
at a festival. "*Amistad* can't overcome
those fiddles, banjos, mandolins. Too crass e'en
for wetback girls," C sang in fandango hum.

"Hey then, let's hit my place and read aloud
from *Slaughterhouse Five*. A great book, and loads of fun."
"Hank, for a working grunt you do yourself proud,
but," Carmen said, "I have one small errand to run

"at Todd's. I really hoped you'd tag along.
A parlay: I'll drive and buy your beer.
In case of bad, I need someone strong."
It works always, sweet flattery, that's no bum steer,

so Hank hopped into Carmen's Nissan Sentra,
which rolled on, powder blue and new. Hank raised
a finger, then decided not to entra
the money question. He didn't want to faze

this beauteous, with-it, almond-eyed gal.
That she'd consider reading science-fic
meant she was no mirage, but one real pal.
He powered down the window with a finger-flick.

And Carmen's errand? To learn just who she'd seen
two nights before, chatting with Hanson.

A Tex-Mex, mid-thirties. The two'd shed spleen
that night, shouting and banging, real man-some,

though ending up as drunken, snugly buds
sharing back-pats and beers, to leer the girls.
Too cozy, Carmen had thought. Like spuds
giving sprout to make potato vine whorls.

His name was "Steamer," she learned in an hour.
"*Jesucristo*, does each guy here have a handle?"
she asked of Hank, returning stiff and sour.
"Not me, just call me Hank, who'd like to dandle

you on his knee as we both read *Slaughterhouse Five*.
Who cares what Steamer's real name is?"
"I do. He's making *guiños* at my cuz. Too jive."
"His name is Carlos; he's in the drug biz."

"*Mi hombre*," C sighed. "Let's go to read some
sci-fi, and on your knee I'll sit to make your
ray gun explode from packing so much fun."
Pure Carmen felt small guilt for her white lie impure.

She had no cuz, nor niece, nor aunt, nor neph.
Such lying came too handy under duress
in this spy biz, with its burgeoning heft.
Except bad Dad and Blue, C stood alone, a mess.

She thought: *I do love math; I could encode
algorithms for where I work.
But dealers don't use code, just items that explode,
cigars, fast cars, cognac, sex, gems, the usual murk.*

Did time stand by for one more Carmen-sigh?
Almost. But in walked Blue, C's half-bro,

to stumble 'gainst their table, pig-drunk, not just high.
(Being half-bro was a fact he didn't know.)

Both H and C caught bottles as they fell.
"Damn, woman, you and me need to get down and eat!"
"Cool it there, Blue." Hank pointed. "Drink a beer, be swell."
Blue focused on the tall cowpoke face turning beet.

He focused again. "You," he said and walked away.
"You?" Carmen asked, watching her half-brother
beat out retreat. "Hanson!" Steamer gave a bray.
Blue walked toward the noise, expelling a blubber.

"I hit his head against a hitching post
about a year ago. Dave claims it's why he went
to Albuquerq. I think he left 'cause most
the women 'round here wised to his foul male stench.

"Fuck 'em, con 'em, beat 'em: that's his game."
"Delightful," C replied. "Like pop, like son."
"Yeah, they do run whole lots the same.
Don't think that Hanson's ever figured I'm the one

"who gave his son that dent in his fool head.
As you just saw, the fool's same self barely knows."
"It's his drug haze, his synapses have fled
for calmer air, where each object won't glow."

Blue and Steamer stood bouncing skulls in tandem.
"Let's leave. I've seen enough, I've got the gist.
Let's go someplace nice, not so random."
Hank frowned. "Tralfamadore would not be it.

But Vonnegut's a genius. He'll be a hit."

Chapter Twelve: In Hank's apartment,
the intimate apparel department, almost heaven

Vaginas, pricks and tits, wet, soft and hard, ah-ha!
That's what you deny thinking (as do I),
hypocrite Reader, my brother, my pard, blah-blah!
Yet C & H must talk, before they munch such pie.

They read some Vonnegut, always a pleasure.
They did some slipp'ry handling and happy dandling,
though who did serve as dandle-ee and who as -er
kept hard to judge amidst their rambling.

Of sudden though, Hank stopped ice cold.
"Kurt Vonnegut is grand, but each earthling must jump,
and I don't think all futures lie foretold."
C gave a wiggle, but Hank stayed slump.

"Now you are talking 'bout my quaint Valentine,
I just know." C inspected Hank's apartment:
its shelves of books, TV, a fifth of Spanish wine.
As Mr. Right, her Hank fit that compartment.

She wouldn't claim the like for her stalker.
For him she'd hit the firing range the last ten days;
each recoil echoed the warning of Don Walker.
How now pretend she had spare time to play?

"I'm buying one big house," Hank said. "Dave knows.
Lies out some ways, ten acres, two-story—
the only such for miles. Come winter the wind blows—"
"To huff it down?"

        "No, there's its glory.

"Was built before sad Oppenheimer's crew.
No radiation . . ."
                         At that, C laughed,
an act she sought to foil the evil brew
that sloshed about. She felt adrift and on a raft.

Was scary to a child born of desert.
". . . so no Geiger needed, but I love dogs."
C blinked at Hank, though not to flirt:
"That's swell, dear Hank. Got dogs, not hogs, some logs.

"I'm happy for you, but—"
                              "But here's my point.
The dogs are gonna be Doberman.
Dave's granddad used to run a poochie joint
training canines for Project Blow Up Man."

"We can't have dogs—"
                           Hank put a finger to her lips.
"And Dave's old dad still breeds some now and then."
C made to giggle at Hank's sexual slip
"No, not more little Daves, but Dobermen."

C crunched a brow, she squinted an eye.
Lorrie was right: both showed a fine wren-brown
and could flit with laughter as if to fly.
Tonight though, they both swooped fast and hard down.

"Just what, kind man, can you be saying?"
"Five bedrooms, two stories. You and Lor could rent
and keep safe. I mean, your landlord's always playing
in Todd's. Have you informed him of this stalker gent?

"For that, he'd let you bust your lease, I'm sure.
Dave nearly always beats him long at pool."

"Hank, Hank, you've made one weird non-sequitur."
Outside, a siren. Carmen jumped, then felt a fool.

"Non-sequitur? You think you'll have me slip
with Latin?" Hank stood too. "I read science fic.
Have memberships." He gave a light-switch flip;
C grimaced and reached for his sci-fi wrist.

She gazed into his Cherokee eyes.
She gazed into his sand-brown bedroom,
kept clean and spotless neat for a studly guy.
"Hank, your care is sweet, but here comes more doom:

"Something else is running slip-slide too,
not just the creep who soiled our place."
"Is it what Don Walker said? The green shoe?
If it had been a blue slipper, I'd hold an ace."

"Do what?" C's voice one octave rose, then dropped in thud.
She let his sci-fi wrist go, he watched her
fine wren-eyes churn out thick desert-swamp mud.
How could her mood go split in such a blur?

"Hey, hey, a blue satin slipper; it's a joke.
I found it on the loading dock—"
"When?"
                "The day that Dave blew all the smoke
and we four rode out to—"
                                "Let's see it then!"

He walked to his dresser to pull out a drawer,
display the same blue satin slipper
Fed-Ex laughed at, the one we've seen before.
Wren-eyes turned hawk, thin fingers went Flipper.

"Drop it, Hank. Don't touch it anymore.
'S a clue, I think." She neared, he gave exhale,
"Naw, was likely lost by some Hanson-whore.
You know he beaches 'em in there like whales."

"Good God, that man's my personal hell."
"How Hanson?" Hank looked from slipper to Carmen.
She looked from slipper to him as well.
She'd ploughed deep earth, though not farmin'.

"Can you fetch up a plastic baggie?"
Hank shrugged. "They do drug screens, so I don't smoke."
"For the slipper, numbskull. I'm not jaggy.
But I'm glad to hear you don't. That's no joke.

"I've got a secret, Hank, not even Lorrie knows.
No telling, promise. You'll think it weird."
Hank studied Carmen's lips, for she gave good blow . . .
OF COURSE HE DIDN'T THINK THAT! *C'est moi*, I'm speared.

(The instant I wrote this, for those who stay curious,
was when my galfriend stomped out in a fit.
Well, more than fit: she screamed, she slung, furious:
"Anything I've left here, keep. I don't give one shit!"

Amongst the things she left were pink opera glasses.
She spins them out at Churchill Downs and fancy plays.
And I used them—remember?—two chapts. past,
when C was puffing cigar smoke ever' which way.)

Here, read on. I'll make it up to her and you:
Hank studied Carmen's lips, so hospitable.
Hank studied Carmen's lips, so sweet in hue.
Hank studied Carmen's lips, so unpredictable.

Hank studied Carmen's lips. Get the picture?
Mea culpa for my previous ungainly slip;
I just had to write lewd to get a fix sure
on what dear Carmen might put to her lip.

Curiosity fits me like a goatskin glove.
And though this here tome ain't holy writ,
neither ain't it rife with sex, deplete of love.
So please to judge my glitch an aberrant flit.

Hank studied Carmen's lips, so serious they cracked.
"But your guru Don Walker said it was green,
the slipper, I mean."
         "He's color blind, that's a fact."
"Even in his dreams?"
        "That's how it would seem."

In all this time, Hank studied her lips.
97 seconds. I have a stopwatch,
and though this is poetry, I permit no slips
in verisimilitude, or else I'd botch

said idol of contemporary writing.
Or should that be idle idyll? After all,
P. Pilate labeled truth at best biting,
not at the champ, but at the fatter-all,

the butt, I mean, no matter what that Roman meant.
Truth all too often doth give chomp when we
least expect. Now, it seems, C's about to vent
that Capital T at her boyfriend-to-be.

"Hank, I'm undercover, a spy, not a ju-co
gal whizzing through her math and history."

Hank's mouth gave curl. That meant, you know,
he thought her fabrication some fish story.

"Okay, wise guy. You wanna see my pay stub?"
She remembered she was at his apartment
and then remembered she had a whole rub-a-dub
in her purse, un-cashed from our holy govern-mint.

Her purse glowed metallic red: was the Mex
in her blood. Just be glad she didn't use
a rosary to keep it clasped.—Agh, a hex!
She tugged a pearled rosary! A ruse

to make Hank think her sweet and naïve?
Whatever her thoughts, the blessed thing jingled.
I hardly think *that* noise would make one believe.
And from her purse came a check she singled

to show her doubting Hank, who whistled sincere.
She then tiptoed and let her secret blow
right through the open air, right into his left ear.
"My God," he said. "Let beer turn icy cold and flow."

Hey Reader, did you catch what C whispered?
The fan behind was blowing, so not a word
could *I* hear. Damn! These characters leave me blistered,
Sometimes I think the whole lot not worth a turd.

If ever they'd decide to co-operate,
this tale would scoot along, a through z.
Instead of mashing our noses against a grate
we could finish, take a hike, hell, drive to the sea.

Hank came back with two beers, a fancy pale ale
he'd picked up in Texas heading for Mardi Gras.

(He never made it, but that tale's stale.)
C took one, swigged, and tugged the strap of her bra.

Whoa! We're getting there? We're moving along?
Heading for thermite in their chasms?
Closed eyes, clutched nails, lips warbling out tuneful song?
Some well-timed Kegels, volcanic orgasms?

Oh Reader, don't get lurid and cocksure;
we've watched these characters in action.
I'm getting a notion that slippery and impure,
as far as tonight, won't get redaction.

"There was this sixteen-year-old girl.
Murdered and found with one blue slipper.
I think—" C's right hand gave Hank's dresser a swirl.
"That slipper? True north like the Big Dipper?"

"Exactly. I was first response to find her.
Her fingers were long, she could have played piano.
Instead, she sprawled in an arroyo in a blur,
to partake nevermore of any grand plan, oh

"Hank, it made me sick. I want to catch the jerk
who did her in, more than I want to . . .
grow up, collect government perks,
or speak fluent Spanish like Mom was wont to."

Away in the town that spawned the atom bomb,
small scientist heads were going, "Tzit-tzit."
Is this something onto which we should glom?
Oh hell yes! They're brewing a world of shit.

That long-fingered Mexican señorita
had the fatal misfortune to overhear

them talking while Hanson mixed her margarita.
The moral? Don't get fancy, stick to beer.

But enough of them and their brewing woes.
Let's check back in at Hank's bedroom
just in case my notion's little toes
have gone about-face to set amour in red bloom.

The prospect *is* building; C's wrapped in Hank's arms.
"Hank, just hold me. There's more trouble than I can count.
Tonight I need to cuddle and calm my alarms."
I knew it, Reader! No spewing sexual fount,

instead we're in for Sermons on the Mount.

Chapter Thirteen: *Two pops, two sons, eight beers, one gun*

We were about to watch the fun
in that last chapt. when Truth broke in.
And as with Frost's birches sloping in the sun
we bent to icy talk, not hot carnal sin.

Apologies for that, though Reader dear,
I fear this chapt. won't flow much more risqué.
But here I plead, ma'am or sir, do not jeer,
do not skim, or fearsome plot will flit away.

But do go on, light a cigar (You'll at least
derive some Freudian pleasure.) or brew
an espresso. (Bring out your glad beast!)
Do sit back comfy; do read this forthcoming stew.

Let's start out mellow, with Dave and Dad.
Hank's right: Dave's dad's young Doberman bitch
has dropped a litter of ten. Dad's glad:
he can sell them five Franklins at a pop, no hitch.

As Dad was sitting and planning on how to spend
his doggy fund—new tires for son Dave's truck?
A trip to the Pacific, where he'd never been?
—young Dave harrumphed till Dad's fancies unstuck.

"Hey Pops, you want a beer?"
                            Dave's dad gave frowns
at that filial show: Dave's sappy gesture
did surely haul some favor fast in tow. Love sounds
had fled when Dave's teen years made show. "Yes, sure.

"And toss tamales in the microwave.
When your mom died I searched out her recipe
for eight long months. She hid it, sure that I'd crave
and marry her widowed friend and drink chai tea.

"That woman's hair stinks, and she thinks Roswell
is Mecca."
    Dave trotted back with two beers.
"You're too hard-headed to marry. Why's her hair smell?"
"Incense. She never gave up hippie days. It's queer."

"She lesbian?"
     "Hell no, Son, listen.
She's hot in bed, for a gal eyeing sixty."
Dave's blush turned red enough to glisten
and match the setting sun, though not so spiffy.

"Aw Son, don't hand me those virgin dapples.
I've seen that new woman you're dating.
Her eyes glow queen-size and her tits—"
         "Pineapples."
Dave's dad laughed. "You're not overrating.

"So full, they make me want to reach out,
like the phone company used to say, and touch."
Oh Reader, can you see how our little sprout
young Dave got bent perverted rightly enough?

Some pun on genes and jeans here might be apropos,
so might plutonium mixing heavy water,
so might a magpie if we espied one of those,
but not—listen up!—a virgin led to slaughter.

For Dave and Dad appreciate well enough
all women. Thus, don't twist your creep alarm up:

their boy chatter just chats. It stays all bluff.
"Um, Dad, you think Hank might buy, say, two pups,

on cheap?"
Dave's dad tilted his bottle:
"I knew something was up when you went to fetch
this beer. Hank lonesome? Need dogs to coddle?"
"It's his girl and mine. Some pervert's acting a wretch."

Dave then explained one scrawl he'd seen, and two
the girls had shown in pictures. Clanging bells
had rung for him and Hank. They'd thought of Blue,
of Putter, of other creeps and skank. But hell,

those jerks could find plenteous many girls
to slap. "This isn't slapping, Son. It's dark.
So I'm guessing Hank wants them to give a whirl
at livin' in his new rancho house? Spark, spark."

Dave's dad perked as the microwave gave ding.
"All right, I'll talk with Hank. I can still sell eight.
Go fetch them tamales. If I'm going to lose bling—
that's what you kids call it, have I got that much straight?"

Dave smiled. This was no time to correct his dad
on lingo. "You're with it, Pops. I'll go get
the tamales. But they always make you sad,
so—"
"It's because I never want to forget."

This was true enough, though Incense Hair
had plowed sinewy inroads of late.
With Kama Sutra diagrams in her lair—
her bed, I mean—she roamed Dave's dad from toe to pate.

She and Dave's mom indeed had been the best of friends.
A week before she died, "Take care of Chelsea,
she needs a man to tame her wild loose ends,"
was what Dave's mom relayed to Dad, in loving plea.

Dave toted four tamales back with two cold beers.
"So. You moving in to make it a harem?"
Today, Dave's SOP seemed blushing to Dad's leers.
"That's okay, as long as you both don't share 'em."

"Dad!"
        "And remember our family tradition.
Don't marry till you're a wise, ripe thirty.
Pineapples or no, you're young, in no condition.
Good 'nough for five generations, good 'nough for thee.

"Don't croak out 'love.' You've known her just two weeks."
"Almost three!" blurted Dave. His dad took a sip
and ate a tamale lewdly to make it squeak.
How I can't say. Mayhap through his arthritic hip,

which Chelsea massaged so hard to unhitch?
And speaking of hitch, this thirty thing needs
explaining. Go way back, jump a time ditch.
We're extracting lots of Dave's previous seeds.

We're in Virginia just before there was a West.
We're there just before the Civil War, in fact.
Dave's forebear—let's give the greats a rest,
but there would needs be six getting in the act—

was enchanted by a blonde-haired German witch.
(Such was his claim after she stole the farm.)
Forsook, he headed Gold Rush West without a stitch.
Made it to Santa Fe, where he again was charmed.

"Eighteen and stupid," he heard folks say
after this new lady, a redhead, took his cash,
his horse, his favoritemost gun, and galloped away.
He got drunk, of course. Hell, he got downright smashed.

He woke up under some mysterious tree.
Was not pin oak nor maple, that's all he knew.
He banged his head upon its bark: one, two, and three.
A ghost voice spoke, "You can beat yourself blue,

"but what you should do is to keep from ladies
till you earn some sense for your bruised-up head.
Twelve years will do, before you make babies."
That tale endured. Had ol' six-great's brains all fled?

Not so far he couldn't work into owning
a dry goods store, the largest in Santa Fe
After eleven years of atoning,
he spotted a perk brunette heading his way.

"Mr. McDowell," she hailed. "Preacher Jay
sent me. I just moved from West Virginia."
"West?" He then remembered the sly way
his neighbors had seceded. Was no skin, ya

know, off them, if plantations had to free those black
slaves. "Yes, West. I'm good with numbers,
I need a job. I've got a strong back,
I plowed with Dad 'til the farm went under."

At thirty they were married and soon had Gramps
Five in line of precession. To Dave, that is.
So that's why thirty. Until then, they collect stamps,
I guess. Their pizzles' only job is to make whiz.

(If you believe that, let's locate a bridge:
I'll sell it to ya cheap so you can jump.)
"Dave," his dad now said. "Your gal ain't no fridge,
is she? Sit down and tell me how you hump."

"Disgusting, Dad."
        "Minute back, I was right quick."
His dad gave suck to his tamale lewdly.
"Think I'll watch TV. Least that won't turn me sick."
"Don't touch that idiot box!" Dave's dad yelled rudely.

"I'm giving you life lessons, Son."
        "On how to eat?"
His dad smiled and toyed with a third tamale.
"Nope, how to love wise and true. Take a seat."
Dave did, lest his dad suck the edible lolly.

"Now when your momma wanted some lovin'
she'd stroll to that piano and play 'Für Elise.'
That's exactly how you got stuffed in the oven,
she and me bakin' all that hot love grease."

"Dad!"
    "That's how come your love for music,
though that banjo you twang sure stretches limits.
—Now I'm not saying I want you to lose it."
The black piano sat so dim that its

no-shadow looked just like his dead wife's hair, but
'twas a gray bandanna left by Chelsea. He laughed,
he cursed. "Dave, if I was your age I'd want to rut.
A woman's work is to make men daft.

"That's why you gotta promise—"
        "Wait till I'm thirty."

"Bingo! I'll fetch us both one more cold beer."
Dad snatched the bandanna: incensed and flirty.
He draped it 'cross his nose and rolled a leer.

He twirled it, eyed that last tamale and
rubbed his chin. Chelsea wanted him to grow a beard
so it could tickle her little glans.
—Whoa! Let's shut things down lest they get too weird.

Bandanna fetish? For McDowell men, not queer.

❄ ❄ ❄

It was a dark and bleary night. Which means,
I s'pose, Ol' Sol done gave it rest.
Dave's dad, bandanna in teeth, was last Sol'd seen
Now Ms. Moon watches two Hansons, a harsher test.

Do you think, by the way, sun and moon
communicate? Morse code? Telepathy?
Ah, but I promised no spiritual loony tune.
Still, it'd be nice to think they share empathy.

They'd need it with these two creeps autonomous.
With filth and shame, they're synonymous.
If truth could out, Hanson would be eponymous
with skank. But truth, she doth remain anonymous.

Not bad, eh? Think my future lies in Hollywood
nib-penning scripts? The cash and coke would be delish.
In Tinseltown, my spirit-ban would do no good,
but a sight more sex would show than this poor script's

as yet tossed out. Hey look! Here they both come,
Hansons, dad and son. They'll spew vulgarity
a-plenty. In fact, I'll bet five-to-one.
Twixt Hansons and McDowells lies disparity:

"There's this cunt been coming to Todd's lately."
(See, reader, what'd I tell ya? Could be Pop *or* Son.)
"Mexican bitch, though she talks funny, stately."
"Stately?" asked Pops.
      "Throws foreign words on a run."

"She have a gal friend with big, huge tits?"
Blue Hanson gave a nod and glanced at the moon,
whose silly face irked him, so he spit.
They sat on the porch, and it was June.

(If I insert just one more clichéd word
I'll pen the most perfect sappy love tune.)
Blue's foot jerked. Had he kicked an armadillo turd?
He looked. There, covered in slime, lay a *spoon*.

(I did it! I did it!)
     "Yeah, really big tits.
God almighty, Dad, what's this? Have you turned
to cooking Drain-o? I could get you a fine fix,
primo Columbian coke that leaves real good burn."

"We have drug screens tomorrow, so no thanks."
"They notify you ahead? Not bad, Dad."
"Just one of many perks with my rank.
Still wish you'd—"
     "Working for the gov would drive me mad."

"Well I wish you'd apply. Y'know, you can retire
at fifty if you start at twenty-five."

"Hey Pops old guy, you sure you're my sire?
I got less than three years to thirty, no jive.

"I'd rather have women pay my way
than Uncle Sam. He's going broke, ain't he?
Women, whiskey and drugs are here to stay.
I'll be right back, I gotta let some pee."

Blue walked into the yard to cop a whiz.
"Welfarin' these damned Indians and Mexes
is busting Uncle Sam," Blue shouted in a tiz.
Dad moved his bottle of beer, forming hexes.

A thing crossed his mind that he shoved away.
Was about Pineapple's Mexican girlfriend
and how her lip gave out a funny play.
He snatched at his own, to make it unbend

What comes to you, sharp Reader, through this mist
is right. Hanson had no clue C was his daughter.
Blue walked back on the porch and gave his jeans a hitch.
"Wake up, Pops. Dream of taking big tits to slaughter?"

"Pineapple's what some of the pencil necks call
that big-titted woman."
                         "Surprised they even saw.
Thought they were innocent like before the big Fall."
Hanson senior belched and gave a haw.

"Innocent? Hell, they snatched her and those tits away
before she'd worked for me a full four weeks.
I barely got a chance to see how tit-land lay,
those brain boys wanted to horde all the peeks."

"I heard she was hired up because she saved
that math whiz's kid. Did you know that she dates
one of your motorbike slugs? I gave them a wave
at that bluegrass do last week."

                    "Music? you hate—"

"Two cunts were there."

                Hanson senior gave a grin.
What junior did not tell was that a smooth drug deal
went down, one that saved his skinny rear end
and paid a debt. So he endured the fiddle's squeal.

His third eye—I guess even creeps can have one—
pictured the woman called Pineapple by his dad.
Then it roamed to her Mexican chum, a plum
he just knew would squirm and make him glad.

Plop her down on her tummy and do the old pump
while she gave shout to silly Tex-Mex words
like "*mas*" and "*amor*," and he slapped her tan Mex rump.
Blue got so engrossed with packing her turds

he didn't hear what Hanson senior said:
"Might want to cool it on the drugs. Big tops
have notions drug czars have it in their heads
to expand into spy biz. As if those sops

could decipher equations or even spell
the word 'computer' in English or *Español*.
Still, rumor is there's going to be hell,
that bunches of drug-dealing heads will roll."

Unhearing, Blue dozed on his beach, the sexual shoal.

Chapter Fourteen: My gal Trixie returns,
presto changes her name to Dixie
then to Pixie, gives loud suggestions that burn,
that make your author scream and yearn

At my front door I heard a tapping.
Ignoring it seemed best; I kept on brewing tea.
Thought it was wind, but it became a rapping.
It was no raven nor Lenore, though 'twas a she.

Here's something I should set loose about Trixie:
She's quite the lass, cunning, funny, and gay.
But oft times she becomes a Dixie,
strident as Stonewall Jackson, has to have her way.

Then after she gets it, ooo, love city.
Her little toes flex and I call her Pixie.
Of course it's not that simple, and 'tis a pity:
she'll connive and deviate, even as Trixie.

The rapping, it did stop. *Oh great*, I thought,
'tis a Hollywood director who read my rift.
I better get up or my work will slip to naught.
Then I noticed two glossy red heels adrift.

"How long's it take to answer a front door?!
You cripple up in the week since I left?"
Her hair had turned bright red. I studied the floor.
"Hey look at me! Are you too bereft?

"Heard you were mooning college girls
at Fred's. You need to give all that a rest,

old man. Your middle's past shootin' scamperin' squirrels.
Stay home and write. It's what you do best,

"though reading that last chapt. with the duo sons
and pops, I have my doubts. Where's any action?
And you call *that* 'fearsome plot'? For once
you need to listen: do tough redaction."

"How'd you get in?" I yelled, noticing an anklet
with three pearls.
        "Duh." Trixie held up a key.
"But my computer password?"
          "Double duh. Let
me say I had to misspell Nietzsche only three

"times to pass. Really, Joe, fetch my opera glasses,
brew me a tea, and for once just be nice.
You need my help. That last chapt. blew gases.
It masticated Uncle Ben's white rice."

"It held important clues!"
        "Clues to rhyme with snooze?
Give action! Plot! Make a rocket explode!"
"Los Alamos doesn't—"
        "Whadya have to lose?"
"I guess I *could* make a gravity ray implode."

Trixie jiggled her anklet. My eyes gave swell.
"That's right, Bud. Say, like my new bauble?
Tony gave it."
        At that I gave a Rebel Yell.
"Aw, jealous, old man? Tony's young, you hobble.

"But tuck your lip in. *I* bought it for *you*.
Let's make up." Dixie offered a rub and a kiss.

"Say, that bit with Hanson's lip *was* a nice clue.
You need more of that, fewer boys taking piss."

She gave another cat-rub as I brewed chai tea.
"Um, speaking of Hanson not knowing offspring,
do you realize Loretta's the only poor flea
without a last name? Now that's a real mean thing

to hang on a KY girl. And just what color
are her eyes? You weigh Carmen and Hank in with brown
but hers you leave the reader to mull or
worse. Joe, I swear, sometimes you're a damn clown."

"Her eyes are green, emerald green," I state
with vim. "That gets declared the very first page."
Not wise to place refutation on Trixie's plate,
but there, it's done. I don't aver to be a sage.

"So they are. Just giving a self-awareness test,
a magic mirror's view, so to speak."
The way she bobbed her head, I'd get no rest.
"Go on," I said. "There's something you're dying to leak."

"Our Lexington's Loretta's city of birth."
"How on green-grass earth can you know that?!" I shouted.
"How? Remember you thought so highly of your worth
when you sneaked into C's bedroom and outed

that she was a govern-mint spy? Well I
cat-crept into Los Alamos' personnel files,
slid right by Hanson, who of course was high—
he'd passed his morning drug screen clean with smiles,

was trying to make it with L's replacement
but having not much luck. The girls got to her

the night before, so his lines were a waste 'n' meant
his drool could raise nor blink nor wink nor stir.

"Anyhow, take a guess at L's last name, sailor."
I sipped tea and studied those pearls on her ankle.
"Well, since you don't want to, it's Taylor."
This is Pixie's game; she always tries to rankle

before we hop in bed. It usually works, too.
But not now, for this was crude. "So? Smith or Brown
float just as common. If it'd been McGurk, shoo,
then I'd inspect birth records filed downtown.

"I mean, if my last name was McGurk, too."
"It's called denial, in case you wonder.
This morn, I took a trip to city hall, and boo!
Her mom's first name lay there, easy plunder."

Pixie was flipping back to Trixie. I held
my breath.
          "Linda, of course. Father listed:
Unknown Schmo. You hadn't yet been gelded
and Linda was your gone wife's name 'less I missed it."

I neared the window, hearing some noisy bird.
A cardinal. How in hell can they mate for life?
Whoever could stand it? "Your notion's absurd,"
I snorted.
          "Think I'm just causing strife?"

I should have snorted more, but coughed up phlegm.
"L's eyes are green; let's see, just like we know whose.
And your wife's mother's name sure wasn't Jim."
"Loretta," I remembered weakly. "You ruse!"

I spewed.
       "Why would I do that, if it were true?
Um, your gone wife's mom kept a farm in Danville,
I believe."
       "So? What's that got to do—"
I remembered L and Granny's walnuts. My will

was weakening. Trixie saw it, too.
"She's your daughter. Just treat her nice is all
I'm sayin'."
       My face fell; I felt it undo.
The world was working hard to shrink quite small.

"Um, right before our divorce Linda made me screw.
I was watching TV, the Berlin Wall's fall.
She'd dabbed on patchouli and started to chew—"
"No need for details, old man. Just recall, is all."

Pixie rubbed my arm, and then my neck.
"You've always said that Linda was weird.
Loretta's twenty-six, I did a check,
Berlin Wall—"
       "'Eighty-nine." I'm too tough for tears,

but this news gave my stomach a grinch.
"Loretta listed her mom as deceased. The file
said so, I mean."
       This made me flinch,
since I'd planned to kill off L's mom in a while,

just to make evens with Carmen and Dave.
(Hank's, though, is still living and kicking,
works as produce manager at a Pick 'n' Save.)
But L's mom—my ex-wife?—is Grim Reaper's pickings?

My head flew up in wild cosmic swirl.
Midnight dogs gave bark, a lone owl made hoot—
all those signs of death that send us a-whirl.
So . . . poor weird Linda lies among the roots.

"Wait! No! Lorrie said she's got a younger sister,
who lives in KY, just turned ten years old.
She watches cartoons."
                              "Buster, you missed your
text. Wasn't L who said; that came from your word hold.

"Joe, as good as you are, even Homer blinks."
"Nods," I corrected.
                              "Blink, wink, or nod,
fact is, your info about a young sister stinks,
so think: once truth runs barefoot, it stays unshod."

I was back at the window. I hate and love it
when Trixie's right. It's always good for a fight
and adrenaline, then a cuddle in love's pit.
A cuddle, a kiss, a grunt, a love bite.

Outside, the cardinals were guarding each other.
One ate whatever delight lay about;
the other hopped limb to limb in hover.
Me, I didn't know whether to weep or shout.

"Hey, cheer up, lover. You've gained a daughter.
Let's celebrate. Wanna undo my anklet?"
Seize the day! Pixie's right, we're all fodder.
Alive and supple, I bent with a thanklet

though clenching my butt, fearing a Trixie spanklet.

Chapter Fifteen: Mace takes a place.
Implosion or explosion?

It's the middle of the week, folks, and C
and Hank have sneaked off to the rancho,
which isn't yet legally his, you see.
It's midday; Sol's doing a real dance. O

yes, the old man (speaking of which) holds plenty
of hydrogen to twirl romantic tangos
and romp the sky while acting twenty.
Hey look, the weird old guy is spinning fandangos;

that fits, since Hank and C below are preparing
to wrangle. Hank took off a personal day,
in case you wonder. But Carmen is faring
on govern-mint time: she needs the pay.

She's at the rancho because life's too sinister
for her and L back at. The creep hasn't been
again—they think!—but neither can minister
the least normal function, for fear he'll spin again.

L takes her undies and clothes to work to change;
C carries her Walther to the bathroom.
And Hank was right; the condo owner's made it plain
they both can break sub-lease, even soon, even June.

(That word again! How convenient for rhyme,
how convenient for me when I weary,
but most convenient when it's just that time!)
"Hank, this place glows so huge and cheery—"

C paused to study the polished stairwell;
she hadn't seen one since Santa Fe.

She fancied descending in queenly farewell—
envisioned tripping, so her mirth gave way.

"Why laugh?" asked Hank, on giving her a look.
"Those stairs. It's good I was born Mex, not Southern belle."
"Just as well. They're mostly dumb, drizzly and forsook."
"All that moss and Dixie give their brains a swell.

"But Hank, do tell: can you afford this place?"
Hank grinned. "I performed a Scout's good deed,
helped an old lady pick up spilt flour and mace.
Told her I thought mace was a small WMD.

"She said no, she was baking cookies and cake.
We stopped nearby to have coffee and tea—"
"Dirty old man, always on the make."
"Old's right. She'd lived here thirty years, you see,

before Groves and Oppenheimer set twenty toes
on this mesa. Groves anyway. Oppy'd
ridden Boy's Ranch before the Trinity explos-
ion. The old gal's memory-electrons had copied

each year into her brain. She spun some dirt
about Los Alamos wives, especially Kitty."
"Kitty?"
            "Oppy's mostly only main skirt.
While he piddled, she sang her own special ditty."

"Behind each genius a woman lies screwing 'round."
"Thank Sagan's billion stars I'm no genius then.
Well, my old gal kept getting older. She found
herself collapsed one day in her den.

"Took her twelve hours to stand and make a call.
Decided to move to her daughter's back East.
I helped her sell her things, donate, pack up, and all,
kept this house on market ten months, at least.

"At last she thought to sell it dead cheap to me
so she'd cut free. Her daughter teaches
in Carolina, at Duke University—"
"Not Harvard, but grows cherries and peaches,"

said Carmen. "Once I wanted to double major
in history and Mom's Spanish . . ."
                                        "You still could," said Hank.
". . . or math," mused C dreamily. Hank didn't phase her.
"But this sub-sub spy job gave all that a yank.

"I'm not a very good spy, you know, else
I'd never have spouted. When our jobs were formed,
most real spies were all taken. 'Sno wonder I squelch."
C stopped. "So, Landlord Hank, we'll rent your dorm."

"That's swell. Consider all the land your spa
and walk those Doberman pups; they warn of snakes
according to Dave's talky old pa,
who's kicking Dave out here. We'll both be rakes."

"No chance of that, you're much too sweet.
On second thought, Lorrie does love *Star Trek*."
"But her sci-fi is all TV. She never reads."
"A scholar," Carmen teased. "No common fleck."

She moved to tickle Hank, on spying a whisker.
"You mentioned this old gal left her antique bed?"
C leaned and gave one hair a tug, to whisper,
"Four posts and thick mattresses go straight to my head."

Our young Hank needed no ray gun to point
and burn what Carmen's mint-breath whisper meant.
They climbed the stairs like some Wild West joint.
Not Victorian, not Southern, but heaven-sent.

C dropped her heels with a lime green thunk.
At last! she thought. *I won't really try*
for Teller's H-bomb, just a common ordnance whump.
They kissed, slurped, tangled and tangoed. Quite high

they flew within eight minutes, and one second—
my watch, remember?—then seismic occurred.
The house shook, one post's ball fell—cherry I reckon.
"Santa Maria!"
                    "Holy Robert Heinlein!"
                                        Words

reflecting—not what was on their minds
or bods, but that little panic button
we keep reserved for times when fortune blinds
us, right in both bad eyes, and ruins our ruttin'.

Each gathered an old lady sheet, Hank's green,
C's yellow: the old gal's colors weren't mellow.
They rushed to the window to see what could be seen.
"An explosion? Carrot-colored, but more yellow?"

"*Im*plosion, hued like marigolds and the sun.
Remember I'm a spy and trained to observe.
Took me four days of movies, was almost fun."
"Implosion, explosion, atomic swerve—

something bad."

        With one grand sigh Carmen dressed.
"Wha—?" Hank asked.

          "A good spy should never snooze.
Come ride," she trilled, giving Hank no rest.
He donned shirt, jeans, and shoes. "What's there to lose?"

Just your life, the four-post bed might have said,
being well acquainted with tricks of those labs
on the hill. Two Japanese cities left dead.
But beds keep mum, like mortuary slabs;

still, Hank voiced doubts: "Those pencil heads
leave my brain folds loose. They dwarf sci-fi
with bombs and whirligigs they spread."
"You're right, my hero. Life here flies much too high.

"Atomic's passe, though. Come with, don't wonder why."

*Chapter Sixteen: Hank left—almost—
dry and wondering why;
some boy talk that for once doesn't boast;
the new girl on the block sneaks by*

The marigold ruckus glowed full six miles away.
Took them twenty sun minutes to drive there,
where Carmen's badge got past the MP's okay,
but Hank was left to stand, alone, sans rocking chair.

Now, Carmen's clearance was really quite low,
but her department showed so new, her badge so blue
that the MP—daydreaming of Donna's last show—
let Carmen drive on through. Hank stayed with his two shoes

and four cold beers. The MP and he became buds.
"Listen up, guy, this damn place is weird."
The MP pointed with his can of cold suds.
"Toward where she's driving, the sky seared

like napalm in reverse. Lord knows what these brains
have up. Left to me, we'd use arrows and bows;
the Indians were right."
                              " 'Cept arrows couldn't dent trains."
"There is that. Hey, I see you at Donna's shows."

The MP and Hank regarded Carmen's tailpipes.
"I know! You work the loading dock, 'mI right?"
"Five years."
                    "Don't mean to piss and moan, sail gripes,
but no way I'll stay. This place stings like fright night.

"Today makes thrice this crap has happened.
The colors get mixed. Orange today, four days back
glowed green. Two weeks ago—give me a slap and
whack if this ain't true: blue poured to black.

"That time was worst: a King Kong blob
that acted magnetic."
                Hank raised his eyes
and downed his beer.
                "No shit, guy. My heartthrob
went fritz and swirled like hungry swarms of flies.

"It's what I mean about this place and weird."
A car approached, the MP handed Hank his beer.
Hank turned aside until the car was cleared,
to wonder, *Am I dumb to have no fear?*

The oldster on her rancho had jammed his ear full,
and other than the sexual peccadilloes,
not a one of her stories struck him as cheerful:
Scientists grew snouts like armadillos,

lab workers turned green; limbs fattened, then shrunk;
faces slipped to putty; arms dropped, hair fell.
He recalled her saying, "One year the whole place stunk."
Surely some rumors were bunk. But how to tell?

"Your boss," the MP said.
                "Hanson?" Hank's hand
a fist did make: 'twas quite histrionic.
The MP, staying on track, remained bland.
"Him and that brain in sub-zero electronics

have showed all three damned times. Hey, I thought
his name was Manson."

Hank laughed.

"Got two

more beers."

"Better not. Might get caught.

You know, I saw that creep and creep son Blue

at *Sangre del* in Santa Fe a month ago.
Heard they'd been slapping some young woman.
My friend walked out to better see the show."
"Not to stop them?"

"My friend's pretty low, man.

"I came later, or I'd've—hell, I don't know.
Manson Senior's a tough hombre in a scratch,
I hear."

"Maybe. His son's not so very so.

A skinny guy I know left his face a thatch."

Our Hank, of course, was talking of himself
but thought best not to spread that truth about.
Some matters should stay on a dusty shelf.
Now there's one truth you *can* go out and shout.

The sky where C had gone seemed to pulse.
Hank glanced at his tiny cooler and its beer.
"Here's this: the reason women treat men like mulch
is that men keep slappin' 'em with their spears."

"There is that," the MP replied. "As long
as we are trotting philosophical, I'll
take your one more cold beer. Would be dead wrong
to spin so fine and stay bone-dry the while."

Hank went to his cooler, brought back two beers,
poured one in a coffee mug from that damned Taos.
"I went there once," the MP said as Hank called, "Cheers."
"Spent two week's pay on a recuerdo for Ma so's

she'd feel fancy over Saint Francis and his birds.
The rest went for beer, two tacos and whiskey."
They stared at the pulsing sky, saying no words.
"You think she's safe?"

                "Your woman? It's risky

"for all in this damned place. Hey, you know,
that Manson left from Santa Fe with a Mex who
swung underage hair bleached like rock star shows.
She flashed a da-glo orange dress and bright blue shoes.

"Manson and that sub-zero freak—Strychnine?"
"Strickland."

            "Yeah, the one who's over by the glow.
They wobbled her out like some Texas two-step line."
The MP paused. "Scared kid, putting on a show.

"You know, I got a theory about people."
Both he and Hank gulped beer for thought's pure sake.
"Aping someone is like climbing a steeple.
You might make it up, but where's your take?

"There's only air. And when you reach for it
you fall, and down you spin—to drop, ker-splat!
I mean that Mex kid. Be proud of your own bit,
remain aground, avoid ker-splat!, know where you're at.

Hank studied the pulsing sky. "There is, indeed, that."

❈ ❈ ❈

When Carmen came on site, there were
twenty-one people. No film on observation
distilled that number; her counting came in a whir.
One lipstick dab, she joined, no reservation.

Despite small breasts, she'd learned from dearest Mom
that mincing earns you *nada,* just trash. Brash,
however, earns you queen of prom.
So twenty-two (with her) watched a marigold flash

that pulsed. Dad Hanson and the sub-zero guy—
his name may have been Strickman—stood aside.
She edged close by to keep an open ear and eye.
Strickwhat held clasped a long black box at side.

A prairie dog stuck its head from a hole
then flip-flop tumbled up on the ground,
was pushed—or pulled—to be absorbed by marigold,
which turned deep purple to give a snapping sound.

Yum! Carmen feared it just may have said.
But yet its snap had come so quick and cold
that no emotion truly could be read;
its rumble tolled primeval old.

All twenty-one moved back. C gladly joined.
Such choice no more stayed with yon prairie dog.
C noticed Dad Hanson flipping a coin.
Stricksong laughed and whacked Dad's back a flog.

Whatever their joke, it spun out mean, un-nice.
Strickdick meandered up to give a Cheshire grin.
"A gal got near enough, that thing would clean her lice."
"A prick got near enough, his balls would spin."

"Say, you I like. I won the toss with my good pal
to come and talk with a pretty señorita."
Strickland nudged Carmen's purse. "Heavy for a gal."
"Filled with tequila and ground beef tortillas."

"Cal Strickland's my name. You work on the hill?"
"Sort of. Carmen Brown's mine. Your eyes are green."
"Well, Ms. Sort-of-Brown, I'd perch on your sill
and bat my green just to hop in your dream."

"Maybe we'll meet at Todd's."
                              "Santa Fe's my town.
Sangre del Toro if you ever slip that way."
Strickland's black box burbled. He looked down
then raised a finger. "Gotta go. Wish I could stay."

C exhaled and frowned. She'd had to hold
her breath, a smell so odd moved 'round the man.
If cinnamon could sour or take on mold,
that would the ticket fit. One-year-old Easter ham?

She guessed he wore a sachet aphrodisiac
like crazed Cubano lovesick males. *Change it out, bud.
The present way things hang, you smell sad sack.*
Correcting herself she thought, *He's a loutish crud.*

She watched the marigold glow, still plain.
Its pulse stayed hypnotic, mesmerizing:
a rattlesnake's tail, a monsoon rain.
Bam! Lightning strikes when you're fantasizing.

She felt sand sting her arms and eyes and face,
as if some mean long wind gave blow. But clouds stayed still.
Each stinging grain of sand made fast to race
for marigold like prairie dog: sans any will.

C shielded her eyes to find Dad Hanson.
In this crowd he cut a figure still. Was why
her young mom had found him so handsome,
C guessed. His droopy boxer's eye,

as many worry lines as beggars have
in Nuevo Laredo, made marks. Standing away
was Devins, her hair stacked mean red, no salve,
the mother to the kid Lorrie'd saved that day

back when. C's winding thoughts were soon cut short
by screams. A bone white purse tumbled in spin.
A woman jumped and Strickland gave snort.
C had no doubt, the woman was thin:

she would have joined the prairie dog and marigold
if some fat guy had not made lurch to tackle.
One more grabbed him, so both took hold.
The purse, a blur, spun out toward the jackal,

which gnashed bright orange flames. C began to regard
it as *lagarto tuerto*, that one-eyed lizard
her mom had warned would snatch small girls who left the yard,
to lug beneath a rock and feed his gizzard.

Five people now held the gal in daisy-chain.
As Strickland toyed about his long black box,
a sixth joined in. They tugged, they strained
to hold thin her from slipping off like frayed old socks.

A bang! *Lagarto tuerto* turned purple first,
then black, then disappeared. Sand dropped, along
with the human chain. A hush like a hearse
fell wide. That Easter ham sour smell came strong.

Had it emitted from a box silver and blue
resembling R2D2 of *Star Wars* fame?
That box did whir and tumble out a few
clacks. But C thought it a red herring in the game.

The truth? Did it lie in that oblong box Strickland
toted?
     "Show's over, folks!" shouted Hanson.
Why would these twenty brains heed a creep from hick land?
She wished him hung on some gallows transom,

then shook her head at that un-daughterly thought.
But she could not stop. Now wishing him shriven—
a niggle warned that Strickland and his box ought
to be included—she also wished him riven.

Hey, Reader! Today's the day twelve years ago
when Camille Paglia published her epic tome,
Revelations. Trixie gave that one a go.
Just mentioned the fact so's this chapter'd end high-toned.

Not sure why I give care: our globe's a low war zone.

Chapter Seventeen: Some thoughts on when to piddle, when to diddle, and when Fate leaves you plunking a fiddle

"Not bad," said Trixie, strolling in the door.
"Want to give hand with our groceries?
Kroger ran shrimp on special. Small chore
first, though: your last chapt. made me think of hosiery.

"Wanna know why?"
                                I followed her to the carport.
Maybe not Trixie, maybe a Pixie mood,
I hoped. The sway of her hips stayed hard to sort.
"Why?" I took her bait, already nailed on the rood.

"Why? Contra my advice no rocket did explode,
but glowing lizards, whew, that worked out creepy.
We both know you're the expert on Los Alamos.
But Joe, you left me and every woman weepy."

She put down two sacks and turned.
                                        "You wore
that blouse to Kroger's?!" My eyes doopsy-diddled
at cleavage: 'twas Armageddon and more.
I pulled out shrimp, 8-count; they squiggled.

"Bag boys get lonesome too. They need some cheer.
If I display two lumens from my light bulbs,
so what to you? Some boy'll just go trim his spear."
She bared dark nipples; I took two gulps.

"See what I mean, old man? They're both still here.
But let's get back to that last chapt. you wrote."

I sensed a Dixie emerging and I feared.
Too bad, my own spear had started to bloat.

She marched sharp steps at me. I dropped the shrimp;
they hit and plopped.
        "Joe, you are such a sop!"
Came time to stand for manhood, not be a wimp.
"Why?" I whined, manhood slipping a-flop.

She shouted, "Why? It's been over two months,
and far as I can tell, not C, H, D, or L
has got it on. Don't you want your daughter to hump?"
"She's not my daughter!"
        "Joe, you're a hard sell.

"But in three months, September . . ." She stopped.
"You'll see. Well, write on, spinning your old man
pace. But the onliest one whose pants have dropped
is the creep stalking Carmen. It was a good plan

to move them out to Hank's two-story house.
Who is the creep, anyway? Blue? His dad?"
Was my turn to snort. I pointed to her blouse.
"As nipples peep, so does the creep. He's bad,

"for now that's all I'll say. Hey, let's blacken
these shrimp. I'm in the mood for spicy."
"So are C, H, D, and L. Cut 'em some slack and
let 'em fuck. Unless that word rings too dicey.

"Hey, wanna know why I hope the creep's not fat?"
Of course mad Dixie did not wait for my reply.
" 'Cause I hope Lorrie gets out your old baseball bat—
Linda gave it to her. Doesn't that make you sigh?

"— and gives him whacks that break some bone.
If he was fat, they'd just splat and leave him blue."
She tapped the shrimp. "And blackened."

I moaned.

"Just get them in bed, Joe. Can characters sue?"

"What the hell? Sue? For not enough legs-spread
time? You want me to lump them all at once
in the old gal's cherry four-poster bed?"
"Want *me* to invite Tony over for a bunch

of blackened shrimp and cuddly squiggles?"
"Always you bring that guy up at crisis time."
"Jealous and old," she sang-song giggled.
"Tequila with the shrimp. I'll cut the lime."

Dixie, Trixie, Pixie: I wish they'd take up mime.

Chapter Eighteen: C visits the morgue
where she finds reason rhymeless, hard to absorb

Carmen entered her blue Sentra
after checking its back seat for any creep.
—Just two more days until they gave Hank's entra.
(That word! This car's rhyme throws out far too deep

for any other.) Yes, C holds worries galore
what with the stalker and the talk she and
Hank had after *lagarto tuerto's* encore
of purse, long daisy chain, and all that blasting sand.

Hank told her what the MP had relayed
concerning Strickland and her parental bond
(whose bio-secret also kept her frayed)
both leaving Santa Fe with a teenage bleach blonde

in blue Tex Mex slippers. The bleach-blonde part got her.
Was something she'd not told Hank. (Along with
half the source of her genes and just whose daughter,
this meaning Hanson's, she was. A truth with sad pith!)

How many, she began to wonder
bleach-blonde Tex Mex girls roamed the entire Southwest?
Three? Twelve? That Hanson sodded even one under
gave gash to her brain and left it no rest.

So she requested one more look at the corpse
still kept on ice, just down in Santa Fe.
Today would make C's first trip to a morgue;
one of the white-tie four had business that way,

so he would go with. Was the macho named Ted,
but *la cucaracha* cannot always choose

what crumb to nibble, *Madre* often said.
Still, Carmen dreaded what bluster he'd use.

She picked up Ted at his "secret rendezvous."
He wore a tie so white; he swirled a secret sign
from page 19 of their Spy Manual spew.
It made her want to chug—lots stronger than wine.

"After the morgue, let's go get tamales.
I know a place that's grand. We'll charge it to account
since we're on business, right?"
                                    "Ted, gollies,
Tex-Mex after *cadáver* sounds tough to surmount."

"Don't laugh. The coroner's mom owns the place.
The local joke is how he freshly grinds her beef."
Ted went for somber, re-arranging his face,
resembling Medusa in bas-relief.

"So, how'd you get assigned this dead girl case?
You're new to the department, after all,
and she's priority. Think it's her race?"
"Oh, Ted. Our department's like the latest mall,

so every store within is spanking new."
"Wow, *spanking's* such a word, don't you think?"
"Ted, oh Ted, you hot ladies' man, you."
"Just trying out some chat. Don't raise no stink.

"And still, you didn't answer back, did you?"
"What? Her race? No, I don't think it's just her race.
She was dumped outside Restricted in quite plain view."
"A message? If you're a Mex, keep off this place?"

Brown Carmen inhaled. "Ted, you make it hard not to
veer this car's right side into a telephone pole."
"I know. My three friends think I really got to
find a woman who would give me soul.

"Say! What if me and you—"
                              "Careful, a pole's
ahead. Besides, I have a boyfriend."
"Him, I've seen. *My* opinion? His squat role's
too fake for you. Pretends to be a rear end

"entry type, him and his motor bike."
"Ted, both you and your tie are amazing."
"You think? You think maybe some girl could like—?"
"My eyes stay peeled."
                          "I'm not just star-gazing?"

Ted hit his fist to palm. *Might life no longer flop?*
C punched her car's radio, but it stayed broke.
She cursed she hadn't taken it to shop.
Result? One hour of listening to this lame yolk.

It passed, however, as hours are fated
to do. They parked at the mortuary building,
where some guy with a gray beard un-sated
Bogarted a cigar, a statue unyielding

that grinned teeth-yellow to Ted. "Great! Got my check?
Keeping young señorita froze for all this month
has left my workers and my morgue a wreck."
"She's got it."
                    The morguemeister rolled his blunt—

was cheap, machine made, Carmen gave note.
"Well, Miss, she's thawed out pretty as a desert rose.

Can't understand why I didn't get your vote;
I do—"

    "Our guy's homeopath, uses his nose."

Carmen wished she had a cigar to roll
like morguemeister did at what Ted just said.
"Um, I think 'osteopath's' the word." *You troll,*
she added mentally.

    "Was just messing your heads,

"Homeopaths are homosexual.
That's why I added the bit about the nose.
Just like a woman, ain't it? To get textual?"
The troll was fishing for bonding, C supposed,

but Herr Morguemeister wouldn't bite, just gave
his cigar a tap, as if it were lit.
"My name's Carmen Brown. Ted's the guy who raves;
I'm the chick with your check. Let's all hit

the morgue soon as the DC doctor shows."
"He's here. Been flirting with my assistant
one hour at least."

    Ted gave a honk with his nose:
"Takes him an hour? She must be resistant

"or else he's un-handsome and un-charming."
"My assistant's a he, and so is the doc.
Times are a-changing. Don't mean to be alarming
but cool the fag jokes. My assistant's a jock

"from U of Colorado's football team."
C grinned delighted; she handed over the check.
"Hey, oughta wait till we see the goods. I mean—"
"A little trust can reach quite far."

    "Yeah, show respect."

In walked the three. The walls glowed white; C's nose
gave lift. No flowers. *Well, of course,* she thought.
It smells hospital, not funeral home pose.
Sure 'nough, the Doc and jock got caught

mid-giggle. *I should write about the dominance
of wiggling.* Which thought reminded C of Hank.
"Ready?"
      "Ready."
          "Ready."
               "Ready."
                    "Let's prance."
Was Ted who said that last. C gave him a yank

to whisper, "Now's the time to practice
on having soul. Pretend that I'm your date."
The poor guy turned rigid, a Saguaro cactus.
Surprised her: she'd judged his ego could just inflate.

On seeing the corpse, C discombobulated.
The bleach-blonde hair had stayed as straight,
but Señorita must have ovulated
and gained thirty pounds in water weight.

"Is this the wrong corpse, but in the right dress?"
"Remember, I'm your date," Ted noted.
"I went first response. She weighed thirty pounds less.
Now she looks to be a grade-schooler, bloated."

MM and DC doc both gave out wheezes.
"We should, maybe, re-weigh her now, in case.
Wrong corpse would make a fine be-jesus;
one should never take anything at face."

Herr MM replied, "My lady friend would approve.
She's always harping how life blows tricky."
With scalpel he cut his cigar in a groove.
"Mike here's met her; he thinks she's a pixie."

Together, the two docs rolled the table
to a far wall, where red arrows on a scale
awaited. "When here at first, I was unable
to weigh a corpse alone. Arms, heads, and legs would flail.

"Now I just give a pinkie nudge and roll . . ."
As Herr MM demonstrated, the table slipped;
the corpse's right leg toppled a steel bowl,
from which dark blue liquid spilled and dripped.

The leg then wanged the floor with one harsh thud.
Herr MM lisped, "Pride goeth before each fall."
With grunts, the three men hefted the corpse like a spud.
"I heard a bone go crack."

                         "May be. Will be your call,

"though I already ascertained the cause of death:
suffocation."

            "Strangulation?"

                       "Nope, no bruises.
Just some *love taps*, as my predecessor, bereft
of politesse, charm, and other social uses

"was always fond to comment. Good thing
my fine sweet lady friend never did hear
him pluck that chauvinist banjo string.
She'd've belted him a Dixie rebel jeer."

The girl's dead butt stuck up in cooling air.
"One hundred thirty-two pounds. Sixty kilos even."

The MM lifted a chart and sat in a chair.
"This figure comes hard to believe in:

"says she weighed thirty-one pounds less
when we brought her in."
                         "Maybe a tech tube-
fed her, so she'd fit her funeral dress,"
the one named Mike let slip.
                         "Maybe some local rube

broke in and made to rape, against her dead will,
got her prego." This of course from Ted.
"You two aren't very funny."
                         "She's right. Chill."
MM slapped the butt as if putting it to bed.

In return, Juanita Doe let out a fart.
The four males giggled. "For shame, young lady,
this place is sacred, you're acting the tart,
you shouldn't spoon out gasses like gravy."

Then, damned if the DC doc didn't bend to sniff.
C looked at Ted, who looked at the doc,
who looked at the morguemeister—a real riff—
who looked at the assistant, who checked the wall's clock.

Tick-tock is precisely how it went.
And went and went until the greasy hand of fate,
disguised as one fat blowfly, was sent.
With a pop, MM hit the blowfly's pate—

or so it seemed, for the wounded creature
away did flit. "Cinnamon," the DC doc said,
his nose still on the corpse. "At least your
freezer preserves smell. I'll need to open that head."

From the land of zero DC whisked a scalpel
to give the girl's poor stomach a slice.
Carmen dropped like Newton's apple.
Falling into Mike's muscles would've been nice,

but she fell against Ted. Just as well, for he fell
against her, and for them both, things got blurred. . . .

Chapter Nineteen: a G-String Interlude

Let's leave them propped, Doric pillars on the Acrop,
for a min or so. We need to talk of heavy water.
Was good the Germans couldn't make it, or slaughter
might have purged grandparents a-plenty. We oughter
be thankful Nazidom's quest to blow uranium came to naught or
those fine grandparents' fine sons and daughters
(better ID'ed as our moms and pops)
could never have diddled out you and me. And we're no sops.
Yes, enriched Deutsch uranium might have put us to a stop,
if Hitler and pals had launched V-2s to make a drop
of, say, Big and Little Schatsie. Well, my German slop
would have improved, and I do like schnapps.
But Big and Little Boy were left to Los Alamos
where every finger and most the toes
(Except for Kitty Opp's, whose curled where, who knows?)
worked on defeating Krauts and sending death throes
to Japs. Yep, that completed the big show:
Yankee know-all drubbing out, blow-by-blow,
utilitarian logic and research persistent,
like some Medieval mystery play's rhyme insistent,
to leave listeners numb and un-resistant
to life's overall mishmash of sadness consistent.
'O send us,' that play might shout, 'a saving host!'
But Trinity was no no-see-um religious ghost,
'twas an atom bomb site where a host
of sand got spun to glass
and on consequent a host of Nips lost their ass.
Whoa! You think those rhymes racist and crass?
Hell, you ever seen an atom bomb blast?

That, Reader dear, defines both racist and crass.
It lends these slurs and rhymes vague hope of class.

    So, here's where G-string shuffles on in.
The G-string's not scarlet, silken, and thin.
No, I fear, mariner dear, that no blue sin
will slink up or slip out again.
And if any spirit sticks its snout within
'twill be Shiva or Satan, bounding with a grin,
since Strickland—that name ring a bell?—
has concocted a weapon so darned swell
it could be used to furrow hell—
or if not that fairy place, at least plow a show-and-tell
blood-deep within some worrisome third world land
 and force it to halt any impoverished demand,
to stop its sniveling o'er starving babes and
prego moms ground down to sand.

    But on to Strickland; let's quit this rave.
S is searching out a brand new wave,
a taming of gravity to brand it slave.
He's got some help and lots, hooray,
just like in good ol' pre-atom days
when Los Alamos wives crunched numbers on clacking
computers so their hubbies' big brains could keep on racking
approaches to the one and only grand ka-whacking
and crisp up some humans in that Land of the Rising Sun.
Prez Truman claimed himself the responsible one,
dismissing fretting scientists and their White House petition.
He claimed those burnt cities were his sole decision,
the "buck stopping here" remaining his true vision.
Why then, did we hold trials at Nuremburg?
Hadn't Hitler already glurged his bunker's final glurg?
Didn't the deutschmark stop with his dying whines?

Oh mariner, you can ring this with the loudest of chimes:
Only losers get charged with any war crimes.
Did Sherman stand judgment in Civil War Times?

    More later, for my rhyme's starting to melt.
To back up, Strickland indeed has help.
Devins and McGuire float in the kelp—
the parents of that wayward boy whom L saved from self.
Strickland dubs their project "The G-String Theory."
Now, that letter G doesn't mean girlie, girdle, or god.
It means Gravity.
Gravity held the key.
As you've seen from the purse that did flee
and the prairie dog that went whee,
S might be onto more than a Mall shopping spree.

    So what I mean to relay to conclude
this dilly-dally three-page interlude
is that Professor Strickland was the dude
who led Los Alamos to again develop an attitude
that again might create something . . . Truly Rude.

Chapter Twenty: Back to the stiff, the boring, the obnoxious, and the bored

. . . when C came to against the Ted, she felt unwell.
DC stared down to the gut-slit. "We need a word."

Couple it with a blow, C, recalling Shakespeare's
play, thought. Was it *Romeo and Juliet*?
Not happening here: except for the two gay dears
no amatory advance was dancing yet.

DC inserted his scalpel into the gut;
Herr Morguemeister leaned, then dropped his cigar.
C forced herself to look into the flux.
Tapioca beads that had turned to tar:

that best bright thought was all she could muster.
Did this dead girl have TB, VD, breast cancer?
Though Ted still stood groggy and sans bluster,
was he who formed a question wanting answer:

"How come her cells are fat and black? Is it because
she's done been froze?"
                                  The three med men each shook a head.
Carmen, untaught in cold cadaver laws,
felt Ted's surmise fit just the size. Instead

of films on corpse and autopsy rot,
her classes focused on drug paraphernalia.
She reasoned, after all, such would help her spot
the dealers and users, amidst their regalia.

Morguemeister spoke: "32 years, I've never seen
the like. Please, Mike, go fetch some tweezers.
This girl's much too young and thin—"

"Her spleen?"
"Don't mind us, son, we're just poor medical geezers."

"Just thought I'd throw suggestions in the pot.
Didn't mean to stomp your old guy toes—"
       "Ted, our date,
remember?" Carmen blinked, exuding hot.
A fool's dumbo stop—could she have worse fate?

C sadly pictured finding this dead girl,
In company of a nice guy who'd since transferred.
He'd lit two cigars, a regular Milton Berle.
She'd taken one; did not care how absurd

she looked; the girl, stone dead, would not complain.
"I could have opened a pizza parlor,"
the guy had said.
    "You Italian?"
       "No, plain
New York. With pizza pies there'd be no horror."

While squatting there he gave his cigar loads of twists.
"Those long thin fingers, take a look, would you?
She could've been a concert pianist."
Now C looked down: they nestled plump and partly blue.

The assistant named Mike returned with tweezers
and what to C seemed some mechanical thing
Don Walker'd use to etch his tourist-pleasers,
his crystals radiating goofball New Age bling.

Would standing here with these four doofuses
make her pudenda sprout a tiny extension,
bounce out a pink rude prick? Nickname it Rufus?
Che sera. Carmen had no intention

of becoming a half-baked undertaker . . .
A cinnamon whiff gave halt to her reverie.
MM stood pinching those tweezers like the Maker
bewailing his latest cosmic flop: *I'll be . . .*

will my creatin' ever flip just one thing right?
"That cinnamon again," DC twitched at the stink.
"This girl was soured apple pie she'd fit right in."
MM popped the tweezers and gave a wink.

Joke away, Carmen thought. *Jokes fight the sight*
of clammy young-girl skin. Sir Death awaits us all.
At danza*'s end, we shuffle off in two-step blight.*
So laugh until the fiddler gives last call.

C left dank thoughts on hearing three puffed clinks.
MM and DC were butting apelike pates,
dislodging black tapioca cells from high brinks,
all pulled from J Doe's corpse to drop onto a plate.

"You hear that ring? I wonder how—"
"Let's climb it six centis higher . . ."
Each crumpled his best gorilla doc brow,
while Ted and Mike stood by to admire

how science, how reason could never rest.
MM grabbed a chair to climb altitudinal
and give a regal tug to his corduroy vest.
His plink would have been tuneful attitudinal

if its plunk had not plunked so rat-tat flat.
"Wisdom comes dropping from giants' shoulders,"
be-tied Ted said, "to render things so ker-splat that—"
C gave a sniff: "They thud like falling boulders."

Good news, though! Unless they found a Wal-Mart ladder,
MM attained stratospheric pre-eminence.
C helped him down, to save his old-guy bladder.
"My thanks. This place hasn't seen a live woman since

"Helen Gurley Brown and *Cosmo* made girls badder,
even maybe before ye olde big bombs got dropped."
Carmen curtsied and Mike began to jabber,
"And we complain feminine grace has stopped."

Replied C, "You know, you *could* bring your girlfriend—"
"Trixie?"

       "—Yes. Down here. Decorum seems a flop."
The one named Mike declared: "That tiger would blend
on in. No tellin' what a-bomb she'd drop."

C asked, "Do tell me, MM. Did you learn
Any so ever from perching on that chair?"
"Oh yes. Each metric byte of knowledge must be earned.
First, gasses rise. Señorita's fart still hangs there."

MM twisted his nose toward the ceiling.
"Second, something's deadly wrong, but what it is
escapes me here. You, Doctor, have a feeling
on the matter?"

       DC, too, stayed a-tiz.

No wonder, Carmen realized. He'd been pinched
by Mike.

       "Let's open up the old pineapple,"
DC said, starting his roto-saw sans flinch.
But it was no go. Mike bent to grapple

the loosened cord, while giving a charming wiggle.
Our C looked down to see where it got plugged;

the roto-saw buzzed, DC let out a giggle,
MM gave cough. All in all, C felt mugged.

A brass drain stood nearby on the floor.
Un-etherized, impatient, and sans table,
she didn't care to learn what that drain was for;
So sick of this visit, she hoped she'd be able

to keep her simian legs upright. Why couldn't
she have stayed with history? That tall prof fellow,
Doc Gentsch, almost had her convinced, but she wouldn't,
because in Third Reich class he'd let out a bellow

reminding her of . . . what she didn't know.
Psychology then? Math? English? Some major
that might remove her from this morgue's sad glow?
No, that's wrong-headed thinking, a futile wager.

Was soon she noticed señorita's blood oozing
for the brass drain in the floor. All said, this day
would send her home a-sighing and boozing.
Best looming scene? Her Hank and she could play.

The saw made buzz at poor señorita's head,
C took in acrid whiffs of burning flesh.
Turned out the brain too held gobs of black, not red.
C remembered World Lit. and Gilgamesh:

through waters dark he swam to fetch unending life.
Mi Madre Dios, whoever would want it?
Juanita Doe here was lucky to leave the strife—
Damn, this morgue must be totally haunted

with black light vibes. Dear Lorrie, lend me your crystal.
As C looked on, the girl's skullcap slipped neatly off.

C touched the comfort of her purse and pistol.
In Mike's palm the skullcap wobbled, politely doffed.

"Thirty-two years," MM repeated.
"That cinnamon," DC offered again.
To Carmen, the room pressed super-heated,
not with ideas, but with death's lean grin.

One hour later, two docs, one assistant concurred:
señorita had died of suffocation.
" 'Course, that's what we all die of," DC observed.
"There were anomalies," MM made notation.

"I'm hungry," Ted said as MM slipped off a glove.
"My mom's having a carne special today,"
MM offered.
                "That's one woman I just love,"
Mike the assistant said. "Beef makes me gay."

Herr MM was a glove-snapper most alarmin'.
Four snaps and one grand pop for each Latex glove.
His showmanship, C thought, was hardly charmin'.
Damn, get Trixie in here fast to spread some love.

At that precise moment the front door went whack.
In stepped a redhead petite and oh so pretty
that even the two gays gave time some slack
to toss a look.
                "God, this place smells shitty,"

the redhead said. "Been burning cinnamon
buns in your clavicle scalpel sterilizer?"
The three med guys gave a laugh as if one;
C and Ted looked at each other, none the wiser.

"My dear, do you mean the autoclave?" DC said.
This new bombshell turned. "And just who are you,
besides someone who wants to give Mike head?"
So much, C thought, for women bringing a slew

of decorum to this wasteland of a morgue.
The brass drain gurgled as Señorita's blood
went washing, a flash flood in a gorge.
'Twas being scooted along by happy suds.

The redhead heard the noise and rolled an eye.
"Your mother says come on over for lunch.
She's got a new dish she wants us all to try:
cordero en empanada. My hunch?

"She's stretching toward some sick morgue joke:
lamb-baked-in-pie, like that poor girl, *que no*?
Your mom's raised donations though, so don't stroke;
a tombstone, a Mass, a priest will see Señorita go.

"Say, did you learn anything by dicing her up?"
"There are some anomalies," muttered MM.
Mike added, "Suffocation made her belly-up."
"A cinnamon overdose may have done her in."

At DC's last words, the redhead groaned. "Had it?"
Confused, C did not know, at first, she was addressed.
The blowfly'd restarted its hypnotic bad flit.
"I asked if you've had it. Or are you impressed?"

When Carmen waved her palm over her head,
the redhead rumbled a laugh, "You, I like.
But these four males? Sour zombies among the dead."
"Hey, not me!" Ted gave his nose a hike.

"A metaphor, doofus," the redhead said. "Nice tie.
Your mom pick it?" The redhead gave a tug
to Ted's pink shirt. His eyes zoomed cherry pie,
his feet went stumbling, on a non-existent rug.

The redhead searched her oversize purse
for lipstick so silver-tubed it glittered,
an armor-piercing bullet. But worse
was the ice that tinted each thin lip embittered.

"So you rode down from Los Alamos with
this tie guy?"
    C gave a nod.
      "Poor Babe, you
stand here, an innocent stuck in some bad male myth.
Stay, eat Mom's lamb pie and I'll fade you

"a buck donation for that poor girl's burial.
Mom keeps a charity jug by her register.
Fifty bucks more, the local nuns will turn feral
and dance St. Olga's jig for that wayward cur."

Ted leaned to whisper, "Will the department pay
since it's work-related? Every buck counts
in these dark days."
    Carmen tiptoed to sway.
She really wanted to give Ted a bounce;

instead she turned toward that female red hair to say,
"Can we just follow after you, behind?
Although, lamb pie seems too bland a mainstay.
I need piled habanero to make me blind."

As C spoke, her upper thought was punishment;
In this she shared Laerte's filial dream.

Carmen! Go eat, yet heed Hamlet's admonishment:
Give each man just dessert, who'd 'scape whipping cream?

So gobble lamb, swill tequila, don't scream.

Chapter Twenty-one: Trixie takes a minute
to add her comments of late.
Also, she India inks a calendar date,
and lo! your author's in it

Sweet Trixie'd gone clothes-shopping for her work.
She walked in modeling a green short skirt
that threatened flailing my both eyes berserk.
I gulped my tea to yelp, "You flirt!"

" 'Sa hard job, Joe, but someone's gotta—you
know."
　　　　I gave a whiff. Her perfume swam
to float its pheromones in hot slushy stew.
"Hey Joe! I bought the cutest baby pram.

"Think you could give a hand and wheel it in?"
Good thing my fav cartoon was Donald Duck,
because I squawked and looked about for gin.
"You really think I'm prego, Joe? I only fuck

with you, old man; to dream that your lolly
engorged my loving box—well truth be told
we're both more than a teensy old. Good golly,
Joe, it's for my youngest niece. Get hold

of your male sense. Hey that line about prego moms
in your earlier chapt.? Nice touch. Now and then
you really write. But that drip 'bout atom bombs—
no choice remained. Even your poetry can't spin

a fairy tale sans end. And it was sweet
how you then slipped me in. But guess who's missing

for over forty pages? Give? Tweet! Tweet!
Time's up! It's Daddy's daughter you've been dissing."

I rose in my stirrups (must have been nice
for cowpokes to use that prop) and clenched a fist.
"That Lorrie's *not* my daughter! You stick like lice
to an absurd idea."
                    "Lice? Joe, what a twist.

"Your ex-wife give you something 'sides a daughter?"
We faced on the carport. A typical hazy
Ohio Valley summer's day. "T, you rotter.
I'm not that old; my sperm ain't that lazy.

"And how'm I s'posed to know that pram's not for
you? You sure snugged up friendly with the old
cigar-smoking morgue fart."
                              "Joe, get the door,
and let's store this damned pram before mold

"hard-sets your brain. First, MM didn't smoke
those cigars; he chewed them. Second, I never touched
the sweet 'old fart.' Can't you please read what you wrote?
Besides, it's a poem, not real. And here I rushed

"home to tell you—"
                    "Exactly!" I let the door slam.
"Since it's not real, how can she possibly be my—"
"Adam may have delved, Joe, but Eve's the one who spans.
We women see beyond the page; it's called third eye."

T and I stood inside. She shoved the pram
into a closet. *Doing that won't make it go*,
I thought. "Here, bring reading glasses and your damn
third eye in here."
                    Dixie not Pixie glared. The show

was on. I shuffled papers and found
a draft of the scene at the morgue. "Read and weep,"
were my instructions. Dixie didn't squeak one sound;
her two eyes crossed; her fabled third left in a Jeep

and drove for Dodge. Good riddance, in my opinion.
I proffered my special writing chair, polite
as pie; it's where I won't let any old minion
sit. Would jinx my butt's muse and all I indite.

"So read and weep," I dared to bow and then repeat.
"Glad you are home. Should I fix you a drink?"
"Joe, you gave me one page. Is it really that deep?"
"Fair warning now: there's a good deal of slink.

"Maker's on the rocks should be strong enough."
Dixie waved me off and flipped on a light. . . .

An Interlude: What Dixie/Pixie/Trixie Read

At that precise moment the door burst open.
In stepped a redhead exuding so much sex
that even the two gay guys hopped, hopin'
to slide into her act.

"Good God, this place makes hex,"

the beauteous newcomer said. "It's that poor dead girl
you've kept away from burial, on ice."
The redhead gave a glare at C, then made to whirl:
"We need to talk, before you catch bed lice."

When MM didn't move, the redhead grabbed
his wrist and gave a twist. So much for a woman

restoring decorum, *C thought. MM, nabbed,*
quite humbly shuffled for a far-off room, and

Mike gave giggle then crooked his finger
for all of them to follow. "Now shush,"
he cautioned as they climbed to linger
on a dais. "This'll deliver one sweet rush,"

he whispered, pointing to a window.
Below, the redhead stood with MM. She
shook fist in face, then gave a grin, though
that wasn't what they noted. His pink wee-wee

somehow got caught in her left hand. How very deft,
C thought. 'Sa trick my mom should have taught.
The redhead pulled MM's penis to her cleft,
yapping all the while, though what words were wrought

escaped them all. "She's talking 'bout you,"
I guarantee," Mike said to Carmen. "Jealous
won't scratch her surface. If my boss were a Jew,
she'd be a PO'ed Yahweh raging zealous

"over some feigned golden calf."
                              "Oy ve!"
obliged C, for the redhead was pulling M
M to a desk and mounting to have her way.
"Great heavens!" DC exclaimed. "She'll break his stem!"

At that moment a crash with intense vim . . .

Chapter Twenty-one continued:
Playing noir Detective, receiving a dark Directive

. . . I made our drinks both doubles. Rough,
but they'd set Pixie's sights just right.

She took the whiskey and gave a laugh.
"It's called projection, Joe. Jealousy is your
dumb bailiwick, not mine. Say, am I plain daft
or do all of your characters have to endure

coitus interrupt us? Can't you give
at least one poor and horny sap a break?"
"I bet the sap you'd most like out of his skivs
is MM. You and him could bury the snake!"

"You and *he*, don't you mean? Hey Joe, what's worse,
jealous love or a non-grammatical writer?"
"I'm not jealous! And I spoke of the hearse
guy in fury. 'Swhy my grammar's not politer!"

"You do so *al*ways underline my point,
Joe. 'Swhy I stay, despite your tantrums."
"Instead, you mean, of running to a juke joint
to meet MM, Tony, or some other who thrums

your fancy?"
            "Amazing. You should wear a white tie."
"What's that supposed to mean?"
                          "You really *don't* read
what you write, do you? Really, give it a try.
I'd guess that fewer green globules would bleed

on your sleeve from your fevered, jealous brain."
Slick Trixie sipped her whiskey, I sipped mine.

Nothing like ice and Maker's Mark to cool the strain.
"You're right. I do get jealous. Okay, fine.

"But Lorrie does not—by God—share my genes.
Let's drop it. Hey, you said you rushed home to tell
me something. So bury the hatchet, spill the beans."
"Despite your crazed mixed metaphor, I remain well

"enough to loose my word-horde. I used your AMEX,
and I reserved two flights for Santa Fe
this coming September. No, don't start to flex
those male biceps. We're flying in to see a play—

an opera, really, since you're such a high-tone
writer. I even splurged to order you opera
glasses. With them you'll get a chill in your male bone
is my sweet guess. I also went to shop for a

small present. You'll get it come this fall.
Say, why don't you take a stab at what we're
gonna go see?"
        "Lady MacBeth hosting a ball?"
Whatever it might be, it gave hot fear,

for Dixie'd flashed to Trixie. That
could never bode too swell. It was like, in fact,
. . . the simile evaporates. My writer's hat
is lost, and Trixie's butt is now in act

of smothering my seat's soft muse. Oh damn!
MM portrays just the tip of the berg.
T's always flirtin', messin', roamin', making slam.
The trouble is, she's prettier than Ingmar Berg-

man, slinking everywhere like some film noir . . .
Good thought! "Hey, wanna play detective?"

                              "Say what?"
"Slink about, but do it here and not in some bar.
Let's find my writer's hat."

                    "Joe, you've *got*

"to live real at some life point. That cheap hat flew
when you rode Tony's Harley."

                         "Tony again!"
"Yes, Tony. And you almost got a ticket too,
for flaunting helmet laws. Lucky you, when

the lady cop laughed so hard as that fat bike
went down. Say, why don't *you* play private dick—pun
intended—and guess the opera? Oh you'll like
it so. The songs all glow with your foul mood: prick-spun."

"*Carmen!*" I trilled my r.

                    T gave a snort and laughed.
"*Barber of Seville! Romeo and Juliet!*"
"You're closing in; guess you're not quite so daft.
Go push the pram, let your horn rise, you'll get it yet."

My eyes went wide to moons. "There, Joe, you do
see! *Otello*, old man. The moor whose profound lack
of sense blinds him to love that flows true blue.
Lorrie. Next chapt. Bluth. Write it." T turned her back.

Othello, where's the connection? I'm not black.

Chapter Twenty-two: Lorrie divulges a worry
while she and Carmen pet things furry—
then, an intrusion with little reason and poorer rhyme
has your author re-checking the plot's timeline

They'd been at Hank's one day and a week.
The creep, it seemed, had slink, slank, slunk away.
True to his word, Dave's dad sold Hank, on cheap,
two Doberman pups, who now were romping in play.

They stood in the yard—well there must have been some grass
somewhere growing from the rocks and the sand.
Ms Walburn had four times sown it. She had class.
L and C searched and searched, but cacti filled the land.

Lorrie'd called in sick, a mental, not corporal twitch.
Ol' Sol—unlike his normal spin—glowed out benign.
"That's just what worries me." Lorrie gave itch
to a pup's right ear. "Everything's going too fine.

"Too damned fine."
                              "Don't say that you and Dave—"
"No, no, not him. We swirl sandstorms of love."
Lorrie grinned: "Just can't make my pineapples behave."
"Better than *mi frambuesa*." C gave L a shove.

When Lorrie first learned her secret nickname,
Pineapple, she cried for half a day.
But Carmen devised just the plan to tame
her friend's male woes. Piña coladas paved the way

to bacchanalia and a laughing spree
providing every blessed male they knew

with dirty *nom de spumes*. Lorrie'd said, "Gee,
we ought to give one to my dad, who flew

the coop while I tummy-swam."

                               "¡*Bastardo!*
—Not you, *mi amor*," C quickly corrected,
"but him!"

            "All men!"

                         "*Sí*, with their pricks that grow."
"Glow?"

          "Blow?" They giggled and thus rejected

the pending pineapple disaster. "In
the South, they mean hospitality."
"Penises?"

            "No, Carmen you goof, not them!
Pineapples—fruit, not my duality!"

And soon it looped that Carmen's dad too had
flown the coop before she was even born.
(Though she kept *pater familias* secret and sad;
time just wasn't right to expose her Hanson thorn.)

Beneath Ol' Sol, a pup now bit someone's toes.
'Twas Lorrie who yelped and gave a swat;
it must have been her digits, I suppose.
So emblematic: In life we barely know plot

much less specific whats.

                          "My mom,"
L said, "one time told me my dad was a doctor."
"A doctor! Whoo-hoo! Girl, you could glom
on lots of prescrip drugs." Carmen shocked her-

self by saying this. Much doubt abounded near:
she needed a break from her spy job,
which she'd been working for less than a year.
But day in night out, she'd had to hobnob,

alas, with the scream of the local crop:
each low-life and hard-blow in a
one hundred mile radius. Her life would flop
unless señorita's killer would show in a

few months or so. But what if rumor blew right?
The Mexican drug lords aspiring to spy biz,
acquiring stolen high tech to create a blight
on our fair land and send us all into a tiz?

¡Caramba! Carmen laughed. Her Hank had been placing
employment ads upon her bedside stand.
To speak of that, the two were still racing
back and forth between rooms to assuage glands.

"You think that Dave is really going to move in?"
C asked as one of the pups lunged
for her toes. She dodged; the pup put a groove in
its nose.
                    "Oh yeah! He swears his dad's expunged

restraint and now is sleeping with a hippie
straight from the sixties. Slick patchouli oil
be-dabs her hair and body till she's drippy.
And—just get this—they make something odd with foil."

"Fudge brownies?" Carmen asked.
                                        "No, something kinky."
"It boggles the mind."
                            "Don't it, though.

Bent tantric's not enough. They go ultra slinky.
Dave thinks they're channeling aliens for the Big Show."

The day was moving; Lorrie felt hot and sick.
O'erhead, Ol' Sol impatiently strolled
and turned up yet more heat. O, he can be a prick!
"I hope he moves in soon; I barely can hold

"on. Carmen, I wish I'd never seen that boy
and never gotten that raise. The brains
those people carry scare me. You should see their joy
each time a squeal emits then drains

into a quiet nothing in their labs. "Newton,"
they mouth then hiss a grin. And I don't
think they mean Wayne. God, Hank's Glueton
rayguns and even *Star Trek's* Klingons won't

hold particle accelerators to the creeps."
"Say what?" C asked.
                              "You know, I catch their lingo.
Something over in France has them all a-bleep."
C looked at Ol' Sol, who indicated, *Bingo!*

"Coffee, tea, or beer?" She stood, a pup yipped.
"Oh pup, I'm sorry. You need to watch your toes."
"Amen."
        "Amen."
                "Amen."
                        "Amen."
                                Did something skip?
For sure, pups cannot speak. No, two natty machos

were standing by the house. C spotted a black Ford
Explorer and looked at their faces: *gamberro*

conveyed polite description of the hoard
of scars thereon. Enough to squeeze out woe's marrow.

The female pup barked and rushed, to be
kicked a foot away to yelp. The nasty one's
face showed grotesque in its true glee.
Both Carmen and Lorrie tightened their buns.

Not to be topped, creep two kicked out. The male pup's yelp
skipped dry, hot air. C pulled out her Walther
and jerked it at the jerks. "Let this pistol help
to make my point. The kicking bullshit should halt or

you'll learn how good a shot I am."
"Sweet señorita," Creep One on stage right said.
Did he have more scars than Son of Sam?
"Señorita—" he pointed at the other's head,

"—we both was mauled by pit bulls when we
was ten. We don't kick again. We come here,
amigos giving only nice advice, you see?"
"Sí yes," the second said, "we feel this place a cheer.

"Would be not best to loose, enjoy the sun,
let certain matters stay?"
                              "Which of us are
you talking to?"
                    Both men stared at C's gun.
Crevices deepened their each and every scar.

"Ah, does it play? We heard that you
were *chicas acaneladas*."
                              "Cinnamon girls?
You think we're a duo and sing ourselves blue?"
C gave her Walther a cowgirl twirl.

The first-kicker—he did have a longer scar
than t'other—coughed. "*Mi amigo* means that since you—"
he coupled his hands as if opening a jar—
"*Simpatico*."

> "Lesbian? We hump ourselves blue?"

Both men gave shrugs. "The blue-shoed *niña's* requiem
was sung by monsignor Guillermo. There are those
with feelings who paid. Please, for the sake of them
do not abide to look—"

> "To expose

"your selfs to danger," the one with fewer scars
made to say. He opened his palm and reached into
a sporty jacket. "Take." They slunk to their black car,
on setting down paper by black designer shoes.

Carmen saw one—they faded into nasty twins—
give butt-scratch as they entered the Ford like crabs,
backward. Well, if not high IQs, at least wins-
ome agility was shown on the desert's slab.

"I bet he has fleas."

> "Lice."

> "Scabies."

"Damn, girl, you were quick with that revolver."
"Pistol. You should learn to shoot. In case of rabies.
Tough to tell: am I involvee or involver?"

"Huh?" Lorrie asked.

> "Who were they warning, you or me?"

"They think we're lesbian, a rainbow for us each?"
A pup ran to the paper and squatted to pee.
"No!"

> "*¡Jesús!*" Both C and L hustled to reach

the natty gift left by the natty creeps.
The distant black Ford shrank to a spot.
"Hope that's the last we see of those two peeps.
—Should we?" L bent.

>   "You're the one who's got."

C tucked her Walther in her yellow jeans;
enquiring Lorrie raised paper to sun
and shook to check for razors or jumping beans.
She gave a rip. "Better than a cinnamon bun!"

she then exclaimed, showing four hundred-dollar bills
and four red tickets to some fine event.
A purple Sticky Note, balled like a poison pill,
read, "*Make loose. Your time on fun is never miswent.*"

"They can walk backwards and they can kick,
but writing and speaking sure ain't their bent.
What are those tickets to?"

>   "Othello, spelled in Spic."

L blushed and coughed for a tiny stint.

"Offense not meant."

>   "Of course. We lesbians

would never cast aspersion. But what *do* you mean?"
"It doesn't have an H."

>   "Ah. It's not Thespian,

but operatic. We'll hear the fat lady scream."

"For real? You think that we should go?"
"We'll check the date, maybe change it.
But sure as hell we'll spend that dough.
Unless it's counterfeit, we can arrange it."

C took a bill and held it to the sun,
who's looked on diamonds, rubies, and topaz;
on napalm, iron maidens and sten guns.
No surprise, Sol gave such boring Franklins the razz.

"You're spot on, Carmen. It's at the opera house
near Santa Fe. Top seats, not cheapies in back.
We can take Hank and Dave, give them a rouse.
But I don't get it. Othello? We're not black."

Ol' Sol spewed flares at that. To laugh or hack?

Chapter Twenty-three:
Trixie leaves your author a note;
it certainly doesn't esteem or dote

I've just got to ask, Joe: Can you now need
more proof that Lorrie's your genetic spin?
'I don't get it. We're not black.' Clearly *your* seed
sowed that half-brained connection in.

And hey, *Otello* in Santa Fe . . . Gee,
ya think there might be some droozy connect
coming to play? Remember that we
will fly high, sipping wine aboard a Southwest jet—

say, did your daughter ever check the date?
Don't worry, old man, I've marked our calendar.
Your opera glasses will arrive here soon—it's fate,
accept it, and, dear old pal, we'll upend our

red wine with care that day. No sense in seeing
things double. One bad shock will suffice your ticker.
And hey, complaints to SPCA are speeding,
REGISTERED MAIL, today. That second pup-kicker?

Gratuitous violence. The Author's Guild
will surely levy some fine for you to pay.
Don't those fine folks want you fine writers to build
fine reading morals, the pure American Way?

Ta-ta, I'm off to work. Sweet Tony asked me
how your writing's coming along. A song,
I said. Pure and simple, like a bird and bee.
Ain't it just great how well we get along?

✳ ✳ ✳

Just who's the WE in that note? Trixie for sure,
makes one half. Is the other me, or Motorcycle Bloke?
My writing stings like a bee, my heart floats pure.
Gratuitous? Her Tony's not just one such poke?

With what's about to happen, it's no time to joke.

Chapter Twenty-four: Some sad happenstance
near what used to be a boy's ranch,
but now seems Ted Bundy's outreach branch
of school for boorish charm, sad romance, and ill chance

Inside this chapt. the action comes on quick,
so as your author I will needs be slick.
Quatrains with rhyming couplets should do;
alternating rhyme leaves too much to chew:

'Tis three days later and all through the house
all creatures are stirring including, yep, a mouse.
But this sad case isn't about poor thin him,
although his end will come, so sad and grim:

a Dobie will catch him in her jaws
obeying nature's more obnoxious laws.
While the SPCA may think nothing's ruder,
the Dobies *were* bought to dissuade intruders.

There's one intruder welcome though;
that is our Dave, whose moving in goes slow,
where Lorrie's heart maintains concern.
Dave's valves too hold a deeply glowing burn;

they're pumped to move come Saturday;
they're tired of keeping beat to old folk's play
with Reynolds foil, patchouli, and hippie dippy.
"Next they'll be dancing out Shaman Skippy!"

he shouted to his friends' bemusement.
The further fact that neither wore shoes meant

Dave feared contracting athlete's foot or worms.
When he announced this fact, both pups got squirms.

That was then, but now is when Ol' Sol has risen
up strong, up bold, a sky-teen spewing jism.
Tan Carmen's driving Lorrie to work.
Above, Ol' Sol makeshifts a solar lurch:

as they drive past some crows, a mare, a rock,
a tree, a bush, L yells out "Stop!" in shock.
"I swear I saw a foot tangled in that bush!"
C obliges, though her mind goes to mush.

She starts to back the car, but Lorrie
jumps out so fast, you'd think her called to Glory.
C looks in the mirror: sure enough, a shoe—
It's green this time, not Blessed Virgin blue

Lorrie runs to find one more Mexican teen
lying face-up, cold, eyes open to the scene,
opposed forever to her taking it in.
L feels for pulse, though knowing it's no-win.

Blowflies, abruptly shooed off their hard work,
land back on the girl's brown eyes, without a shirk.
Carmen arrives to swat them off and take a look,
though it's no fun regarding death's shallow nook.

C's nose gives twitch. "Cinnamon. Holy Saint
Francis! That spice is coming to taint
young dead señoritas too much these days."
"Cinnamon? Hanson brags that it pays

"to chew it when he's with 'the plump *chicas*,'
though if you ask me he's trying to reek us

straight out of Building Eight and send our noses
to seek sanctuary with funeral roses."

"Posies. They called them sachets during the Plague."
"Well, the big brains threaten to sue him at the Hague—
nothing halfway for Los Alamos folks.
Wish I could say—" L bends— "they were bad jokes—"

to close the señorita's deep brown eyes,
once more disturbing diligent blowflies.
She then looks to her friend: "What'd you mean
by 'posies' and 'plague'? –God, this gal was lean."

Carmen is on her cell calling her four pals
and their white ties. She thinks of "Buffalo Gals"
and hums it till Ted picks up with a grog-
gy "Hello."

                  "You and dream team need to slog

over to County Road 74.
One more dead señorita, nearly at my door."
Ted tries his best to make an uncouth joke;
it comes out jib-jab. Carmen lights a smoke,

then punches 9-1-1. Her smoke's a Henry Clay;
she's grown partial to them and anyway,
their namesake emitted from L's home state.
What more does she need to make them rate?

"The Great Compromiser," C notes after her call.
"No, the Great Divider. Like a limburger ball."
L's dissing Henry Clay, but just the smoke,
not the historical KY bloke.

The ambulance arrives, the cops screech in—
we've been through this before. Life should be a sin—
maybe in some religions it is, X-ians
and Muslims seem anxious to prove it a hex and

much worse. You'd almost think they'd cheer a hearse.
Life sums up negative, they claim, so check your purse.
You'd get no argument from those standing about
that brown young corpse whose sad last shout

delivered some dun creep the rush he sought.
A white tie bends: "Don't even look like she fought."
Amazing how peeps begin to shuffle
when death's face looks in. Still, no one can muffle

their horror, their fear completely,
so white tie number three continues neatly,
"No blood, no flesh beneath her nails. Nice and
easy, like she's getting ready to sail—sand,

though—" he glances about—"is all she found."
Both C and L inwardly groan: *How profound.*
Now you likely think that this was Ned . . . no Ted!
But sorry, he didn't create that said.

Still, he does bounce his head to judge those glurgs
as pretty sharp. All thinkers don't stay in big burgs;
his friend's bright words sure show that to be so.
"Hey, Carmen," Ted says. "I bet you didn't know

"that DC fellow's still down in Santa Fe.
That morgue jock and him are waltzing fairy play."
So it gets settled. Señorita is shipped
to glamour city where even rivers don't drip,

where boutiques extend like pedicured toes,
unto the foothills of Sangre de Cristos.
Will she find truth, justice, the American Way?
She's bloating now, so not so likely, don't you say?

Time does some passing, not a great so much,
four, five days—I can't keep meticulously up.
Los Alamos has barely spread first rumors—
another corpse, murder spreading like tumors,

found by that sweet Pineapple and her friend—
when bang! on that same road, what should upend?
(Though C and L to this poor chance weren't bidden.)
Two more señoritas are found hidden

by a roadside grotto to that saint with the birds.
Now, oh now, doth fly a flurry of words.
And just what do MM and the two gay morgue
dwellers conclude? Suffocation. 'Twon't quell the gorge

of fears now swelling in folk and big brains alike.
Oh, and two persistent anomalies do strike
the three and Carmen too. Instead of each fat cell
showing white, its tapioca rolls black, like hell.

And then again appears that lovely island spice,
cinnamon. "The creep suffocates, he doesn't dice,
and then he finishes with a little posey,"
MM notes off the record.

                     "Do ya suppose he

has allergies to women's perfume?"
Ted offers this in their team's think tank room.
The others laugh, C thinks of her dad.
Not even he could be so sad—

though Mom did say his utmost charm was sperm,
which helped make Carmen lovely. Thinking thus, she squirms:
"Maybe we should start checking out the hill."
"Those big brains? They've got larger ducks to kill.

"Hiroshima, not a piddling wetback—
don't take offense—is what keeps them on track."
Despite Ted's slur, Carmen sits up, impressed.
"Ted, you really have a mind, why keep it suppressed?"

Ted gives a blink, she blows a kiss,
which sends him off to hermit land, hot bliss
One pertinent observation a week
swells him enough; thereafter, he reverts to freak.

"I guess," C comments, "what Ted said is right.
"All told, that fact could make today's highlight."
They laugh then warble out staid suspects,
all Betty Crocker or Boy Scout rejects:

Blue, Steamer, a dealer named Roca, one
named Pendejo, another named Hot Bun.
None of this matters, for death comes on a platter:
Three more dead señoritas are found, to shatter

Wednesday morning air two days later—
a milk run for Ol' Sol, death's prime inflater.
Still, this earthbound creep deals on metro scale:
leaves seven dead just three months into his trail.

And that is only a start, my good friend!
A slumber party goes off the deepest end,
and five señoritas lay cold in a heap.
Indians, Mexicans, plain white folk now hide as sheep.

If I pen like Shakespeare, I beg you understand:
his fine lingo lieth not at my command,
but this mad heath's stormy plot stacks corpses thigh-deep.
For that, honorable Will and I both do weep.

The town of Los Alamos hath no sleep.

Chapter Twenty-five: Not too much cheery,
the Fibonacci Series, eyes getting bleary,
visitors getting speary, señoritas getting feary

Trixie said this about the last chapt.: "A whopper.
Beat howling *Pater Noster* during dog sex."
With that, you'd surely think I could top her,
but right now she's setting realtor muscles to flex,

split-levels moving as if there's no bust.
Well, fine with me, we might be flying on my card,
but we're dining on her In God We Trusts.
Meanwhile, let's take a peep at Hank's back yard . . .

'Twas he, sci-fi buff Hank, who offered up this clue:
"The murders have filled the Fibonacci Series.
Anyone note?" Both pups stopped chewing a shoe;
L's dry tea bag did float. Already weary

with toting clothes and CDs in, Dave tugged an ear,
his real intent to tug some part on Lorrie.
Above, Ol' Sol scooted along without one jeer,
his brain keeping young, those below growing hoary.

At last, Carmen exhaled: "Hank dear, I'm grieved.
Explain just what you mean."
                              L gave a shout,
"It has to do with yoga and green plant leaves!"
"The leaves are right," said Hank. "Yoga, I doubt.

"It's numbers occurring in nature, in sheaves
like one, two, three, five, eight, eleven.
Two previous numbers make the next; they weave
to show how nature grows ordained by heaven."

"Dearest Hank," C, astute in math, cleared her throat.
"If what you say is true, it'd be fives, eights, thirteens."
The others closed their minds to Carmen's number moat;
as normal humans, math gave burble to their spleens.

Hank raised his hands, the pups began to slump,
Dave's dream of dug-tugs slunk off to dissipate.
"But if your meaning stays true—" C gave love-thump
to a pup— "the next number to participate

will be eight: lots of señoritas to tether."
"I wonder," Hank mused, "if they have to be
Mexican."
                    "Or young?"
                                   "As long as they're together."
"I thought the brains were creeps, but geesh, you three

"are proving them quite tame. Can we please talk
about *Star Trek* or the Dalai—hey wait!"
L glanced at Dave and took a lewd mind-walk:
she wished him not so skinny—bed bait

is what her mom would warn, and Granny would abjure.
If Lorrie ever had a sister she
would have tri-knotted her pigtails to ensure
her Mom's Handsome Man Caveat might never flee.

Soon Carmen's toenail gave L a ragged nudge.
"Ow! –Oh yeah. Hank, what was that big word you said?
'Paparazzi?' "
                    Pouting, Hank did barely budge,
but aping apes, he grinned and scratched his head.

"Fibonacci."
                    "Yeah. Our main heap creep, Strictdick,

has replaced *Newton*, his favoritemost word,
with that one. Just now it gave a click
to me when I got, er . . . somewhat deterred.

"So . . . Hank?"
                    "I'm thinking about the sun
and wonder: What number of murdered young women
has it seen in the two billion years it's spun?"
"A pleasant thought for Saturday."
                    "Yeah, a lemon."

"Fibonacci, Liberace," C cut in.
"This talk of death leaves us all too strained.
Let's take a hike and leave Mister Dark to swim
in corpses stunned by Fibonacci's acid rain."

The pups wagged tails and frolicked to agree,
As Dave, C, and L stood, Hank's bad mood belayed.
Would Sol send down consoling beams creating glee?
Not if what we've seen before remained his way.

The trio gathered water, a pistol for snakes,
nine of Lorrie's ultra-fine vanilla whey bars,
and her good luck blue-eyed crystal. "For Lord's Pete's sakes,
come, Hank. Turn your foul mood off like day stars."

A look at Carmen's eyes, then her legs,
then seeing the bulge in her yellow shorts he shook
his head: a P thirty-eight, not lipstick or eggs.
No matter; she had him hooked. It wasn't just nook-

y made him that way. "Okay, but if all of you
are packing guns, I'll need to get my Colt."
"No gun pack I, Bub. To global peace I'm true."
"Aw, Lorrie, you're a butterfly ready to molt."

"You got it backass, Hank, but I'll accept
what I am sure you meant as accolade."
Hank got his Colt. Since he did not want L bereft
he also filled a water gun with lemonade,

to carry out to her. "You may as well
join in."
                  She took the orange plastic gun
and gave a squirt. One pup wigwagged its tail
and licked, then slobbered, snapped and spun.

"Lemonade," Hank explained. "And not too sweet."
L wiggled her nose just like the pup;
this sent poor Dave comatose with heat;
'twas not caloric or thermal, but rut.

They strolled out east, away from noonday's sun.
They'd trekked but one-half mile, when darling L
raised up her water gun. "Damn, this ain't no fun."
Her straight KY talk told it was hot as hell.

"Not back like in KY with its humidity.
And here the skies stay clear and blue, but whew—"
Our Lorrie, Girl Scout deluxe, showed no timidity
but shot at lover Dave, and aiming true

splashed his thin mouth. "Even this lemonade is hot."
A pup barked twice. They looked. A swirl of dust
arose ahead. As long as the auto was not
a Ford Explorer they kept simpatico trust,

whoever might come. Soon they could discern
a pink car tossing tan dust upon their driveway.
"Dave? Hank? Does one of you hold a secret burn
for cosmetics shipped straight from Mary Kay?"

"Huh?" answered one, "Haw," jawed the other he,
"did she leave off her animal-torture jive?"
Both pups began to bark at a lonesome tree
shading a lonesome rock beneath. "A hive

of bees? A nest of snakes?"
                                "Dave, do you mean
the car, Mary Kay, the rock, or tree?"
                                        Dave ran
to the barking pups and pulled both off clean.
Was good: a rattling meant some snake's rave plan

to strike. Hank joined to aim his Colt, but Lorrie gave
a shout, "For why?" All three combatants
did heed her notion. If jolly Ol' Sol could shave
and think, not just rise up for matins,

he would have applauded Lorrie's laissez-
faire. Not all snakes are Satan (nor satin), shoving
an apple down poor Eve's throat. That myth goes mazy:
would any gal heed some snake instead of loving

her man's warm worm? Size counts? That's crazy.
The task left for the four was to track back, Jack.
As they did, the pink car became less hazy:
white writing rode its door, two women stood slack smack

amid Hank's acreage, thin figures watching.
"Miz Walburn called," Hank said, raising hand to head
for focus. "She thinks the lab is botching
again. According to her, better red than dead."

"Then she can vote sap Blue." Dave spat at a skink.
"Your logic? Vote Red if you wanna be dead?"

"Hush, you two. No political spats. Think
and hold your tongues. We've got guests ahead."

Sol only got hotter. No thoughts today,
just the usual shine and spin, tuck and roll—
much more than the approaching four could say
about the women standing, arms a-fold

across their skimpy vegan chests. Lorrie had
no need for jealousy. In fact she thought
of jogging to a cupboard for this sorry-sad
pair who now bowed like karate champs. Carmen caught

the pups to clip each on a leash. One kick
in this damn heat would trigger a potshot.
Who needed headlines that read: *"Sun-crazy spic
spy guns down two!"* But her worry turned to naught

for: "We're from the SPCA. —Aw, those
two dobies are so cute.—We're hunting down a
certain Joe Taylor, a lowlife creep whose
specialty is abuse. Good he didn't drown a

pup, but only kicked it. Me and my friend
are going to bash his balls flat in. Oh here:
my ID." The woman speaking could blend
with vine-ripened tomatoes; her hair was sear

and red as if it might could host a piglet roast.
Our wary Carmen knew the charm of plasticized
ID. She took it, gave it her spy-gal utmost
to see if it were fake or bastardized.

The redhead sniffed. From her oversize purse
she pulled a silver tube of lipstick.

Looked like an armor-piercing bullet, but worse
yet was the ice she rolled on each thin lip.

"My nickname's Pixie—"
                              "Do you have a
twin sis in Santa Fe? Cute and tiny?"
"Trixie. She owns a medical plaza.
Calls it Dixie after our sis. Way tear-briny

"and sappy, you ask me. But that's my sis.
It's got a morgue in it. My good sweet Lord,
just getting embalmed would already shitcan bliss—
but in a plaza named for yelping rebel hordes?"

"She owns the morgue too?"
                              "Of course. The old guy's
employed in name by city, but his real titty
is my sis. I go dif for my sexual sighs."
Her svelte vegan friend purred like a kitty.

"Oh, this is Toni. She and I have worked
for years hauling in animal abusers—"
"And some women-abusing scum and murk
too," Toni roared. "Gamblers, druggies, boozers—"

"Anyway, back to this pup-kicking dweep.
I've got a picture, if you care to see."
C and L nodded, so out of her family keep—
I mean her purse, which may have held eternity,

it loomed so spacious, wide, and deep—she yanked an
old photo, black and white. Can they still make those?
She passed it to Lorrie. The guy looked tanked and
what's worse, his honker surely could expose

half this green globe to snot-making disease.
"I've never seen him," Lorrie said.

                             "Of course not,"
huffed Pixie. For some reason she looked pleased.
"Damn, didn't think Los Alamos would be so hot,"

she said then, this Pixie from the SPCA.
She passed Carmen and the guys the photo too.
"Nope."
        "Nope."
                "Looks like a dope."
                         "That's okay,
Hank. Your moniker fits him like a shoe."

"Say, how'd you know my name if you're not from here?"
"The SPCA has an invisible hand."
"Like Adam Smith's?"
                    "I said you'd throw down like a spear."
Well, Lorrie *was* sharp: she knew about *Star Trek* and

herbs, crystals, some witchy spells from her mom,
who'd first tried to allure L's poppa back,
but soon laid on curses thick enough to glom
him to some forlorn and icy railroad track.

Lorrie had learned about Mister Adam Smith
from a ju-co business class, which she hated.
Those money-monger faces sent her adrift
to EMT, where blood never abated.

At least the blood was real and very dear
to those who owned it. In business class
one maxim had been taught amply clear:
ALL went for sale; ALL sold was crass.

So here she was, admin. secretary
at Los Alamos, Building Number Eight.
Which, alas, made her feel like an actuary
predicting señoritas' death chances, of late.

"So sharp," repeated Pixie, stepping forward.
"And bright green eyes to boot. You can't tell it
from the photo, but this guy's eyes tend toward
parrot green. His squawk helps him sell it—

"his line of bull, I mean. Well, if you see him
give me a du-ning ring. Here's my card. I
push real estate when I'm not catching flim-
flam like this. Be sure to peel an eye.

"He's just the kind to leave a daughter jammed."
The redhead took the photo and handed
it to L. "Keep. I've got lots, like cans of Spam,
as tasty and bad for you as a banded

"rattlersnake. You folks here 'bouts fry 'em up?"
"Why, I believe you're from ol' Kentucky,"
said Lorrie. "Your words, you tie 'em up
like they're too many for your mouth. Lucky

"we met. We'll keep a watch for this Taylor
wise guy. It's my last name too, you know,
though I don't reckon he's kin. A wandering sailor
in Kaintuck just ain't that likely."

                              "Lorrie, stow

the folksy KY. You're giving us bellyaches,"
said her oldest roommate.

                              "It's contagious,"
said Lorrie. "This woman's KY talk takes

me back to Mom."
                    "Don't be outrageous,"

replied Pixie. "A mom I'm not. But a pop
I might just know. Now and then. In defense of
men—a ride whereon I do not often hop—
it's possible that some pops don't make sense of

"some daughters 'cause they've been kept in a veil
of ignoramus by the mom. Give it a thought,
young miss. Daddies of course have to be male,
but even absent ones ain't always wrought

"of prickly pricks. Some are—"
                            "Sorry to bust
the old home revival, but stuck like a nail
on that hill a car's been parked—long enough to rust."
They looked. Fat and black, it made their hearts flail.

Then handsome Hank added this nasty note:
"Looks like a Ford Explorer."
                            "Good, that is not.
That's what the creeps who kicked these little pups drove.
You really want to give four *huevos* a shot?"

C asked the two thin women, who grinned
like they'd bashed a birthday piñata.
"If only we could make sure it was them
parked up there—"
                    "Oh honey, I got a

"pair of pink opera glasses in my car
that just won't quit. Saving them for *Otello*
in Santa Fe—watch the fat lady hit the bar
to warble her warbs, like a bowl of Jell-o."

Ms. Pixie strolled to her car, her hips now swaying
as if she'd eaten spicy beef carne and
cheddar. "Pixie's top agent, I'm just saying,
back at the office. And I'm her right hand

"woman. We work for the SPCA
from a volunteer base. Ball-bashing is
a perk. The solid American way.
Any creep who gave these pups a thrashing is

"deserving of mashing." This long speech derived
from Toni, who sent both the gals a wink,
as much as to hint that if they survived
their two bull males, she'd happily dress them in mink.

Pixie strolled back. "Here they are. Focus
and let us know if either's the same guy
If so, we'll ride and throw some dominocus
on 'em. Say, you have any idea why

"they're up there lurking? Got a crush on one
of you pretty señoritas?"
                Was the wrong word,
considering death had left so many undone.
C focused, acting as though she hadn't heard.

"It's them, all right."
                "Well so, we've got to go."
Pixie retrieved her red binoculars
and said ta-ta. "Hey, *Otello's* a great show.
Let's have a drink, converse, be less ocular

"than today." She and her right-hand woman
slipped in the pretty pink car and drove away.

The four observed their dust. "She's a showman,
all right," said Hank. "Sure had a lot to say

"to you, Lorrie."
                    "Yeah, she acted like she
knew all about your no-see-um dad, too.
Hey, how'd she know what we're gonna go see?
Otello, down in Santa Fe, I mean. Do you—"

"We're going to a play in Santa Fe?"
Hank asked.
                    "A play? Does that mean a tux?"
asked Dave. The girls explained: "It's not a play,
you won't need a tux, the tickets came from flux."

They stopped talking to look up and see
The SPCA women speeding in a groove.
Their pink swirl swarmed like maddened bees
intent on stings, but the Explorer made cold move

and left the rise.
                    "Too bad, no S & M
for today." Dave gave a sigh. "May as
well continue dragging my last stuff in.
You three gave me some help we could go play as

"soon as it's done."
                    "Got to call Miz Walburn."
"Got to feed the pups."
                    "I left an iron on."
Dave's face drooped hard. "Aw, Dave, we'll all take our turn
and help. We're all just jokin' and firin' on

"ya." Above, Ol' Sol rolled, no doubt conspirin' on.

Chapter Twenty-six:
a hometown altercation
that cools then heats;
some more dead peeps;
a paternal invocation

"You're not the only one with a credit card,
old man. I made three big-time sales last week
and flew out west for rest. Don't take it hard."
"Toni!?" I shouted. Trixie gave my cheek a tweak.

"Quite clever, eh? Don't fret, I'm not going lez.
No need to up your dose of Viagra.
You know, all things considered, bed sounds pleas-
ant."
    "Midday?"
           "That ever stop Niagara?

"But Joe, just truck right back to your writing;
I have to meet with sweet young Tony anyway;
We've got some urgent matters that are . . . biting.
Say, at least your daughter should get some sexual play . . ."

"She's not—"
        But Pixie stopped me with her hot kiss
and slicker tongue—she'd chewed a peppermint.
Monica and Bill, them I'll not dis,
but when Pixie gets going, my upper vent

gets spent. So writing was forsook,
forsaked, forsocked. Off went my slippers
and pants, out came my rocks. I could barely look
at the clock. Noon-thirty. *Well, one for the Gipper,*

I thought, and made manly to tip her.

❊❊❊

Time keeps for no couple, no matter how wound.
An entire week passed in Los Alamos,
and I fear more bodies were found.
The señoritas got a breather, for most

of the eight were white and pale—even one
male showed in this bundle. You can bet
that lots and sorts of agencies had spun
their way to The Hill. The best they could get?

That unhappy, non-news word, *anomaly*.
Speaking of that, the DC Doc and
Mike churned, an item hot. A homily
on tolerance was delivered by jock and

Doc to the white-tie guys, especially Ted,
just after he let slip, "Anomaly is
like two fine bitches humping in a red hot bed."
This at a morgue to-do where the cadaver biz

then took back seat to angered, dancing Mike
and his doc love. They swept through the corpses
like Girl Scouts taking a butterfly hike.
What happened then was a real *iste lorpsis*,

which makes doubtful Latin for "local spat."
And while I won't claim that one and all
made up with a hug and sweet butt pat,
a peace did descend, as with Adam, post-Fall.

Put tolerance aside, what else did come
from those autopsies and their investigation?
Same old two things: anomaly and cinnamon.
Natch, right soon sprouted social hesitation.

The movies, churches, and cocktail parties
off limits zipped, as did any gathering.
Still, some considered themselves hardies
and stopped at Todd's for suds and blathering.

Our Carmen knew how well alcohol loosed
lips, so much better than the afterglow of sex.
That old saw, *omne sunt triste*—to once more goose
my favorite language, works a surefire hex

to shut most mouths from dilatory musing.
You know that redhead whose name almost rhymes
with "whiskey"? Even she stops her rusing
after enacting body grind—at least most times.

It was hump day, speaking of that two-backed
act. Hanson made his habit to ingest
three pickled eggs, one tortilla, and a six-pack
before hitting the sack. That wholesome food fest

plus some young-titted Mexican cutie
always set his mouth spewing fizzle,
for on reaching that point his onlymost duty
lay in dipping and wetting his pizzle.

He wasn't unlike his son in this aspect.
And lo, Blue was skinny-bellying the bar's
far end while his dad tried to win respect
from a señorita of 21 stars—

I mean her birthdays. Travelling from UCLA
(where Oppie nested his pre-bomb home)
to Los Alamos, she wanted in the worst way
the streets of Day-Glo City to work and roam.

Some man of science, this dolled-up she surmised,
would set her whole career plan geiger.
Such uranium diggers—don't be surprised—
work like gold-diggers: metal-seeking tigers.

Carmen sipped Coke nearby and twitched an eye,
though higher heed she paid to her right ear.
She chose a table close enough to spy
the whispers from her smarmy dad who drank his beer

and spewed his bullshit lines. Despite Ted's said,
C had become downright convinced and sure
that each and all the mounting corpses led
to just one place: the lab's purported pure

research. Believe in "pure"? You're thinking's screwed.
Those sterilized lab coats, milk-white and virgin,
can harbor viruses immoral, many-hued,
each one intent on infectin' and urgin'

research that spews a blurred statistics river:
"Tweak just one number here, and two over there."
Lo! Cometh results to please our Lord Grant Giver.
The truth? Research doth a pious "pure" pew oft share

with holy men and philosophes by scads,
(except for Kant, his strolling mind and bi-valve heart),
who soak on sly their own ethereal doo-dads
with furtive shots (tequila, lime and salt)—those tarts!

John Stuart Mill, he preached one thing sure:
the most bananas for the most monkeys.
Just so, "pure" oft doth swoop in deep manure;
just so, "pure" research attracts its grabby flunkies.

To illustrate some more, regard those crisped bodies
across the sea, in Land of Rising Sun.
The Boys so Big, so Little, turned fire-bombs shoddy,
made flame-throwers seem just carnival fun.

Or, mayhap, check out Messrs. M & J,
those psychologists dear who planned—but did not run!—
a torture program for the CIA.
All done in idealistic, thoughtful fun.

More facts will bare when in two days Miz Walburn shows.
She's visiting the rancho for lots of weeks,
From Hank's bad news, she's assumed good-old-way glows
resuming on The Hill, more death-and-seek

fun games for über brains. But for now, C paid
her mind to secret Dad. He stayed chit-chat
deluxe with the buxom L. A. maid:
"You read about the God Particle? Shit, that

is just where we are at." Dad took a gulp
of beer, his fifth. "Come with, I'll show
you one."
                    "Say Guy, you think my brain's a pulp?
No one's seen a boson-Higgs. Barely its echo."

¡Caramba! Carmen thought. All right, Chiquita.
Even though you spewed it backward
and though you should stop to breathe and heed a
true warning and not too soon jump sack-ward,

you still run smarter than my secret dad trots slow.
Her Hanson dad blinked twice. *Oh Carmen, you too might*
stop tight to sniff a genetic fact or so.
You did arrive from Dad's pool of genes. Buzz, buzz, bite,

replied our Carmen to that intruding niggle,
then tuned her ear again to eavesward-dropping.
Be damned if she didn't hear a giggle.
What was with her crappo dad? Must be whopping.

She stopped to think: Did not the señorita
just prove him fool? But there she sat and
wriggled and giggled, ready to eat a
well gee, tamale, or flop her pussycat hand.

Just eight mins. later—C's a counter, remember—
the girl and Hanson stood to leave the bar.
C noticed Todd go cold like December
and drop a five in his mountain nun jar.

She shook her head, went over and handed
him one more Lincoln. "Hank told me about the jar,"
she said, since Todd's look demanded
an explanation. He smiled; she got in her car.

A GPS—you're up-to-date and have one,
I hope—would reveal this situation:
car following car following truck . . . someone's
travelling toward a bad initiation,

there's *my* prediction. Hell, another's just
now turned up! Sweet Carmen's svelte foot pressed
the gas. She fretted things would be a bust
if she conjoined her finger in profane quest

with her P-38 to end in patricide.
Such acts had never done the olden Greeks much good,
and time nor ocean wouldn't likely glide
her matters better. Nothing's pure, she understood.

She hadn't read Kant, but I've got to tell ya,
I cannot think that a real concern. Pure is
as pure does. Just by giving a smell ya
can judge where pure, and where manure is.

To scan some more: a fourth and fifth vehicle
enjoined the line; their drivers drove with motives skewed
and mixed. Not all of them from bars did trickle,
so shove that thought, unworthy and rude,

off from your cranium. I might as well tell you:
amidst them drove our Hank, who played guardian angel;
then Blue, who figured for dibs on Dad's young screw;
and then two creeps whose motives dangle.

(I'm sorry for that last rhyme, dear hearts,
but Pixie just drove off, and it's ten after two.
I'm lucky to have contact with all my parts
after one hour of you-know-what with you-know-who.)

Are these the creeps we've seen before?
No. Just as this world fills with impure smells,
it fills with creeps willing to spread their gore.
Arriving in ones, twos, threes—their number swells

without the aid of Fibonacci or any
algorithm. First in line, the señorita
has crossed that secret border many
front seats have seen. It's hard to beat a

pick-up's bench seat for Cupid's play;
deep bucket seats, I conjecture, were made
by moms to keep their daughters from harm's male way.
In car two, C opened her purse for a Rol-Aid,

since driving on a lonely—sort of!—road bared
the chance of shooting her pater familias
into an ulcer that not only flared
her tum to knots but warped her one to two ilias.

Her dadkins took a turn that led off from
The Hill. One mile or more and C made out
a lover's lane that every high school chum
employed as means to hear wise mountain trout

who always kept so calm that each and every kid,
annoyed and bored, would take up anatomy.
C made a B in what studies she did,
but plenty earned an A to lose a *flat* tummy.

Merdre! C exclaimed, forsaking maternal Spic.
She slammed on brakes, she doused off headlights.
This lane hadn't been so short, was some alien trick.
All three cars behind took likewise frights.

And since this caravan has stopped, let us take
account of what each vehicle carried:
The L. A. gal had an autograph—was it fake?—
from Richard Feynman. Hanson himself harried

a long black box that he caressed as if
it were some personal item that shouldn't be
declared. C's pepper spray gave off a nasty whiff;
her P-38 hardly made folks go, "Gee!"

Blue brought along a cold six-pack of beer.
Hank, in puppy love, cradled dark chocolate.
The two mean creeps bore nothing of cheer,
just weapons enough to make kids gawk a lot.

And right here comes a point of surprise:
Dave's dad and the hippie with smelly hair
already sat parked ahead. In their gold truck lies
a telescope, a jug of wine, a pair

of pink handcuffs—Dave's kink comes honest—
a star map, some Alpo, and three Dobermans.
These five Darwinian creatures were on a quest
for alien craft, enough to send a sober man

a-scooting back to Todd's, for double shots.
Oh and they'd not forgot aluminum foil:
ten yards unrolled to X two hot glow spots.
Chelsea assured Dave's dad their toil

would not slip by unnoted. Mr. McDowell—
some called him Mac—had shaken his head
and gone along. He'd thrown the towel
in since his son left Chelsea in his stead.

The three Dobermans barked. "You think they've
landed?" Chelsea asked. Mac munched a
tamale. Chelsea'd kept the recipe to pave
his top love form tonight. She had bunched a

plastic bin crammed with them and three ham bones
to stave the four away if landing aliens
had need of private consult or maybe a jones
for crystals to run their craft. What was salient

on earth or even love's lost lane might change
in one half hour. Or even second. Poor Chelsea
did not realize how incipient the range
of this did play, for as she exited to pee,

a purple flashed one hundred yards behind.
"They're here!" she shouted giving a joyous jump.
The Dobermans were not so very kind,
letting off growls, snaps, and body bumps

against the bed of that gold truck. Belonged to Dave,
the truck, I mean. It knew this lane quite well.
"The cops?" prosaic Mac gave ask. "You'd best behave
and get back in. They're nervous and raising hell

for people out so late."
                              "Area 51!
Spacemen, Mac! Bring my Tupperware bin!"
"Aw Chelsea, you're setting my babes undone.
We'll look. It's just some kids in kaleidoscope sin."

Light show, kaleidoscope was nope. But sin's a win,
since Hanson had just doused the L. A. girl
with his oblong box. The one-eyed lizard stepped in
to gulp her down with dusty purple swirl.

She only had brief time to yelp, "Miss Gray!"
before she shrunk into a thing quite like a bean.
Garbanzo or pinto, her choice had flit away.
Miss Gray was an art teacher kids called an old queen;

she taught distrust of males and science
with carloads of feeling. She chaired, in fact,
California's first Bucket Seat Compliance
Act. Her concern for virginity did extract,

by march on Sacramento, mandatory
automated seat belts and deep bucket seats.
Fat good done for L. A. lass; her amatory
foolish heart thought all men of physics neat.

Life, friends, ain't boring; in fact, it's roaring.
Since I'm stealing lines, therein lies the rub.
The brains of Strickland et. al. had been soaring
to prep their G-string weapon to leave but a nub.

No more untidy corpses with blackened cells;
all fleshly matter fizzled down to a chick pea.
No more Fibonacci counting, what who could tell;
this sleek, improved Higgs boson filled them with glee.

In moonlight, Hanson bent to lift the pod
that had, as student, aspired to science's sea.
He looked to the moon and gave it a nod.
(And people thought his heart never skipped in spree!)

"Damn," he grunted, for he had to use both hands.
Said pea pod weighed one hundred-fourteen pounds.
At first, he foolishly and proudly had planned
to carry the L. A. chick pea around

in pocket, sort of a memento glory.
The thrust of L. A. gal's condensed gross weight
now changed his story. But here lay one whore he
just couldn't let fade. She sat out here as fate.

He finally managed to drop her in his boot:
her black hole density there scraped raw his skin.
He found he had to limp. A randy hoot!
He'd strut like Dillon, doing desperados in.

An l.e.d. shone on his limping dance.
"Damn, Dad. That little cunt musta give your
blue balls a bruising."
                            Hanson stopped his prance,
to catch up the oblong box. "Blue! As I live you're

a nosy mess. The little bitch ran like a shot.
"Go chase her if—"
                        "Hanson! Hand over the box!
It's government property and you're not—"
The three Dobies burst as if they'd seen a fox.

Flashlights and guns scattered and dropped.
Though one creep did pull off one single shot,
it jumped for the moon, then did a belly flop.
Soon any pant not ripped became white hot

to trot. Even Area 51
and spacemen would surely be preferable.
Behind thick bushes our Carmen spun.
"Ah, Mr. Mac," she sang. "You're inestimable."

Above, the moon, as wise as the sun,
gave silent chortle and beamed on a purse
L. A. girl had dropped before Hanson's fun.
Was just one dead tonight. Things could be worse.

Vehicles sped off, two denting C's fender.
"LaFitte," C cooed. A Doberman with
a crimson collar lunged to upend her
and lick her face enough to leave her spiff

for any alien ball that Chelsea planned
whenever First Contact arrived. Curtains

of Reynolds foil plus a tamale stand
proclaim our culture best, Chelsea thought for certain.

"Hey Carmen? You okay?" Hank gave a nervous shout
as all three Dobies jumped and licked.
"Hank? What—"
                    "Why in hell are you two out—"
Mac yelled.
                "It's not aliens. I've been tricked!"

"Did anyone see a girl in that last truck?"
"No, he was driving alone," Mac said.
"It was damned Hanson. Alone, the stupid fuck."
LaFitte sniffed out a purse. It too lay lonely, red.

The dobie nudged Carmen. "That dog's always liked you
best."
        "Chelsea, for heaven's sake, she brings him
treats . . ." While the two squabbled like lovers do,
C found the red purse. Its contents were slim;

she quickly exclaimed, "What in the world?"
and beamed her flashlight on a large pink frame
encrusted fakely with diamonds the L. A. girl'd
enshrined around Feynman's handwritten name.

"Not spelled right," noted Hank, who peeped over
C's shoulder. "Only has two n's, not three.
He worked here on the bomb. A longtime keep-over
who froze O rings on national TV.

"Right after Challenger exploded. We were babes."
"So was she." C shined her light on the girl's I. D.
"Hank, that purple flash . . . it didn't mean Jesus Saves.
Just once, I wish this life kept clean and tidy."

"What is her name?"

                  "Rosa Traci Johns. This is

a student I. D."

              "Rosa!" Hank yelled. "Traci!"

He grabbed at Carmen. "We've got no business

not looking." He then prodded Chelsea, spacey.

"Come on! We need to see if this girl is hurt!"

Or worse, thought C, recalling the snuffed prairie dog.

For one full hour, the four called, the dobies lurched.

But Rosa Traci stayed hidden under a log

or boulder, bush, or in the trees.

"You sure that purple wasn't some abducting

space alien?" Chelsea asked timidly.

"Please!"

          C pleaded. "That was my damned dad conducting

"a creep experiment with that creep machine."

"Your dad?" the three yelped out in unison.

Bernstein could not compose refrains more lean.

"Yeah, Hanson's my dad, I swear by moon and sun,

"though he sure doesn't know it. He knocked Mom up,

she had some goods on him, so they got married,

and I got raised a fine U. S. citizen pup."

"Aw." Chelsea opened the Tupperware she carried.

"You poor babe. Have a sopapilla and some wine."

"You fried sopapillas too?"

                    "And ham bones

for your dogs. I recommend we all dine

since no space aliens showed and that poor girl's gone zone."

C clutched the purse. "You sure this one is fake?"
she asked of Hank. The two explained to Chelsea,
but Mac munched twice then said, "Let me take
a look at that fancy autograph and see.

"Old Feynman was a joker. Wouldn't put
it far past him to misspell his own name."
"Too many jokers here'bouts. They're all afoot,"
C said. "But this girl's death is no damn game."

"Death? She could have just run off, you know.
Wouldn't blame her, with all that ruckus."
"No," C inhaled. "Smell that cinnamon blow?
Some bad game's afoot, and it's out to fuck us."

Thank you, Sherlocketta, she thought and sipped
Chelsea's sweet wine. You've got your killer,
just like you've got your dad. But both have nipped
all proof away, a sealed room thriller.

Instead of *The Tightly Locked Tea Room*
this case deserves a different name.
Gone Lost in Nighttime Mesa's Open Doom?
As C pondered, a male voice acclaimed:

"Damn, Chelsea, these sopapillas ain't bad."
"Aw, Mac, that's the sweetest you've ever said."
For real? thought C. She looked at Hank and was glad
her sci-fi guy was alive. *But poor Rosa's dead.*

The moon, if she had swooped, would have patted C's head.

Chapter Twenty-seven:
It worked, but who was she,
who were they,
why'd you do what you did,
why'd they say what they say'd?

"So you didn't send them, don't know who they
were?"
   Hanson asked this of Strickland, who had
eyes only for the box: "Just show me the clay,
that's what'll make our Army lads glad.

"Let *them* go fumble and worry
about who tried to steal our little black jewel
off you." Cal Strickland smiled. With a flurry,
Dad Hanson bent to enter in duel

with his left cowboy boot, which dropped in thud.
With grunts he made it topple, using both his hands.
"And here she comes, as slick as gully-wash mud.
She won't be dreaming any more science plans."

S heard the blackened chickpea thud. "You mean? . . ."
"She kept on yapping 'bout the boson Higgs."
Cal Strickland closed his eyes. For fifty times it seemed,
he'd told this dolt, whose mind was drying twigs,

the name was Higgs boson. Reverse played
out better for the idiot's brain. S knelt to stare.
"She drove all the way from UCLA.
Told me she studied physics over there."

Cal Strickland made a mental note to donate
twenty bucks or so to the department chair
for scholarships. He lived not insensate
to human suffering. The chickpea lay bare

and black where it had cracked the cedar floor.
He couldn't budge it, though hardly more than a fleck.
"You know, pal Hanson, I always thought it a chore
to read philosophy, history, and such dreck.

"What Oppenheimer got from his Hindu
shit strikes me as bland as stale paprika.
But here and now I want to shout with that guru,
that Italian fart, Euripides, 'Eureka!' "

"Uh, wasn't he some Greek?" Hanson mumbled.
Strickland stared at the chickpea, shiny and black.
It would be a pleasure to claim he fumbled
and blast the G-string at this security hack.

He eyed the machine on the edge of his table.
"Maybe you're right, Sir Hanson. Greek. But for now
let's test our little gal to learn how stable
she sits. Don't want her puffing up into a cow."

Cal Strickland bent and gave a sniff. "Cinnamon,"
he said. "Reminds me of my mother."
Surprised by that, Hanson blinked. He'd been
sure Strickland arose from some test tube or other.

With joined clean hands, they gave Ms. Chickpea
a heft onto a rolling table. Strickland
eyed Hanson's shiny black bowtie with glee,
picturing it, alongside Hanson's adrenal gland,

as one be-shrunken, ebony garbanzo.
And what about, say, peppering in some red
to leave this goof a Technicolor James Bond so
he'd fill a tea cup at some headstand of some bed?

A task to ponder.
               "What're you thinking?"
asked Hanson as they rolled the cart along
the sterile hallway. Strickland, without blinking,
said, "Need to investigate Cheech and Chong

"who tried to steal the food right off our plate."
"I think they could have been some Spics or Mexes."
"That narrows things down in this fine state."
"They could've been Indians, too. The sex is

"all I could tell. Too dark. There weren't
no alien spaceships lighting last night's sky."
Hanson rubbed his butt as if he'd burnt
it atop an oven while baking apple pie.

Was bitten by LaFitte, which clearly showed
how good at judging character that dog
right truly was. Remember how he licked C's nose?
"Enough damned minorities in this state to hog

six grant foundations three decades or so."
Cal Strickland huffed and gave the table
a shove toward the elevator to take below
where Devins and McGuire would be able

to count a radioactivity
output. *This thing is almost a damn black hole.*
How useful, he mused, *how attractive will it be*
if it munches New Mexico up like a mole?

Ah, science! You know, it's really a sin:
we can't live with, nor without it.
In that sense it's a whole lot like men,
at least to hear the feminists spout it.

This song replays reverse on the tongues of men;
their lower organs grandly spout it.
The war of the sexes will never end,
but like the Shakers, we wouldn't live without it.

Outside, Ol' Sol shone, ozone all about it.

Chapter Twenty-eight:
No wait!

Don Juan José Carlos Castaneda
watched as two men showed rips in their pants.
Other than drugs, one thing only played a
ding-ling on DJ: hard cash made him dance.

"I sent you for a box, not to sashay
with packs of dogs." He turned to a bodyguard.
"Shoot 'em. No wait! I got a better way.
Our dogs need training. Take 'em out to the yard."

The bodyguard frowned, one man peed his pants.
"No wait! Disgusting. Oh hell." Boss Moe—
he liked to be called this after once in France
he saw a film about Mafia—you know

our guy's cosmopolitan and can order
beer in five tongues—anyway, Boss Moe,
who'd travelled over many a border,
reached in his desk for a cigar to blow,

made change of mind and pulled out a Glock,
then fired four times, then walked on over to check
his groupings: off a bit, but nothing to knock.
"Take 'em both out. No wait. Say, what the heck,

"I need some exercise." Boss Moe, no common speck.

Chapter Twenty-nine:
Miz Walburn lands, on both wise feet.
If Fibonacci no longer holds the line,
where else should our hero(ine)s look for complete(ion)?

Was Friday. Thunderstorms had delayed
incoming flights, so Hank perused news magazines
and drank hot tea. After the four had played
in Taos, Lorrie transformed into the queen

of steeping tea. Bagged or loose, green or black,
she claimed it brimmed with antioxidant,
"and costs lots less than coffee from some Taos shack."
Carmen guessed L's genetic pop had bent

her up that snooty way. "Maybe your secret dad
derived from British royalty or such?
Maybe that's why your mommy got so mad?
Her fine Brit earl was really a four-flush?"

Whatever, Hank found hot tea to his liking,
imagining it gave him savoir-faire.
He even began to ride nose-up when biking
till Dave laughed it down again with a stare.

No bike today. Miz W needed a truck.
And Hank's, though worn, rode comfy enough.
"I'll bring her and evidence back, with luck,"
he told his pals. Was Hank a seer, or just a bluff?

Time will blab. Erstwhile, two brats gave scream through the lounge.
Had Homeland Security slept? Each brat

had surely dug in three junkyards to scrounge
—explosives no, but a puce virus that

could disable half the West and Mexico.
"Jumping Holy Saint Francis!" Hank exclaimed.
His magazine showed a face that a Texaco
station's oil, retreads, and gas had maimed.

Black eyes stared back at him. *Boss Moe*, the headline read,
How Does He Stay So Clean? A joke, a pun?
Hank read the words set under that so-ugly head:
Reputedly Mexico's main drug Hun,

Boss Moe, as he likes to be called, was born
Don Juan José Carlos Castaneda
in Nuevo Laredo, "untimely torn"
from his madre, else he would have stayed a

shopkeeper or maybe even been a padre.
This, at least, stands the legend he gives out.
And Boss Moe really does take care of Madre,
(see inset photo) whose mansion lies about

ten miles off from Nuevo Laredo.
Ooof! One of the brats hurled a stuffed black cat
that hit Hank's ear. Some strychnine-laced Pla-doh,
inside a tub, stirred by tails of plague-ridden rats,

would be just what the drug dealer ordered
to send these brats to coffin's quiet end.
At present moment, their manners bordered
on a cock fight this drug lord might attend.

Hank found the picture of Boss Moe's mom.
A looker! Not even fifty, she

had popped the Boss a year before her junior prom.
Caesarian birthed just like Macbeth, he

went on to build Mexico's largest drug
empire. Immensely popular, he gives
to church and poor. No common lowlife thug,
he loves flamenco; opera sends him shivs.

He's planning a trip north to Los Alamos
for a donation to Bradbury Museum.
"What kids today should know is science most,"
read a quote. About the coke he kept mum,

Hank made note. Wait, it wasn't Macbeth who
got ripped. It was that other Mac who thrust
Macbeth with *his* mean gory sword. Reporters, do
they ever check their tips?
                                    "Not waiting long, I trust."

Hank jumped. Was Miz Walburn, holding a bump
on her forehead. She gave a frown and rub.
"Those screamers there lent me this lump.
I lent them Ex-lax cookies. They'll sit in a tub

"for days." Hank grinned and took her paisley bag.
"Be careful, Queen Victoria gave that to me
for my ten-year birthday." Hank's mouth gave sag;
Miz Walburn cackled out in glee.

"Dear Hank, you're such an easy mark.
But I did lift it off Kitty Oppenheimer,
who owed one huge favor to me. Was no lark
to skirt around her snits. Turned me old-timer

before I reached forty.—And you! Now you have
three roomies. I'm certain I'll like them."
She gave a backward look at two bad lads.
"Let's scram. My cookies act with utmost vim."

The shorter brat already was tugging
his cherry red pants, hitching them upward
as if they might assist in plugging
the inner cookie life jug-jugging forward.

A stench not so much wafted as did erupt.
"Oh hurry, Hank, grab that suitcase, we really
must leave before this entire room turns corrupt."
In open air by the truck, things were less mealy

and soon they drove. "Can we do a stop
in Santa Fe? I need to leave some things
with my friend there. He's almost ready to flop
from his lovely new fiancée's button stings.

"By chance, do you know where the morgue is?"
"Another joke, Miz Walburn?"
                                        "Dear me no.
Morguemeisters make the two-back too. This one's in biz
because of me. A week deflowering virgin snow

"left him to contemplate the afterlife.
Oh, I once played a hellion in that bed
with those four posters." Her sigh rang rife
with memory. "And then, he took it to head

"to be a doc. You see a connection,
you work with logic better than I can.
He went dissection, I, my direction.
He's stayed the type always sitting in jam.

"Engaged now to some red-headed firebrand.
I promised him good meds for his lolly.
Told me her name is Trixie. Can't understand·
why hitch yourself to names displaying folly?

"It plights what harmony trips through this world."
"Do you mean, why marry her or why
did she keep that name?"
                                    "Either presents a burled
knot, dearest Hank. Consider the earthly sky:

"it neither toils nor spins and all that biz."
Miz Walburn paused as Hank elevated an eye.
"So literal, dear. Don't huff a Cyclops tiz."
"I'm just doing what you said, though wondering why."

"The sky's simple, though every color there is."
Hank ran through some sky colors in his mind,
from yellow, purple, black, to pink. "Uh Miz
Walburn, it's no color to someone blind."

They drove, and Miz Walburn gave a titter.
This lad's thought patterns would toss out some ruby
right alongside his mindless sci-fi twitter.
She loved him for this. Forever true, he

kept quite clever, worrying egg before hen.
"—Look, our first saguaro! Now there's a deep
old mystery. As child I thought them dead men
sent back as spies and soldiers to ever keep

guard on the land. But when Oppie and Groves
killed that sweet boy's ranch operation
I knew cacti clumped like defunct iron stoves,
and offered this land no salvation."

"My roomie Lorrie thinks they're spirit gods—
those three over there are bending to talk."
"I thought that Carmen was the lass you unshod."
"Right. Lorrie's the one makes my pal Dave walk

the line." Hank pulled on over. "Something odd,"
he said. "I'll leave the truck running. Be right
back."
    "I'm going with. I'll get my rod."
"A gun?"
      She laughed. "Expecting a cacti fight?

"My witching rod, to find gems or water.
Used it to locate Kitty's wedding ring one
night. She slipped it off when she was hotter
than that blessed Bomb. Oh she could sing one

"lovely tune when she pumped in a hot funk mood."
Miz Walburn retrieved a pale, forked stick
that stuck out like a bone of something crude
and dead. She gave a desiccated flick

at Hank, whose moustache twitched sans guile.
They walked. The three cacti indeed had bent
like glum conspirators who might compile
a stack of doctored tax forms to be sent.

Hank pulled his cell phone out to take a pic.
Miz Walburn quivered her witching stick as
if palsy had hit. Old folks these days roam thick
as gravy, but a lot can do the kick-ass,

so watch out. *There's* the moral. Or not. Say,
her bony stick is really giving a jiggle.

Is she gonna find some clue that will play
a role in our whodunit? Or just give wiggle

on life's sad road? Let's pause. I'll cover all your bets.
Come on, guess. Wiggle or Clue, Clue or Wiggle?
Just mark C or W on the chad, and let's
be clear: I'm not from Florida, so no wriggle

will take place. Gentleman Joe is what they
call me down at Keeneland's fine racetrack
whene'er I go. So you'll stay certain: fair play stays.
No need to cry out foul, demand your money back.

Yet do you wonder, why this interim play?
Sweet Reader, we both know how Trixie's back
doth stack with hackles; why, she'd pop a stay
if women still wore whale bones to rack

their figures. At very least she'll pop a bra
when she gets cold wind of Miz Walburn's low,
vocal blow against the grand name "Trixie." Ah la,
I'll need to placate, and that's no unearned go.

Will cost me plenty. Twenty times twenty
times twenty might not even equate
the dough I'll need. My guess? I'll need plenty.
How many Hershey's kisses overcome hate?

We've seen already what that candy can do
when left in, inopportune place. How many?
A semi-trailer from PA might salve the rue.
How much? Too much. Lots more than any

overworked AMEX card of mine can do or sheave.
So phone, e-mail your bets on in. A credit

card works for me. Send help, or I'll need to leave
my home and hide on the streets. Suspicion? Head it

away. The game's not rigged, I swear to you.
I have no more idea what's under
those three cacti than where you got your shoes.
On Bourbon Street, right? Ha-ha. No such blunder.

I'm not some drunken, drugged, New Orleans con!
Such scheming lies outside my blood's clean circuit!
And I'm too minor for any Mafia don.
So don't be suspect and think, *My, how he works it.*

Nor should you think, *He knows, his muse's flame is on.*
Homer's muse might nod, mine sinks in catalepsy.
(Of course, I'll need some skim once the game is on.)
A blank computer screen is often the best she—

my muse—can do these mornings. Hot black tea
can barely budge her. So, a fifty-fifty chance
right now you'll win. There, please let me renew my plea!
Your ten-buck bet will help me enhance

my life with Pixie after she reads this chapter.
As mentioned, there will be a carrying fee.
Please don't leave me to hang from a rafter!
(Though Rolfing might just cure my bum left knee.)

Have you decided? Oh good Lord yes,
I can just smell those PayPal bets coming in.
Be sure to include your home address
and send your winning bet running in.

I'm tempted to take a break, sniff some brandy,
but I'm a moral, upstanding type of guy.

And though my stalling might come in handy,
I'm trusting you to move quick, not shuffle by . . .

So Hank, to get on back, to return to our tale,
is taking a flock of pictures. What bearing he
intends—I swear—leaves me windless, without a sail.
The crone? She's out there digging, tearing the

desert up like some frisky Labrador pup.
Bones or bullion, there's no bingo surety:
treasure or junk, who can know what is up?
Just stay certain: this plot's been writ with purity.

Two minutes to race time. You gotta bet to win!
C or W? Clue or Wiggle? Wiggle or clue?
Come on, friend, give Fortune's Wheel a spin!
C or W? Clue or Wiggle? Wiggle or clue?

Come on! Place bets! Don't throw your—or my!—horse's shoe!

❇ ❇ ❇

Well *that* was disappointing. PayPal's tally,
the cut to me of what was taken in,
is $84.80. I've tried to rally
by promising a graphic novel's shakin' in

my future. The PayPal folks are tough though,
and my account's already history.
I'll keep my word. I owe a half of you some dough,
so let's unwind this flighty mystery.

"You want to look at my new cactus photos?"
On hearing this, Miz Walburn turned her witch stick to

Hank and thought, *Today's kids let a Roto-*
tiller plow their brains too slick to

give thought a think. Why stare at photos when cacti
present themselves to touch and prick? Still, to please the
dear lad she praised his pics. "Close to exact, I
suppose. Say, Hank, no need to tease the

new photos from negatives in darkrooms
these days, is there?"
       "Oh no, I own a printer."
"As well. My heart could never send balloons
on smelling chemicals. Soon as I'd enter,

my love sachet would shrivel, despite the yummy
red lights."
    Hank blinked. It was like old folks
let oxen plow their brains, leaving a mummy
behind. He gave consider before he spoke,

omitting talk he deemed too randy:
"So did your stick find mineral or gem?"
"Don't know. It found a pile of dandy
black pebbles. Odd, I can't heft a one of them.

"Let's see if you can."
Hank could, with strain.
"They shine just like polished obsidian.
Think I'll lug one to C's mom's old swain."
"What strength! You remind me of Gideon."

"Who?"
    "A trombonist. Who's your rock-hound, Hank?"
"Some old Indian who yaps out prophetic dreams.

Can't hardly shut him up. He's tall and lank,
if you are wondering."

        "Lank? Tall? Some final screams

"for my love sachet would be just the thing.
Let's take all eight back. Instead of Manhattan
I'll sell him my sweet thing, let him poke my ring."
Hank blushed. "Miz—"

        "Goo up my sheets of satin.

"I trust that you and Carmen have already slid
on them."

   "Miz—"

      "Hank, it's such delight
to stand near you again. So innocent. Did
you ever figure I lied about the night

"that Einstein dropped on by to hunt snow snakes?"
"Uh, sure. You hunt them in broad daylight."
Miz Walburn gave her witch stick a shake
as Hank grinned. "Science fiction's left you a sight.

"Let's pack these load stones to your Native Am
friend. May be some diamonds, rubies or pearls
within."

     "Or may be some nasty Hill scam
in them." They stopped. Possibilities made swirls . . .

Sorry folks, but I must needs sit on your money
a short while longer. This chapter's inconclusive.
I can't pay off one way or t'other. Honey,
recall, tastes sweeter when it stays elusive.

So don't lick it off. We'll wait for less abstruse if—

Chapter Thirty: You don't mind

"If you don't mind!" Sweet Trixie yelled e'en while I gave
her foot a hot oil rub. I knew it'd be this way.
After reading the last chapt., she's stayed a-rave
for two long days. I've broiled lobster, rode the Parkway,

rented a motorcycle—nearly crippling us.
Needless to say, $84.80 flew
off first hour, first day. And Harvey Hippo's a bust.
That's right: now we're at Cincinnati's Zoo.

"That old hag's got to die."
                              "Miz Walburn?! But—"
"I don't care if she's the damned Sphinx, Joe!"
I swear that Harvey winked, or I'm off my nut.
"She's lowdown and slutty, a meddling minx ho!"

"She's one hundred and two years old!"
"The reason more. To live beyond a century
reveals bad taste." Trixie turns to the hippo.
Another wink? "Wait! That biddy may give entry

into the sexual rink for your sweet daughter."
My nose gives twitch. Repeat a lie enough,
and you believe it.
                     "So hold that old slut's slaughter
until the opera in Santa Fe. Some rough

old times will hit your quintet then. You too, dadkins.
Let's eat. H Hippo inspires better than your muse,
but now my gut wants meat. Why not let your glad kin
sweet Lorrie climb the pole, not moan out lonesome blues."

Ah la, when T hippo-struts, keep off her shoes.

Chapter Thirty-one:
Cinnamon at the morgue,
strange happenings in a gorge;
your author writes two rants;
he may as well have jigged a dance;
a potential cat fight turns to prance

Hank parked before the Santa Fe morgue,
located in a plaza named Dixie.
Out front, an oldster's cigar-puffing gorge
reposed sun-broiling, bandy legs shifting. "Risky,"

Miz Walburn made to note.
                              "Are you talking
cigar or sun?" Hank raised his brow.
"Old man sun can't be helped. He keeps on stalking
till we're evicted from this globular now.

"But way used-back, MM gave only chew
to those penile things. His Trixie trollop must be
one sexy handful."
                      "He's storing overflow stew
of corpses from the Hill. He might just be

fast veering daft from that."
                              "Hank, what's got him worried
shows woman wrath. But I've tucked up a cure
here in my paisley. Was good we hurried
and did not get stuck when you mucked up your

"truck wheels in that sand."
                              "Those stones were way too heavy

to tote to the highway."

                      "I did bring some extra."

Miz Walburn tapped the paisley. "A bevy

of women will gather to sing 'Sex, tra

" '-la, if you please.' But should you dare use it,

fight 'em off. You're built of good moral stuff."

Miz Walburn gave Hank's shoulder a thwack abusive.

"Take it, you'll tote those stones for miles without one huff."

"Why, Emma!" The cigar man fought to stand.

Miz W inhaled. "See? She's crippled him!

He's not that old."

                      "I thought that you and he planned,

after your virginity—"

                      "Mine? *His* tippled in!

"Was Vietnam. A virgin in college

that day and age just wasn't right. Make love,

not war. Good slogan, though a raw harsh edge

slipped in if Cupid zapped with fake rake's love."

The smoking cigar fumes swirled toward Hank's truck,

still puffing sludge. Good thing that Sigmund Freud

lay dead: each puff produced a wanton suck.

"MM! My dear, you never could avoid

"a strong woman. That why you loved on me?"

MM ignored her razz to sniff about Hank's truck.

"Cinnamon," he moaned, as if in plea.

"That's what's that smell! A Cuban male in rut!

"Our saintly stones! Quick, Hank, lend me your hand!"

Hank did and Miz Walburn gave it four whiffs.

"Blessed be Sinatra! My dream about the land
plays right. Saguaro *will* save us from tiffs

"by birthing these love stones!" She looked in back
to see MM ascend the truck's thin running board.
But not to inspect Hank's brand new gun rack!
No, his nose gave whiff and twitch at the hoard

of shiny black stones. "Cinnamon! Whatever
are they?" He tried to budge just one but couldn't.
He leaned back to count. Eight. "Wherever
did you find them?"

                    "Beneath three cacti that wouldn't

let us drive past. They bunched to huddle,
they seemed like chanting monks worshipping great
saints' sacred bones that they'd exhumed to cuddle."
At Miz W's words, MM beamed in hope. "Eight!

"Won't count my blowflies 'fore they hatch, although
maggots can mount in warm corpse-time too."
"MM, diverting as a flaming match, although,
please heaven, let the death slime shoo fly shoo

"on this visit. Tell about your upcoming spouse."
MM's thick shoulders scrunched. He peeped at a pink car.
Hank looked. His memory went fritz, unable to rouse.
Not even thirty, and his brain cells couldn't jar?

The morgue's front door popped open with two great whacks.
A thin redhead sprang, leaving both sides ajar.
"You're Emma! I see you still hit on younger jacks.
My soon-hubby told all; it's past, no need to spar.

"I stand in peace, my name of folly and all!
I hold great hope you've brought my olden stud new life,
He's so obsessed with deaths his lolly and all
love-thoughts have fled. 'Give due to the almost wife,'

"that weird Saint Paul guy said—"

                                 "Eight stones, my dearest!
Eight deaths last night in Santa Fe."
"Your dearest? Not for these two months. The nearest
I've come to love is watching those two gays!

"They're in the morgue, they're prancing around that
dead señorita your mom collected the cash
to in-grave. Aren't you ashamed? If she found that
girl's blue hat on an old dead drunk she'd bash—"

"Shoe. A satin blue shoe, but we had to
hold *it* from the casket too." MM turned to
the stones and sniffed. "For evidence. Sad to
bestow such status on girl and shoe. I yearned to

"enlist the Mountain Nuns to sing their chants
around her coffin ground. In case, you know, there is
some god whose dictates present other than rants
on queers and race and what slim-shaped berries his

"disciples munch at sacrificial breakfast."
He turned to Hank. "Everyone calls me
MM, and this is my beautiful steadfast
gal Trixie. Never more loving lass—"

                                   "Oh balls, he

"hasn't doled out love sauce since—" Trixie
heaved up a sigh and gave a jerk of head

toward the morgue. "Since that tangled pixie
from Los Alamos was shipped here sad and dead."

"But, dearest, now with these cinnamon stones—"
"Obsessed!" The redhead turned to Miz W and Hank.
"A month ago for breakfast, French toast. He moans,
'Anomalies,' complains my toast stank

"like Mexican señorita—"
                    "We found it!"
The morgue's front door emitted two gyrating
men. Mike, a drama queen, yelled, "He'll expound it!"
"We pulled Juanita out to check. She's hydrating!

"Or may as well be. She's gained a kilo
since the Ted goon and that sweet spy lady
left out last time." DC beamed, a hero
Mike, strutting like the young gay blade he

was, exclaimed, "It's swelling up her gorge!
The cinnamon smell and weight gain both."
"Mike," MM admonished, "we run a morgue,
no chicken coop. You know though, one ray of hope

"still shines through. Give a sniff to these eight black
pebbles, which perch too darned heavy to move.
Last night those eight who disappeared were porky fat
BBQ fans who likely chewed all the hooves."

They gazed at Hank's old truck.
                            What moves believers?
What sparks insight in music, science, and math?
A graviton? Gene mutation? Up-your-sleevers
prestidigitating? A hot then icy bath?

Though answers lurk dark-robed and hidden,
mysterious notions strike, insight deluxe:
Just so, all six moved forward, as if bidden
by godlike design to counteract flux.

"Hey now! Let's cart them to the morgue to weigh,"
suggested Mike, while leaning for a sniff.
"Cinnamon, all right."
                              "It was yesterday
those eight went stray. A purple flash, no tiff,

"no shouting, nor flame. That's from a neighbor
who witnessed it." MM gave one pebble a punch,
received a stoved-in finger for his labor.
Mike gasped: "Hot damn, look how they all bunch

"that plywood."
                  Hank pointed out a dent
in the bed of his truck. "That's where I plopped the first."
Like every pick-up owner, Hank's heart went
drip-drop enamoring his truck. Ventricles burst

when that so evil dent gave way. He'd moved plywood
and hefted, with many manly grunts,
the seven pebbles left. "And six weigh out nigh good
two hundred pounds. Those paired unseemly runts

"come in at less than one hundred."
"Four fat BBQ men, two fat ladies,
and two young daughters." MM, with some dread,
gave count and touched each pebble showing shady

despite midday's sun.
                          "That one's for sure the runt,"
Hank said. "I flopped it in second to last."

Mike trotted for a gurney, singing, "Time to punt."
"A Colorado player," DC beamed, fast

to eye Mike's flailing arms and salty hams.
Miz Walburn looked from the running lad to
the pebbles plopped in Hank's old truck. "This damns
The Hill," she spat. "These goings on, I'm sad to

say, share its nasty marks. Something low and shady—"
Mike loped back with a gurney. Miz W
watched both this new gay doc and MM's lady
eyeballing muscles.
                    —Hey gals, if it's a snub ya

desire, fag hag's your game. Not a good profession,
if you ask me—of course you didn't.
But here's a ponder thought, a counter-lesson:
Rosa Traci Johns—Who's she? There's my unbidden

true moral. She was the UCLA chick
who got all shriveled by that guy who's a prick,
the Hanson prick who promised she might flick
or even kick a Higgs boson. Her science shtick

got her dropped under. Not a likely problem
fag hags will face. Too bad PayPal shut me down,
or I'd take bets that such a goblin
won't harm those misled gals. A gentle gay frown

creates their worst fate. So . . . man that I yam,
recant I will. That rant was wrong. Want another?
Steer clear of science! It's a flim-flam sham!
Just think, my sister, my brother:

Without science we'd endure no spam—
not that lovely luncheon meat that deploys
its nourishment in children's luncheon cans
to strengthen bones and sight in girls and boys—

no, I mean those email communiqués,
those incoming bytes that stuff your inbox
to make your eyes, ears, and nose flail away,
then slowly send your colleagues seeking de-tox.

Without science . . . a somber voice doth ring . . .
Without science . . . a country of people would sing . . .
Without science . . . a legion of knells would not ring . . .
Without science . . . a load of souls would not fling . . .

The Bomb, The Bomb, The Bomb, The Bomb, The Bomb.
The Bomb, The Bomb, The Bomb, The Bomb, The Bomb.
The Bomb, The Bomb, The Bomb, The Bomb, The Bomb.
The Bomb, The Bomb, The Bomb, The Bomb, The Bomb.

Perfect in meter, wondrous in rhyme,
a mushroom cloud that quaintly billowed high
a Geiger click of hearts erased from all space-time.
Enola Gay, a dove high-fiving Japan's cry.

But *yet*, does science not accomplish good at times?
In answer to this, just look about.
As sure as I sometimes snap off fine rhymes,
science sometimes slides a keeper in, no doubt.

Machines to roll cigarettes, chemo to dry lungs.
Drilled oil to move our cars, smog to make our globe warm.
Grease to fry catfish, antacids to soothe our tums.
Aircraft to fly so high, bomb shelters to stall harm.

My second rant's undone. I really am thwarted.
I rub my desk, construe complaints,
but each and every doth get aborted,
as if my mind's beset by KY haints.

Without science . . .

Stop this poor cogitation! Back to our sestet:
Both Hank and Mike uplifted black tiny stones
onto the gurncy, needing four hard treks
because of their heft. "There by the phones

"are listed the weights of the missing eight,"
MM noted. Hank and Mike gave eight grunts:
so much in so little wouldn't abate.
Each pebble got weighed, and to be blunt

their weights did jibe with the waylaid fat peeps',
exceeding only by a cool ten percent.
"Juanita's first increase went just that steep!"
Mike did note. His conjecture churned intense:

"The Hill! It's that boson Higgs particle!"
He shouted as his muscle-fingered hands
spoke syllabic flutters. "I read an article
about it on the web."
                    Hank took a sci-fi stand:

"It's Higgs boson, but I bet my Kirk shirt you're right."
Mike twitched his muscled nose; Trixie stepped in quickly:
"Hank's that sweet spy's boyfriend, Mike. Don't show spite."
"How'd you—"
            "My KY cousin came thickly

"here tracking an animal abuse slob
named Taylor. You met her. If you're right about The
Hill then—"

        Miz Walburn's head gave small bob.
"Trouble, dear?" Trixie warbled. "Should we shout the

"words your way? Maybe something in my name,
the *X* or *I*, throws off your hearing.
I don't trill my *R*, so that's not to blame.
Still, something in that name of folly is blearing—"

MM stepped forward: "Regroup! Let's have lunch
at Mom's."

        "As long as she won't serve us cats,"
Miz Walburn noted. "We're scratching up a bunch."
Her right brow arched at Mike, then Trixie: "No spats."

"Hey please, you five, don't mention Juanita.
Mom thinks she's resting in a Catholic grave,"
MM begged. "My mom's menu will complete a
peace for sure, will stop all our raves.

Ah, wine and food, the honey that saves.

Chapter Thirty-two:
A rant resumed (your author can't help it);
that PayPal bet exhumed (though someone quickly
   shelved it)

They'd each drank a margarita at lunch,
though Miz Walburn'd sipped a nice red wine,
so they returned calm, no eyebrows in bunch.
They found Juanita had truly grown like a vine;

in consequence, many words and phrases were dealt:
"Strickland," "Manson," "jerk-ass," "dick."
"Gravity," "depravity," "abbreviated longevity."
"Long black box," "heavy black rocks," "sick."
[I sorrow for the varied line-length and snickety internal rhymes.
Like all bad artists, I claim, of course, that reality determines my form.
What a wretched place, then, reality must provide! It's our norm?
Little wonder musicians, scientists, and poets choose to hide.
Life truly blows absurd. But . . . back to phrases and words]:
"*Lagarto tuerto*," "lots of people *muerto*."
"Higgs boson," "Boson Higgs," "God particle," "clothing article."
"Blue shoe," "son named Blue."
"Blue hat," "family spat,"
"Hiroshima," "Nagasaki," "Trinity," "infinity."
"Potential," "exponential," "explosion," "implosion."
"Fibonacci," "Liberace." [This from the DC doc whose dad was closet gay.]
"WMD."
"WMD."
"No damned way."
"No damned way."
"No damned way." [Said twice for WMD and once for being closet gay.]
"Can't they invent something nice on that blasted hill?"

"Teflon." "Heart valves." "Super Glue."
"Spam." "Spam? The jellied, salty ham?" "And Tang."
"Devons." "McGuire." "Think they're involved?" "Why not? Both for hire."
"Large purple flash," "no wounds, much less a gash."
"A gravity gun that swirls?"

That last came from Hank who recalled his joke
to the Fed-Ex man. Maybe he'd hit cash.
He retold the scene of which Carmen spoke
after they'd spotted the great purple flash:

"Our Hanson held that same oblong black box
the night Rosa Traci Johns went missing."
"Who?"
          Hank explained.
                    Lord what a pox
on fame: *Astray in woods, perhaps while pissing.*

Poor Rosa Traci is flat-out doomed
to be forgot. Such remains the so sad lot
of science's guineas whether mushroomed
atomic hot or cured with a needle's shot.

When Hank finished, five of seven began to yell.
Juanita, she kept prim and quiet—good lass!
Oddly enough, Trixie had nothing to tell.
You'd expect that redhead to toss a load of sass.

Redheads suffer pain more, you surely know.
It seems the red hair gene and the pain gene
spin from identical DNA glow.
Well, stranger twists of fate stand to be seen.

Roentgen discovering x-rays is one.
The apple falling on Newton's head's another.

The coconut that fell and killed Dr. Liz Bunn
just as she was about to find her brother

and together they were just about to concoct
a cure for cancers. If only their tastes
had run to pineapples. A bush can't drop
that far nor fast. This and many such wastes

spill through this world. But the cup can be
half full too, you know. With this brave insight
let's return to our seven to see—
all but Juanita knew things flowed not quite right.

The essence of their noise castigated The Hill.
"From your very first missive to me, I knew well:
That blessed Hill has spewed another poison pill
—and once more it's straight from the flames of hell

"Is humanity's fate to gulp and swallow?
Did you know that Italian squirt Fermi took
bets that The Bomb would ignite air, leave us hollow?"
A regular peas-and-carrots mumble shook

the morgue's high seven windows. Reason came
informed as a shout, from a source that
no one might expect. Trixie, all the same,
tossed logic with these words from her brain's vat:

"If these damn stones were truly roasting on
Barbecue Drive back here in the city,
How is it that they wound up coasting on
the Interstate?"
                          Juanita, out of pity,

let slip a burp from her gorge. Hard to keep
her down, evidently. "Spooky action

at a distance," Hank said, doing his best to reap
from science fiction.
                              "Juanita's reaction,"

said the DC doc, "can easily be explained."
"Not her," Hank said, "but quarks and their
spin. A twin far away can instantly change,
according to its mate. Just like they planned their

"moves in some occult, strange, and mystic way."
"My KY cousin and I do like that.
A realtor, she visited the other day.
I knew before she called. But a shoe like that

"fits a whole different bunch of toes than these rocks
in hiking twelve miles through town on their own."
Trixie had edged beside Juanita to take stock.
She gently touched the gorge that indeed had grown.

A small, compliant burp crept out.
"Cause and effect," MM said, taking Trixie's hand.
"Just so. And sirs, I fear cause has now stepped out
entirely with these stones, to make our land

"lie *terra incognita*." They all
took look-see at Hank, even Juanita,
whose eyes had long ago taken a caul.
Hank's mouth opened, wanting to speed a

bit more about those spooky things that happen
over *Star Trek* parsecs. His silence spoke defeat.
Poor guy, it was like someone had slappen
him silly. Bright words could not come clean and neat.

Take lesson from that and the pineapple bush
that neither toils nor spins. Nor does it drop
death from the sky to crush smart brains with whoosh,
Pineapples, unless grenades, grow a healthy crop.

Our bet? I must hold escrow till this plot gives hop.

Chapter Thirty-three:
Carmen struts her stuff,
yours truly cries enough's enough
Miz Walburn saves all by telling sexy fluff

When Miz W and Hank drove from Santa Fe,
they placed by a steel basin three great thimbles
of penile magic for MM. "No other way.
His stick's just not that flashy nor nimble,"

Miz Walburn stated as they pulled away.
Her Hank, of course, gave blush. "But larger problems loom.
That Hill always crushes good wholesome play."
Miz W's eyes glowed prophetic: "Doom and doom.

"Those corpses smell of more than sweet bun spice."
"Just what we've all been thinking," Hank replied.
Disheveled, they arrived un-neat, un-nice
at Miz Walburn's house, where all five tight sighs sighed . . .

Next night they sighed at Todd's Deep End, the five of them,
for by morning Miz Walburn had nostalgic went,
recalling Todd's had opened on a GI whim
one year post-Vietnam, where Todd'd been sent.

No sooner had they sat down and ordered
when in walked Hanson, Carmen's lowlife father
who looked as if he on some bender bordered.
C huffed on seeing him, caught in his bother.

"Watch this," was her sly comment. She bared a
breast, it was her left one, and a nipple showed.

"Janet Jackson?" Hank guessed. He spared a
lewder comment though his eyes could not stay stowed.

C's nipple? It showed to make a point
(poor pun aside) about C and her dad,
a.k.a. Hanson. C strutted the joint
and stood before him. Her nipple sent nothing rad

to him, nor did her frown, nor did her smile.
Back then she walked, to cover herself, for she
admired Confucian propriety. "I'll
bet you I could do that all night."

                              "Whoopee!"

Dave yipped, which earned a whack from Lorrie.
"I guess it's 'cause I look so much like Mom.
She *did* coerce the marriage. I'm sure he's sorry
his bachelor life ruptured awry, an atom bomb."

"But he's got Blue, his son!"

                         "Blue's a bastard."
"We all know that."

                    "No, certifiable,
not legit. He tells everyone when he's plastered.
Beer and drugs leave him quite reliable.

"My point is this. Unseen, I've been trailing
my Hanson Dad for several weeks, since the
UCLA girl took leave in a flash, sailing
off with the Blessed Virgin M. Hence the

"interest I show in my creep-o bad pop.
Well, three nights back he drove to Santa Fe,
to 'Barbecue Drive,' as Trixie at the corpse shop
would say. There, the flash he made wasn't Santa's way

of eating cookies and cream. Pops drove back later,
stole through the yard and did some hot grunting.
Eight times he rolled out a heavy weight or . . .
those stones. As Mike would say, I'm not punting,

"but still I wonder: those cinnamon stones may
be, in fact, our barbecue fans, and if we went
back to Lover's Lane, young Miss UCLA
in likewise stone might lie there giving vent

"to that same spice. Just as death anointed
Juanita, those ultra-heavy pebbles
might be the new, improved, death appointed
by yon Hill's gravity gun. I bet it trebles

"their output."
        Into the bar two thugs soon strutted.
Astute as ever, Hanson looked up
to wave them o'er. His smile abutted
into a frown the moment they hooked up

and started to talk. "It's those same creeps who gave
us opera tickets," L leaned to whisper.
C gave a nod to confirm. "They need to shave,
but true, 'tis they."
        "That man's face is blister,"

Miz Walburn said.
        "It's Boss Moe! From the news-
paper!" Hank told about the Mex drug czar.
"Hey! He knew about Juanita's damn blue shoes!"
"Oh hon, that was in the *Santa Fe Star.*"

"The Santa Fe what?" Carmen balked. She tugged
her blouse again, post-fact embarrassed.

"Oh hon, whatever it's called. My memory's mugged."
"Those cretins," C said. "The Press are bare-assed

"traitors. They sham like Hollywood writers."
"Novelists, too. They all lie."
                        Who made that boff?
Sweet Reader, did you hear? Like two fighters,
The Boss and Hanson were squaring off.

Turn my back to watch them, some nasty redactor
tosses aspersions at my fine comrades
and me. All best beware! At least one spare actor
in Todd's bar can be popped while this purple fad's

out flashing its snout. Well, the damage is done.
I'll keep an eye on those so-jive five,
but let's stroll near the two who first won
my hard attention. Beer's about to arrive,

so my guess is that Hanson and Boss Moe
have calmed. "Maybe someone gone and took 'em,"
the less ugly thug said, grammar filled with woe.
His boss's head went snap. Less Ugly's words shook him.

He gave bad glance to Lorrie and Carmen.
"Those señoritas been nosing around;
Paid them a visit, one pulled a gun, not charmin'
like *chicas* should be. Think they're our rock hounds?"

"What girls? I only see two pineapples."
"Pineapples?"
               "You mean her *pechos*?"
Less-ugly asked.
               "You two jackals!"
The Boss stared at Lorrie's breasts. "*De hecho,*

"they *are* like two piñatas. Too soft to
bust, though."
        "Yeah, give 'em two sucks and a tug.
"There was this girl once, I'd climb her loft to . . ."
Moby Dick's cetology makes readers shrug,

so I won't imagine ninety lines
of Hanson's titology faring much better.
La Leche League supports the best of wines,
but as we've seen before, The Boss's fetter

is money and drugs. Still, once more he's glommed
on Carmen. I don't like his look at all:
C surely didn't utter the comment that bombed
us writers. Scram, Boss Moe! Halt your visual maul.

That Carmen's a sweet girl, just doing her job.
("Rather he maul your daughter?" I hear Trixie say.)
Damn you, Boss Moe! Why does such evil throb
on this green globe? You live as proof that God is nay.

Back to our five: their remark about writers
I forgive. "That ugly man," Miz Walburn
gave say, "he looks so rough that he elicits burrs.
I doubt a mom could give him kiss. Takes lots to turn

"a momma's love. Groves was pig-fat, Oppy
stick-thin. Feynman was cute in his hot young
days. They made the Bomb; still, moms got sloppy
over them. But that one? Who's ever sung

"a lullaby for him?"
        "Actually,"
Hank said, "he bought his mom a grand casa

outside Nuevo Laredo. Factually
then, you're wrong, Miz Walburn." Hank, un-pasha

like, fiddled with his beer and gave a sigh.
(*"See there! I told you that the old slut was mis-wired!"*
Mad Trixie's taken to reading quite nigh
my shoulder. She claims this will keep me fired

to do what's right, that being rubbing
Miz Walburn out for her nominal slurs.)
"It's not the first time, Hank. I've been flubbing
since birth. It's the human condition that spurs

"us on to greater things. Those brains on The Hill
craft tubs of flubs for humans to overcome."
Hank demurred, "Good comes too, they have good will."
Lorrie added, "Tang instant, a marvel unsung.

"There's Tang from the moon trip, there's ICBMs,
the Stealth Jet, and that cute smart missile;
there's hydrogen bombs to ride high on them—
Hank you're right, good will's innate, almost prehensile."

(*"Joe, can you yet doubt that she's your progeny?*
Her caustic tongue came straight from D. N. A.
Joe, there's not an ounce of misogyny
in you. Give Lorrie a break. She's your fuckin' a

daughter!")
A ruckus showed at the door. Blue banged
in and walked straight to his dad, though his eyes
watched Carmen. Pops straightened at Blue's harangue,
stood and went to the bar, began yapping with guys

were leaning there. Boss Moe and his Less Ugly yapped
with Blue, who finally sat and ordered a beer.
In nineteen seconds—my stopwatch stays strapped
to wrist—Cal Strickland walked in and took a veer

toward The Boss. Then Blue got up and walked to a
señorita. A tall pale man strolled in
to sit at black Bishop 4. Hank stalked to a
lone stall in the men's. Todd rolled in

enough dough to tip his Mountain nun jar.
A fat guy from northwest Texas farted;
two women and one man removed from the bar.
A thin gent in a blue suit departed.

Two young girls came in, nodded at Hanson.
No don't, Carmen almost yelled out.
But seeing two GI's utterly handsome,
the girls slipped toward them like water spouts.

Lorrie—was she in a snit or claustrophobic?—
stepped on out. Hey, is IBM's Deep Blue making
all these chess moves? These jumbles come so aerobic
that if I were stopping time and taking

a poll of readers' thoughts, they'd all surmise
a Master Match was now in play. Life's a bowl of
cherries, much wiser poets write: a surprise
to me. More often it seems a scroll of

instructions written in cold-coded Urdu
that humans must decipher and perform
instanter. One wrong move might slur you
for decades—should ever you slip back to norm.

Let's purvey this bar-cum-chessboard's purview:
Hank in john: closet gay bathroom sex?
Strickland to Boss Moe: needs peyote to chew?
Tall guy at 4: has pale biceps to flex?

Hanson at bar: "How 'bout that game?"
Blue to señorita: "Hey babe, you want some coke?"
And now look: outside it's started to rain
yet there stands Lorrie. Is this some joke?

Miz Walburn's head lolls down to her chest:
Great God Hydrogen, is she fixing to die?
C's studying Blue's butt: surely not incest!
Dave sniffles and drops a tear from one eye.

Allergies? Or did love splat on this rainy night?
Todd tosses five in the Mountain nun jar.
Hanson greasily yaps. Sweet Reader, see my plight?
If this much goes on in one Los Alamos bar

in just one part of one normal then rainy night,
can any mere mortal dare sort it out?
And I have yet to map that farter on bar's right,
the man and women he moved about,

the blonde who saw The Boss and hid in fright,
and that thin blue-suited gent who walked on out.
Red wine, supplements, hikes—try as I might,
what I seem to be is grossly mortal. My snout

can't sniff one solution to this sad mess:
Mayhap I'll give up writing to become
a balladeer, though I must here confess
my voice can't warble like when I sung

in high school glee club. Wait! I spy movement!
Miz Walburn raises her head from her chest.
She's not dead yet!

        "Where am I . . . who, I meant . . .
. . . no, where? Oh, Todd's. He used to serve the best

pineapple drinks. Where's Hank? Where's that Lorrie?"
Carmen reached to calm the centenarian.
"They'll both be back soon. Tell us a story."
"Story? This room spun like a planetarium,

"but now it's better. Get Lorrie and Hank
back and I'll tell about the well-endowed
physicist. I mean, honey, he had a crank."
Carmen gave two blinks. Miz Walburn's eyes plowed

until they spotted Lorrie outside in the rain.
"What's she doing? How can you let her stand
there?"

       "She gets misty, looks for castles in Spain,
when talking about her dad."

               "Go, give hand!"

Miz Walburn ordered Dave. "Bring her inside."
"And you," Miz Walburn turned to C, "Get Hank."
As bid, the two did. "Now, settle for a ride,"
Miz Walburn said when the four enjoined in rank.

" 'Twas a dark and steamy night without condoms.
Well no, let me start over. The wine
was red, they young, hot jazz fell upon them.
In silly youth, they stood certain they tapped life's spine.

"It was after the war, after the bomb.
My handsome scientist had just read a paper

that sent him a-whir. He had one big stromb-
oli. I would have been much safer

"had that not been the case. No regrets
though. He's the one who helped me make
my daughter. So we danced the dance, but he gets
quaked by a paper from a goggle-eyed jake

"named Gödel. Now that man's mom, what do
you think she thought of him and her husband,
with such a name? That's one hard shot straight to
the heart. –At least he wasn't called Bobby Bland."

(Trixie gives my shoulder a right hard pinch.
"What's with this hag and names? She want to
research the next O. E. D.?" I don't flinch
but keep on writing.)
                    "That paper bid avaunt to

"his entire mind. That's okay, his pecker—"
Miz Walburn grabbed Hank's arm and gave it the eye—
"well, I won't exaggerate. A double-decker
would fill the bill." Black Bishop 4 made quick to hie

over and hear a crone talk so dirty.
Todd, too, ambled by, spotting the old lady.
"This Gödel paper was really flirty
with multiple universes. It seemed shady,

"but I'm no physics whiz. Gödel claimed
there were portals and edges—"
                              "*Star Trek!*"
"Hold your spaceships." Miz Walburn drained
her wine and never spilled one red speck.

She, Chaucer's prioress, and the Wife of Bath
the circus rounds should make! "These portals and edges
could instantly form a bright shining path
to other universes, make stable wedges,

"if one plotted the right electrons and math,
I guess. Well, Oppie was busy fretting
his two a-bombs and their nasty wrath.
But Groves, a general, was always abetting

"a better weapon than Ivan down the block,
so he bestowed my love his very own lab.
Lord above, you should have seen that man's cock
engorge when that came out. All crow, no flab,

"it gave a jitterbug hop." Less Ugly bought
Miz Walburn wine. The sweet little thing
that Blue was chatting shook her head and sought
to leave his confines. She took to the wing—

just like Time, that snitty flapping bird—
to hear this old thin woman's story, too.
It seemed that each Miz Walburn word
was gathering a listener or two. Well glory, you

hear an old dame warbling of a penis,
vagina, bombs, and sex, it taxes your
brain. This old-timey, wrinkled brash Venus
there flaring out sex fast as Faxes sure

gave inspiration. "His new lab showed stainless steel
and porcelain. Walk in, all you could see
was glow. Musical vibrations, you'd feel
as much as hear them. Made me want to pee—

"or have sex! Then one day we lay on a table—
ooh la la, I felt *absolument* French.
My lover was so much more than able
Him, that glow, that music, made me clench."

Now Strickland, young Blue, and even Boss Moe
strolled over. Strickland envisioned his mom;
The Boss thought a prima donna had let go
an aria when Miz Walburn's "ooh la" came on.

Blue was chasing the chick with sense enough
to walk away. Miz Walburn took a sip
of wine and winked at Less Ugly, whose gruff
scarred face manufactured a grin. Hearts went skip.

Sweet Reader, look! They all stood in one hot spot.
You ask, Where's Hanson? Lurking the edge,
his perfect slot. Worried he'll need to trot,
he always faces the door. Took that pledge

after C's mom tricked him into tying the knot.
Let's let him quiver. Miz Walburn's cooking her stew:
"Oh such a table, oh such music, like as not
it wouldn't have happened without that brew,

"for my sex gears waltzed over forty. *Ooh la la*,
we both sang, rocking off this universe.
The cool stainless steel made us go ah-ha-ha
each time we churned. Sudden music burst!

"Galaxies spiraled! A star! A comet!
Black holes tugged—even though no human
knew of them then. My moistly hot love grommet
went tight until it took the whole room in.

"He shouted in an alien warble,
I answered in that same astral tongue.
When later I considered it, a garble
was all I could evoke. But *then* a blue hot sun

"flashed out before my eyes. One last love spasm
and he was gone. Vanished, kaput, zero,
nil. Alone atop the steel, my love chasm
quivered and felt one bit left of my hero

"come swimming bravely up to do what life
will best will. He, I knew, had flown to that blue sun.
Did happiness greet him there? Did he learn less strife?
No answer. But for sure he'd left this sparse true one

"universe. Poor Gödel was right. I had to
sneak from the lab. I donned my man's coat and hat;
they're still in my upstairs closet. Glad to
leave them with you, Hank . . . The old goat. And that

"tale manufactures a slew of morals." A sigh
left Miz W's lips; her chin gave lift. "Gals, always
take a raincoat with in lab." Nearby women high-
fived one another at that. "Male strays

"can't always help wandering away. Forgive,
but don't forget. That blue sun which calls them
may or may not afford a better spot to live."
Each male around gave grunt to hack up phlegm.

"Be cautious of science. It often sports traps."
Some nodded, some sipped their beers, some gave
itch at that. "And you lovely daughters without paps,
do stay brave. He might show, green eyes, haircut, shave

and all, intact." L and C wiped tears at that.
"But most important, 'Drink up, poor Shriners!'
We're here today, *mañana* we'll be kersplat.
Life's to grab. Nothing's worse, nothing's finer."

The entire bar whooped and knocked their bottles
at her platitude. Though late-night wisdom
comes cheap, that's when it's needed full throttle;
so who could care if the mix should slur? A misdem-

eanor at worst. People may slight and mock
Omar Khayam, but note: his quotes exceed groats.
My own wimp moral? 'Tis no great shock
Miz Walburn garnered those drunken votes.

"Aw, Miz Walburn, did you just make that up
for me?" L asked, her clear green eyes a-mist.
"Imagine, one night with Kirk, then a blast-up
to rotate the universe and give it a twist."

Sweet Reader: I leave you temporal astral bliss.

Chapter Thirty-four:
Trixie changes her mind,
getting yours truly out of one bind,
only to find . . .

"O Captain! My Captain! Our fearful trip is done!
The rocket ship from port has slipped and sailed!
The great In-Out—at last—has been fair won!
So bless you, Joe . . . at last you got two lovers nailed.

"It takes a woman to admit she's wrong.
I was. That aged gal hefts strange bucolic class.
Let her thrive one more decade, strutting strong."
Trixie huzzahs all this with loads of sass.

She should, she made another hotshot sale.
Well, two in fact. A fancy church, a bar.
Result? Miz Walburn stays no more in Trixie-hell.
Good. To me, Miz W presents a shining star.

Did you key on how fast she pegged Boss Moe?
That newspaper and Hank had both judged wrong:
the casa for The Boss's mom is only show:
a tax write-off. His madre swears he should be strong,

become a Catholic priest. Despising the drugs
he panders, she cares not a whole lot for
his so-called *amigos*, though that Less Ugs-
ly she always yet simmers a warmish spot for,

while hoping Less's *hermana* will act a
spiritual *sor* and turn her so-ugly

hijo into a priest. She's even tracked a
bishop and a *brujo* down, juggling

beliefs. In this, Mom's like us one and all,
hedging bets to waylay our earthly grief.
Miz Walburn's east-coast daughter might could act a Paul
and flip Boss Moe around. But this tale is brief,

like life: some winding paths must just on winding keep.
We have escaped—Sweet Reader might I include you?—
hot Trixie's wrath. No Sylvia Plath, delving deep
in ovens unlit, Miz W won't turn blue!

Celebrate! The old gal plans on staying
till Labor Day. Does that ring a bell-o?
Should we buy her a ticket to what's playing
in Santa Fe? Of course I mean *Otello*.

Having a true crone there could bring some luck.
I'll call the box office and buy a seat.
Santa Fe opera, it's always the shuck:
river-strutting with dressage does compete.

Ring-ding. "Santa Fe Opera Co."
                                   "Hello,
I'd like to purchase one ticket for the
first Saturday in September, for *Otello*."
"Ma'am, you—"
                     "I'm male."
                                   "Sir, I deplore the

"mistake. This is your lucky day. We have
one ticket left, front-center, second tier."
"That I'll take. She's old but I trust she'll behave.
No suicide jump, you can have no fear."

"Sir, you're funny."

"I'm a comic writer."

"Aww, that's so sweet. Anything I may have
read?"

"*Pineapple* will—"

"You're the blighter
who's keeping my boyfriend's dough! They have

"rules, you know!"

"Not true! Inconclusive
evidence won't allow me yet to pay.
I write so hard to finish that I'm reclusive."

"I see that you can come to Santa Fe."

"Evidence awaits there. The book'll be
done by my birthday."

"Just when is that?"

"January."

"Next year?! My Tim's forsook; he
may drown while you stroll out in your top hat."

"Tim?"

"My boyfriend, you jerk. Not that you care.
Enough! How is it you want to pay for this
ticket?"

"Paypal," I say.

"Figures. Your share
comes to three hundred fifty."

"Something's amiss!"

"We have a last ticket fee."

Sounds unfair,
even improvised to me. I take a sip

of tea and rattle off my number.
                              "Hey there,
that account's been closed. You're a real trip."

Crap. I hope Trixie's not been using my
AMEX. I spill that number over the
phone. This dominatrix is abusing my—
Wait! I'm inspired. "Your Tim's a real rover, he

"could likely find a place in my novel."
"Are you bribing me?"
                              "Not at all, Carol."
"Did I say my name?"
                    No answer. Let her grovel.
In fact, I'll leave her grunting like she's feral.

Last ticket fee, my ass. C, chirp a death carol.

Chapter Thirty-five:
Boss Moe makes a contribution,
some peeps hope for absolution,
some for restitution,
some remain in convolution

With fanfare, Boss Moe showed at the Bradbury
Museum. He was making a huge donation
to science for the kids, and few did worry
about his dough's rough source. Sanitation

worked for the Boss just as it does for science,
the Mafia, politicians, preachers.
Money laundering's a major appliance;
My guess? At best it often features

some small good done. This moral bit has made
ground beef of me. I'm starting to see
why we turn to comics and fifty shades.
Sex, giggles, football, barbecue, and glee—

therein lie the golden keys.
                              By the door, Boss gave
a terrifying grin. Great God Hydrogen,
his teeth, it's true, have scars. Not much can save
his poor sad face. Still, didya catch the estrogen

surrounding him as he debarked from
that fine Italian car? A real footrace.
Magnetic attraction. Women derived sparks from
his presence. Moral? Cash exfoliates a face;

gold's glow works wonders on the human race.
"*Señors . . .*" The Boss pronounced by the doors.
Two newsmen white-eyed and increased the space
between them and that mouth spewing spores.

Kerosene would improve The Boss's breath, as laced
as it was with awful, fearsome microbes.
Biochemists, with one tongue-sample placed
on Petri, to Mesozoic could send their probes.

". . . and *señoritas*." Boss M continued to grin.
Less Ugly stood nearby, pistol in pocket
in case some rival cartel remembered some sin
The Boss committed. Jerks always want to sock it

to others. Oppenheimer was slapped by HUAC;
McCarthy and Hoover whipped on Hollywood;
local preachers strap stray sheep to racks;
bigots strive hard to kill for Big C Good.

"I come this loving town where there atom
was smashed. . . ." Say where? Sweet Reader, you likely wonder
what's going on. Turns out the spooks had some
quite real info. Drug cartels wanted to plunder

secrets of science, expand cartel horizons.
The Boss has thus made this donational trip
for face-to-face, eschewing use of Verizon
or email. Last night Hanson admitted a slip:

as we have seen, The Boss ain't one to give
two Hail Marys and a Sign of the Cross
for absolution. Still, he let Hanson live.
Now Strickland has approached bountiful Boss

with that same intent: a working model
of *lagarto tuerto,* the G-String gun,
might be had if Boss M's wallet gave waddle
to spill cash enough to stun the sun.

Hey, what's Ol' Sol been doing? Watching, watching.
It's his métier, damn his hide. He's seen
lots more than pineapples. He's seen grand botching.
His job, as solar center? Render clean.

Heat desiccation works best. This G-string gun
has posed a problem, but it's nothing Sol
can't handle. Hiroshima's workload wasn't fun,
but Sol has wafted steadily through its death toll.

Now Strickland reached to pat The Boss's back.
The Boss has handed Bradbury's curator
a handsome 50 grand check to stack
a science timeline. "An incubator,"

the curator announced, "to milk our youth
back to brass bolts and tacks of science."
This curator hadn't learned beauty is truth;
that much was plain. On shoulders of giants?

Not mixing metaphors such as those.
His lazy tongue, like a politician's,
dressaged his words in fancy silken clothes
to garb the chamber. Faux rhetorician!

Our Carmen, true to her word, has stuck to Dad
like shoe glue. Shoe glue? Well after mocking
that curator, my spouting clichés would ring sad,
so I gave one a twist. Besides, much more shocking

was happening before our C's deep brown eyes.
Her dad had bumped Less Ugly, who dropped
a shining pistol reverse manna from high.
The curator heard the clunk and hopped

on gun metal's sad faux pas—nothing like
a loaded pistol dropped beside some blue blood's
thin-strapped gold Gucci to drive a steel spike
through any room. Lest champagne fizz to mud

the curator proposed this party game:
"Let's split—no pun intended," —he giggled—
"into two groups: Fission and Fusion, the same
as bombs."
                    How Carmen's mind niggled!

Maybe a job as actuary,
she pondered, could deliver her morals.
As the crowd split, obedient statuary,
into two groups, C noted hushed orals

exchanged by Less Ugly and her dad.
Two Van de Grafs gave hairdos a party spin,
Two holograms twisted about, mimicking mad
lad gravity's pull turning this universe in

on itself. "The Higgs boson has us a-titter,"
the curator announced. "Every day we find
new ways that particle will make life fitter."
C mouthed: *Like toasting girls to cinnamon rinds?*

She saw The Boss and Strickland changing glad
hands too. *That UCLA girl was way too thin;*
Juanita Doe is still getting fat. A sad
situation if their killers aren't brought in.

Yes, Carmen had driven back and searched lover's lane
to find not one thing more than an earring
that Chelsea had lost: a ruby spaceship, inane,
but hardly as frightening and searing

as what might be adrift in this wing-
ding donational celebration. *Stiff chin*,
she chided. Then . . . she caught a flash of bling.
Was some poor male's protruding prick in spin?

Bro' Blue? *Madre Dios*, who invited him?
He stood near, chatting up a Boss Moe discard;
his eyes, though, stared their gray sin
straight through sis Carmen's Madame Curie ward-

robe. Girls know when looks float as love taps
and when they leap as leers. Bro' Blue's did the latter,
she feared. Blessed Virgin M, was he the sap
who scrawled those lewd red notes? A mad hatter

for her half-bro'? She fumbled in her purse:
Saint Francis would protect her from dropping
her Walther as Less Ugly had. What worse
than sharing a brand name with a whopping

drug dealer!
             Listen: Carmen's employer—who-
soever it was—as new guy on the block
endured no lack of instrumentation. New?
A purchase order will buy it. Just sock

the bill to Congress. Thus, in her purse, she switched on
a mini-directional-sound-seeker. It
went by a fancier name, but she'd hitched on
that one to irritate Ted—who got meeker, it

turned out, the more she flirted and annoyed him.
Almost at times she wished she had a spare
girlfriend who'd give the lad a nighttime spin
"*Otello*," her mini-seeker crackled. From where

did that bump jump? A local FM?
So, twisting on what passed for squelch
she turned from Boss and Mr. Dim
toward Less Ugly and her dad. A nice Welsh

pop like Sean O'Connery would have been
the nines. Well, Mom did what she could. The gene pool
had floated no birthday piñatas. Spin
your wheel and hope for luck and not a fool.

Mom played her game well enough. As an
Illegal teen she'd turned much to carne,
so Carmen—"The opera house has an . . ."
All this interference added up to blarney

as far as G could tell. Defective
receiver? She checked it: *Made in America.*
Not good. Sad thought, but no use wasting invective.
"The prima donna's stand-in is Erica . . .

"The Boss holds much amor for her gray eyes."
Wait! That couldn't have been on FM!
She tapped the sound-seeker. *America still flies!*
Don't switch your stocks to Dim Foo Dim!

". . . She sings on Thursday for the local crowd,
so not that day. Friday or Saturday—
The Boss likes lunch, so no matinees allowed—"
Opera? These creeps? A mad hatter may

have thought this tune up, but . . . C looked to
Blue, unhooking his belt buckle.
Mad hatter it is, she thought, *all cooked to
a KY burgoo. Lorrie'll chuckle*

when I— "Saturday then, your boss will see."
"I hope so, señor, he does not tall stand
to take twice-time failure pleasantly."
C turned to listen to the triple ugly man

who talked now with Strictdick. Wasn't Boss Moe
his name? "A seat in front balcony
will hold a ratting rat. It would be one hot show
if none again can never ask, 'How come she

" 'can that did did?' "
                                        "Hell, I'll take it all out."
"Draconian."
                        Where'd Boss Moe get that word,
C wondered, picturing his ugly snout
hard rooting through wayside words, but the image blurred.

"Just think of it as my encomium
to you," replied the Strictdick. The Boss's face fell.
"What's that word mean? Bring plutonium
results, *hombre.* One section burnt will just work swell."

A shifting red curtain caught C's right eye.
Blue, she was certain, and the discarded lady
were shifting behind. She gave her mini a try:
"Just one lick of your gash will taste like gravy."

"Get down and do it, Blue. I'll secrete a stew
just for you."
   Blessed Francis and his little birds,
C thought, switching her mini off without ado.
Hi-Tech can spew some downright nasty words.

Exactly! Sweet Reader! Go buy books! Be a nerd.

Chapter Thirty-five-and-a-half:
just one fast dash
to sweep up some trash

This side path won't take long, I assure you.
But debts must all be paid! Don Walker went, well,
walking. Last night a coyote was lured through
his dreams, tail-tolling warnings like a mission bell.

Was this about the daughter of his dead love?
The coyote listened to dream-howling
coming from a hill; each note skipped high above.
Too bad ol' Don never read J. K. Rowling,

for he'd have known his dreamland was shared
with wondrous He-Whose-Name-We-Dare-Not-Speak,
a.k.a. Me, your writer. So he just stared.
Go take a hike following your mid-morning leak,

dear Don, a ghost voice sang—I wonder whose?—
and this dim dream will soon show crystal clear.
Take Los Alamos back road and don't wear shoes.
So Don was now up, shaking his old man spear

and pondering the shoe advice. He never wore
them. Was that some anti-dream dream warning?
Fine, Reader, so I bungled my little chore!
Still, here he is, tea-making despite clouds forming

in his hard head and in the far west too. Look! Out
he goes to make the trek. Far off, I hear
two loud rice-burners rev, two kids give shout
to mishmash rhymes, though all the beer

they drank last night doth slur sap rhyme to turds.
Ho! Don steps out onto the road where he picks up
a rock to throw at omen-bringing birds.
You've thrown your last, you foul, aged pup!

Yeah you! Remember that geode you gave hurl
when sad poor I was writing my writerly job?
Atop my head still sits one large knave's burl!
That's right, step out, let your hink heart give throb.

What's that high noise? Oh just two kids a-riding
some motorbikes. Don't pay a mind. Meditate . . .
Screeeng! Around the curve they come a-sliding.
Look! For once Don Walker really does levitate.

In one hour, state cops will find just four bloody shoes.
The moral? Never cast stones at what others do:
twisting your mind thus guarantees the blues;
it fills your earthly sojourn with run-over rue.

Reader! Emulate what I teach, not what I do.

Chapter Thirty-six:
Pixie shifts to Dixie
takes a stand, makes demand,
lest roiling love sift down to sand

Dixie's banging the kitchen's coffee pot.
Oh hell, I fear there's not— "So mean! So petty!"
I hear her chant as I endow the other pot.
Great God Hydrogen, I'm *so* not ready

this early from the bed, but I sore need some tea—
and English Breakfast, not antioxidant green.
"Hello, my pretty!" I enter with that plea.
"O Joe, my only Joe! So low, so mean!

"How could you leave those four sweet kids without an
upright old counselor, someone wise to
this world's sad penchant to flash and spout an
engulfing snag that opens gashes for flies to

"make feast on naïve tender legs, toes, and feet."
"Tender! Naïve? Kids? Hank's fought a war;
Dave's way too old to think a tickling neat—
unless enacted on his raw taut fore-

"skin. Carmen's employed in espionage
and hopes avenging dead mom on live dad.
Miranda's proven capable of triage."
"Miranda? Oh Joe, your daughter's name. So sad."

"Luella, Loretta, Lorrie. You me upset.
I mean, your upset makes me upset and I

don't even know why you're upset as yet."
"You killed that nice old Native Am! How can I

"not be upset! 'Emulate what I teach'?"
'Not what I do'? Joe, do you *ever* read
what you write? Reach out for what you preach?
Some wise old crone for sure is what you need."

A pot clanks. I eye the English Breakfast
over D's crusading head. "Sometime things seem,
but aren't," I cagily assert. *Good. Trek out fast
amends.* Tricks aren't just for Trixie, I deem.

"Um, could you . . ." I motion toward the box
of tea. Her eyes slot narrow. Am I going
to suffer one more lump? Not the fox!
"Kindness is as kindness does," I'm stowing

my fear. She hands me one red packet of
tea. "So you're saying that nice Don Walker's
not really dead?"
                    I should make a racket of
this, should I not? Each fork in plot offers

a bet. PayPal's a capitalist endeavor.
Convince them to reopen my account
and we'll both rake in bucks. However
it comes, it surely will do one good thing: mount.

Parnassus, I'm thinking, and all its fine muses
might just turn me and ol' PayPal bitch rich.
Hey, in these days no one ever refuses
a scheme that'll yank them from the pitch ditch

of poetic endeavor. But for now my prob
lies in sight before my own green eyes.

"In that case, Joe, sit down and I'll fob
today's work off on Tony. That guy's

almost ready to stand on his own. Natch,
he'll never crack as many deals as me,
but then, what poet's ever gonna hatch
a jug and book of verse as good as thee?

"Eliot? Stevens? Thomas? Berryman?"
"Omar," I add.
            "Who?—Sure, that *Rubyiat*.
Oh Joe, I say, you stand the very man
to send all poesy a-sail. Give it a shot.

"But here now. I do wish you'd stop and tell
just what your thoughts could be in placing that
wise old man in harm's mean way. If even he fell
at his ripe age—"
            "Our wills are not intact.

"The muses, fate, and chance all lead us
where'er they may. But his intent and mine kept good.
'Walk,' that dream told him, and dreams may speed us
ahead, yes, but just as oft into some dark wood

"they throw us may. Alas, free will—" I brew my
English Breakfast till it's deeply black—
"is like a hummingbird that fast flew by
too quickly for the human eye to track.

" 'Free will's a bogus question,' warned Nietzsche."
Pixie pinches my tea bag. "Joe, don't get upset,
but honestly, can you really reach a
conclusion from a dead man whose name as yet

"you cannot spell?"

                   "I do hold some authority,"

is my reply.

             "Fine then. What were you thinking

about? The Miz and Don have seniority,

and you need reason's voice, with the evil slinking

"about. Los Alamos seems a nasty place.

Why not take your daughter to Bandelier?

Get Don and the group out of that lab race."

I gaze into P's eyes. I often fear

tectonic shift will drop another Reelfoot

swampland in them, mire iris with cottonmouths

and other viperous creatures that would put

me—and her too—into a zone far south

of temperate. Nietzsche said—I keep this twixt

you and me, for dearest Pixie need not hear—

that our minds are nests of vipers mixed

about. What wonder we ever get clear.

"Good plan," I say. It's too early for beer.

Chapter Thirty-seven:
One old guy—me—doesn't get his way;
another hikes a lot and has things to say;
Miz Walburn shoos the kids away to play;
free will, does it go or does it don't go Nietzsche's way
on this—or any—blessed day?

Not quite a week since Boss's big visit.
Don's walking the Old Taos Road—is what
the locals call it, though in Taos, is it
then rather Los Alamos Road? Like as not.

Such sends us no surprise. Einstein and his
relativity—has ever man
or woman lived who's not had it command his
or her life? Toe-mae-toe, toe-mah-toe? So, a plan

of one small hike, say up Los Alamos Road,
and see what goes. This thought struck Don Walk-
er. That be-damned dream had proven one tough load.
Toe-pain alone had nearly made him balk.

Don sat on a rock and thought of Carmen,
his close to step-daughter. In that damn dream
hadn't she been facing down some harm and
hadn't he lain flat on a road, trying to scream

a warning? [*Reader, I've no idea*
how this sad scene emerged. Did you see it?
This old fart fought in cold, snowy Korea,
so a G. I. flashback? I'd rather believe it

than allow for free will, that spooky jazz.
Get up, Don, walk just a bit farther.
A real fine, slinking sinewy razzmatazz
waits up ahead, and it ain't no garter.]

Don stood, thinking he'd walk up to that bend
ahead. Like a crossroads, it tugged at him.
Don sat. Don't crossroads bode an end?
That's ok. His life was waning thin.

Don stood, thought of his father, an electrician
hired on at Los Alamos in the war.
Half Mex, half Indian, Dad's suspicion
ran high about what lay at the core

of all those brains gathered in a new-made
town. Don sat. After Hiroshima, kids were served
pineapples, Hawaii's Pearl Harbor repaid
back in full, plus interest. The Japs deserved

it, some people said. "The gringos will have had
dreams from this. Watch their eyes," his dad told him.
Don stood. As summer skipped to winter, a sad
diaspora stirred the town. Don's gringo friends

went off. Don *had* watched their dads' eyes: a splinter
divided them. A kissing girlfriend
told him her dad had lost his only center:
instead of dreaming atoms to no end,

he rode far canyon trails into sunsets.
Don sat. One scientist had died of "the poison"
after his experiment went west.
"As old men they are leaving, as boys on

"parade they came," Don's dad said of the eyes.
Don stood, he sat, he stood. Would it never end?
Stand up, sit down. Was he a puppet in disguise?
If so, did blood cells and microbes give tend?

He glanced down. He glanced up. He glanced nigh.
Emitting sighs, he stood to round the bend.
As he did he jumped and danced—yo so high!
A rattlesnake slithered on the road. No godsend.

Two youngsters on Japanese motorbikes
went skidding in patterns like constellations.
Clothing, blood and skin spread in spikes
across the highway. Not mere intimations

of kind Sir Death: the sassy guy rode in bare,
and galloped off in likewise, leaving kids and snake
to wander toward that gruesome place where
even rock, then sand—entropy will never slake—

come to rest. A motorist happened by,
flipped his cell and gave 9-1-1 a ring.
Ol' Sol, o'erhead, released not one sigh;
he'd seen it before, same old, same old thing:

The ambulance did its rat-a-tat-tat;
Jack Spratt and wife jumped out, not the least dazed;
their ready soles hit tar, hot, angry, and flat;
Don Walker watched, sad, sick, amazed.

Jack Spratt and wife had stowed two body bags
they'd waited to use in affirmation
of county taxes quite well spent; Don said he'd shag
when a Native Am cop offered motoration.

"Say," Don intoned, from he knew not where,
"know a sweet Mexican girl named Carmen Brown?"
"Oh sure," the cop replied. "Her roommate has a pair
of pineapples that make young men drown.

"Don't get me wrong. They're both upstanding
chiquitas. Live out on Road Nine with two
fine fellas. These times economy's demanding,
and rumor says a creep did stalk them, I'll give you

understand. Morals come, morals go. The sun
and coyotes sort that flow."
                              Very Injun,
Don thought with a nod. *Say, what trickster spun
that slur into my brain? Hell, let him have his fun.*

"Which way's Road Nine?" Don asked the cop
"Ten miles ahead, go right. Still can give
you a ride."
                    Don glanced up. *That sun won't stop.*
His mind was made... for Carmen to live

he needed to find her fast and give warning.
The time for thinking was over and done.
Action post-noon, thinking pre-morning.
That snake had sent its sign: evil to come.

His leather pouch held a fine yellow quartz.
Don showed it to Ol' Sol, who did comply
by shining gaily, sadly—whatever warts
from emotion's pool humans cared to apply.

The cop and Don did ponder, then spent a sigh.

Miz W stepped onto her porch and looked
up high. Sunlight gave off shine that bent a
quite curious way. How often had it cooked
just such an angel's—devil's?—brew that sent a

poor creature drifting through these hills?
Or wherehowever. "You four," she turned to yell,
"Why don't you leave me and my old-age pills,
go hike in Bandelier? I won't even tell

"if you sneak back with a souvenir."
                                    The four
had eaten sausage, eggs, and pancakes.
The girls, both bloating, wobbled for the door.
"By my count," whispered L, "swimming five lakes,

"and hiking eight miles to climb nine wood
ladders won't dent the sausage fat alone.
Some Indian spirit would have to send a fine good
ghostly fright to fling these sausage pounds ozone."

Then laughing with Ol' Sol—though as we've seen
he makes one rough-tough stoic biding high up
there—the four, in C's Sentra, figured that obscene
might really take vacation, hiding high up

in mountains yon, or low in some valley
far off. Miz Walburn didn't buy that fancy.
She'd sailed around the Horn, so no such sally
deluded her. Life rolled scat-cat chancy.

Obscene sent lurks around each corner;
it rarely—never—took the time to rest.
Each minute produced some poor mourner;
a ten second gay window might rise at best.

But what she could, she did, and that was to bake
up cookies. Tough hombres might scoff at how
such efforts slouch when streaming missiles make
ferocious tracks across this life's uncertain bow,

but cookies, they're what we got, and oatmeal-
pecan to be specific. No laxative
got kneaded therein. Cooling, their smell floated real
enough. I stood there, tempted to get active—

why sure, I'd arrived!—and tiptoe through and grab
a few but soon I heard, "Don Walker! Is that
you?"
        "Miz Walburn? Glad you're not under a slab.
Had heard you went back east into the rat

"race there." Don Walker snorted, snitted the air,
"Pecan oatmeal soon. But come in, dip some snuff.
They'll cool."
            "That peace pipe sounds mighty fair."
"And needed. Things round here have gone too rough."

"That's why I came. A dream—"
                    Miz Walburn turned
to roll her eyes, but then she caught herself:
How dare I scoff? Have I not learned
that many books abide on life's long shelf?

More shame to me. (Not a bad stance, I'll tell
ya, but you just try to hold it for more than
one sneeze.)
            "—a dream that something near all hell
was wobbling out like a blind lizard man."

Miz Walburn offered Don her tin of snuff.
"Blind lizard man?" With cough, she shook the tin.
"Sorry. Sometimes I trip in my own Taos fluff
I spew for tourists. But maybe just now that's in

"the perfect vein. My little Carmen *niña*
—you know I almost married her *madre*—
seems to be about to get between a
rock and a . . ." Don scratched his ear-nub . . . "*padre*?"

He pinched some snuff that cleared both ears and eyes.
"Oh, Don, you mean a rock and a hard place."
"*Sí*, yes." He blinked. "This snuff's tequila high."
Miz Walburn grinned. "It keeps me in the race."

"A cop told me that she lived here with three others."
Don squeezed his fists to give another blink.
"She does. This was once my place. All four need mothers."
"My Carmen needs something. I fear she's at a brink."

They hit the long front porch and then looked up.
Maybe a buzzard, or was it an eagle?
I couldn't tell; anyway, my mind kept booked up
with hiding. Don said, "Look! An eagle. So regal."

"I love to watch 'em fly. They soar so higher
than buzzards."
                    "And flap less often."
"They certainly inspire me to aspire."
"They wing with grace nothing can soften."

Sweet Reader, how can they do it? Is my work
in code? They squawk this much on birdie detail,
what will they uncover about the jerk
who ransacked Carmen's? Enough to send him to jail?

And further, what about that singing play,
I mean *Otello*. And then those eight black rocks?
If these two should detect and blab I'll need to pay
out so much dough I'll be down to my socks.

My writing goes slow, revealing not too much.
If my left brain, or is it the right, were able,
I'd take up singing—or guitar in a clutch,
to warble my way for a Calumet stable.

The horsey people hereabout have bucks,
for them I'd croon old staid folk songs;
rich people love to slum amidst the mucks.
Who knows, I even might right some wrongs.

Write anything, I think, other than verse.
"Good God," a guy last night did shout, "Don't say it rhymes."
"Why yes," I answered.
                              "Brother, go drive a hearse!
Go get real work!" He backed away. In these sad times

we poets can't stir even bar conversation.
And I was flat down after that PayPal gal
went shrill and belly rolled—not in admiration
of my humor's bright sharpness but . . .

Hello. The oldsters are spewing new *Whazzup*
even I don't know. What am I, some poor clerk?
Some dumbo writer whose work's a botch-up?
Might they discern how my and L's genes lurk?

Say, don't I hold exclusive rights as creator?
If God exists, surely He, She, It
feels my same way. *Paradise? More like a crater
you wretched creatures have dug. Must I see it?*

You there, yes you with all the curves, Eve.
Just 'cause you yank and tug on Adam's wong
doth make no reason he ought to believe
he can give chomp to all that fruit. It's wrong!

Agh! Those damn Dobie pups are yapping;
I may not hear what news the oldsters are leaking.
Their mouths could be smacking important flapping.
There, that's better, just some spy device tweaking . . .

Well, ladies first, to prove I'm not *all* about balls:
"Don, I've got to tell you: Carmen knows who
the creep is who left those awful red scrawls.
It's Blue Hanson. You know how she knows it's true?"

Don, reeling from the snuff, just shook his head.
"She saw him down at Jill's ordering pizza.
If you think that seems light, this gives it lead:
was pepperoni and anchovy—who eats a

lot of that? The cook told her they keep a tin
of those salty nasty little fish just
for him. Her own half-brother! It's a sin!"
Don shifted the snuff. Doing that must

have rung his squawk alarm. "It's only her mom
who saved that gal from rotten D.N.A.,
but still I—"
                    "The second nasty scrawl was glommed
on a Jill's box with that same combo in a

"creep-o note taped on her front door. Perversion
enough without him mixing kinship.
Betrayal of what yet floats sacred. Subversion,
inversion, all atop a garbagey thin strip

"of pepperoni and anchovy . . . Lord, his breath!"
"Betrayal," Don said, "fills the air. I dreamed about
a white man in black face singing of death "
"*Otello!*" Miz Walburn shouted out.

"Say what?"
                "An opera coming soon in Santa Fe.
We're heading there. Some patron sent a ticket
by mail. Synchronicity, I want to say."
Snuff dribbled her chin. Don wished she'd lick it

off. "Might ring more like some evil cabal."
Cabal? Injun? From where do these maggot words
derive? No trickster I know thinks that small.
"I mean some evil scheme. Life often sets its burrs.

"This morning a snake coiled and I jumped
while two kids on motorcycles went into skids.
Death made a hopping visit and dumped
snake, motorbikes, and those two boy kids

"onto his creaky cart. Don't know how I
stayed off. I've looked over my shoulder
every ten minutes since, thinking the plough I
missed would surely lurch like a boulder

"and drive me under just as deep. But my
almost daughter is why I'm here. That song
vision held her in it. We Indians can fly
and control our dreams, they say. Wrong.

"At least not me. But those dream voices
sure did talk the future right to me.
If I was some crackpot writer, the choices
of my plot would show clear and bright to me."

Perchance, Sweet Reader, you think I'll comment?
No. It's flown beyond my poor control.
These wayward actors make me vomit.
On tiptoe I'll just ease some snuff for my soul.

"You have company?" Don Walker asked, a-twitch.
"Just you," Miz Walburn said. "The four kids have left."
"Thought I saw a hand reach out and grab a snitch."
Don glanced at the side stand.

                              "My snuff? I'd be bereft."

"Was wearing a tiger-eye cameo ring
I've seen before." Don Walker stood to inspect.
Ow! Hell! Those damned Dobermans from spring!
They both are in my face, and standing erect.

"What's got those two puppies yipping so?"
"Your snuff bandit, I bet. Listen to them sneeze."
Don Walker's right. The dogs went into fast-mo
on licking me, so I flicked off each. More snuff, please.

Miz Walburn walked out to peep. I pressed against an
old chifforobe half-leaning on the porch.
"Just listen to those poor things. Wait an instant!
Don, you suppose there's a poltergeist? A torch

"since childhood, that's what I've carried for one.
Here, let's leave it more snuff, then revisit your dream."
They headed back in. Scooping snuff on thumb
I snorted enough to make a wrestler scream,

then sneaking close to hear, I sucked all up.
"Well, like I said, this guy in black-face
was singing how his murdering hands had mucked all up
what he loved so very best. Purple sparks whacked space

"and a whole wall of cannon balls collapsed
in thunder banishing his song. Just as well,
he flung it warbly, like a bird relapsed
into dipping this snuff in mescal."

                    "Oh hell,"

Miz Walburn coughed and opened her mouth
to tug a mother lode. Don did the same,
and monkey-like, I dug too. We all headed south
to dump the goo, but then rejoined the game,

a second load of dusty stuff.
                         "My Carmen stood
on a balcony, I guess, while those sparks
flitted their way about. There's the whole goods,
dream's end."
                "That black-face man . . ."
                              "The warbling lark?"

Miz Walburn nodded and I did too,
though my move stayed clunky and hid from sight.
"He was so ugly, I woke up. The visual stew
of his wretched face . . . some gnarled writer's blight,

"is best account that I can give."
—Oh is that so, Donnie? If you old farts
left plotting to me, matters would live
on happily. So stop inserting troubled parts!

Please leave my work less gnarled. Here's one pure fact:
I then could stroll with pleasant demeanor.
"Oh Don, I think it's time for us to act.
Cookie?"
            "Wouldn't mind. I haven't seen her

"in over a month, you know, and now this dream.
Damn, these cookies are gooey with lots of
nuts. Boy cookies, is what I mean. Protein."
"I'm baking others for *Otello*. With shots of

"more potent stuff. And Don, we need to find
a way for you to get there. Your crystals
just may turn handy. Shine one and blind
the so-ugly man."
                    Don grabbed a distal

cookie, though he'd gobbled so many that the
center was barely there to see. Me, I'm just glad
a center holds anywhere. This old bat, she's
thrown down on me. But tickets to *Otello*? Sad.

Such lies beyond her flinty nails. Sold out,
remember? In that I hold control.
No need for *this* fine author to pout:
when Miz Walburn flips her cell, *he's* on patrol.

"You know, Don, I have contacts. My dear
sweet daughter had a college friend who's high
with Santa Fe's Opera House. So here,
let me give her a ring." Don munched and sighed.

I dipped more snuff and gave a snicker.
The last ticket was mine, and yeah that lousy fee
was too. My eyes gave off a flicker.
Do you suppose Carol was the so very wee

lass who ding-rang-ding that sorority bell
with Miz Walburn's daughter? Blackberrying
is where Carol's gone, ploughed deep into hell.
That's why I'm not even worrying.

Ring-ring. Or not. "Can you believe it?" Miz
Walburn turned to ask. "Their hold tone plays
early Beatles.—Oh hello, may I speak—is this Liz?
Miz Walburn here . . . Oh she's fine. Carolina stays

on her mind. Liz, I'm so glad it's you.
I sorely need just one ticket for *Otello*
on Saturday. You do? I knew I could count on you."
Hello? Hell no! Hello? Hell no! Hello?

Miz Walburn turned to Don, who was eating
the next-to-last cookie. "They have one!
And guess what? You'll have balcony seating
right next to me! This tale couldn't have spun

"out better if Willy S. had penned its fun."

Chapter Thirty-eight:
The oldsters tossed their spam;
now your beloved writer must avoid a jam

"You should be happy," Trixie tells me as
we sip espresso. (Not good for my heart
but I must needs escape the volumes of gas
those two old farts ballooned to upset my cart.)

"Happy and grateful. Admit it, stuck is
what you were. Don't they say, writer's blockhead?"
I inspect her eyes: strangely shifting muck is
what I find. "And your last half–chapt. left no one dead!

"There's something. That gravity gun's been doing
a number on New Mexico's population."
"The two a-bombs over Japan weren't shooing
off flies," I say.
           "Hey Joe, get some stopulation."

"Some what?"
           "Stopulation. Some let-it-go-ness.
Those sweet two oldsters popped you from a jam,
and those sad two bombs stopped the scary mess
of invading Japan. Hardly flimflam

"you must admit."
           "Must I? I guess."
"Your daughter—now don't be making a face—
stays our main problem. You must confess
she's getting short stick in the narrative pace.

"Do it for her, if not for me." A rough love bite
is what I then get, right on the neck.

Trixie giggles to grab my love stick, right
in Starbucks, under the table. What the heck.

I rub my neck, I gulp espresso.
By the great god Charles Dickens, I order
one more. My heart's already a mess, oh
I won't deny it. Trixie's hint may border

on obsessive, but Lorrie's just the gal
to calm this matter down. She has my genes,
after all—at least according to my ol' pal
Trixie. So let's just see how Lorrie cleans

up this plot's Mexican jumping beans.

Chapter Thirty-nine:
Two creeps collude;
L gets to intrude

Smart Lorrie'd salvaged pink opera glasses
a Doberman was toting about.
This saved her from enjoining hardy masses
on E-bay's bidding bouts. These glasses gave a shout,

for real. Had that demented animal rights
female forgotten them? L wondered if ever
she gave that low abusive creep the vengeful bites
she'd threatened. Right now, L herself felt clever,

perched high in a primitive cliff dweller's cave.
The other three stood one wood ladder below,
arguing if someone could show a jealous rave
like in Othello. *Read the news, watch TV. Blow-*

by-blow, there's that and more, L thought and lifted
the glasses, focusing on a nearby ridge.
The state's two greatest creeps had thereon shifted
an oblong telescope a dirty smidge.

It pointed at a family of four,
two teenage girls and two downtrodden parents.
The ridge lay one half mile off or more.
Perverts, L thought, for it did seem apparent

the creeps were gawking at posterior
and frontal teen gal cleavage. But bam! A purple
ray leaped to leave the cute fam inferior
and dropped aground, as four smoking durples—

that's how L thought of them, though I'd call
them smoking balls, old-timey grapeshot.
Still, she's my progeny, if Trixie knows all,
so I don't think she would concoct some word on spot

to finish rhyme so lamely. Genes do carry
integrity. Whoa! L saw the creeps focusing
their box again, on her three friends. To parry
that purple ray she needed hocus-pocusing.

Ten feet she leaped, to pull them down behind
a chunk o' cliff. No noise, no zap, so she
and trusty pink glasses peeped out to find:
an empty ridge. She then explained to the three

what Strictprick and Hanson had done. "Look!"
she ordered, shoving the glasses at Dave.
"You see those four hot durples?" At first Dave shook
his head, then gave his hand a hardy wave.

"Yep, I see 'em. They're still down there smoldering."
"Just what are durples?" Hank had the nerve to ask.
The look the three sent him was moldering:
too much sci-fi his education left to bask

in realms of dark ignoramus, quite clearly.
"Durples," answered his patient girlfriend,
"are of a family of spheroid—or nearly—
objects of unknown or unclaimed blend."

One more purple flash ignited the horizon
like wild heat lightning, which is a misnomer,
for it's a real distant lightning comprisin'
the normal stuff. "Someone else hit a homer,"

observed Lorrie. "Think we should go down
to the parking lot and inspect the spheroids
while they stay hot? I'll bet a wedding gown
to shroud that metaphorical hemorrhoids

"is what we've got. And Preparation H
won't ever cure them."
They climbed down to look,
and Carmen bent to whiff: "Hey guys, I hates
to tell you, but cinnamon is what the cook

"baked with. Could Strickland and my foul ex-dad
be bright enough to—"
"Devins and McGuire,"
L cut in. "The Curies and X-rays made us glad;
that marital duo set out mischance for hire.

"Those purple rays, they sure aren't made to inspire."

Chapter Fo(u)rty:
Wherein the number four
explodes some spores.
Will they sting like bees?
Spawn hot love sprees?
Emit squared, synchronous debris?

There are four lovely Gospels written by
four lovely Apostles, if we can trust hist'ry.
A good great many ships go down, all smitten by
four winds. How wind worked was a myst'ry

until I watched Mr. Greenjeans. That man
wore four sweaters that reached out and touched,
though I bet his master wardrobe plan
called for five until one got smushed.

So that left four. There are four directions,
by last reliable count: North, South, East and West.
There are four heart chambers to make connections
that let blood, love, jism and hate gush, sans rest.

The Russian Revolution had four great comrades:
Trotsky, Lenin, Stalin, and Sen. Joe McCarthy.
Our Civil War had four military lads:
Grant, Sherman, Stonewall Jackson, and Lee.

Buddhism professes four noble truths:
that first about all earthly suffering
stirs muck enough to rot most global youths.
Oh, face it: humans need some buffering.

Here follow four great lies to do the job:
"I'll love you till the twelfth of never,"
"A pretty face plights true," "Man has no need to sob,"
"Floridian voters pulled the right lever."

Oh, four more, why not? "The good get what they deserve,"
"The truth will set you free," (Nice irony, yes?)
"An honest man's conscience will never swerve,"
"Bad deeds are always punishéd. (The best.)

And lo! There were four Beatles. A four-leaf clover
sways better than any early Beatles song.
There are four horsemen playing rover
for the Apocalypse, that bringer of wrong.

The Greeks had four elements: earth, air, fire,
and water. Though those guys played awfully bright,
the periodic table has since re-inspired.
Science! It gives us second, third, even fourth sight.

There are four classical virtues—those Greeks,
again: it's hard to beat 'em. Prudence, a tough one,
I rarely show it. Justice, for sure the meek
never see it. Temperance? Ten drinks I'm done.

But fortitude? Hell, I'm still breathing, amn't I?
And look at you, reading these wayward rhymes.
To those fine four, the Christians—never say die—
added faith, hope, charity. In these times

we need all we can get, so I won't bitch.
In fact, I'll add one more: othershoeness.
That's right. Before you cast the first durple, hitch
your tight self up to another's blueness.

You very well might just learn something, friend.
If not, assault rifles are easily purchased.
They'll bring disparity to a sweeping end.
I suppose that's one road of virtue-worship.

There are four seasons, and I feel sure
that each doth offer delectable charm,
though *my* bucks shout that winter tosses manure.
There are four dimensions affording harm,

if you count time, which makes the whole sad point.
Five, if you count gravity. Which brings us
about to a Los Alamos beer joint
named Todd's Deep End. Let's see where it flings us:

Ah, four white-tied gentlemen, wouldn't you
know it, have just stepped in. Todd sees them,
and donates a twenty—of virgin hue—
to his Mountain Nun tip jar. Lately, it's gone slim.

Too bad our Todd couldn't have plopped in
four fives, but he runs a business, not a
synchronicity support group flopped in
some dank corner. Those four fives he'll need to spot a

twenty's change. If these guys order sarsaparilla,
that'll cement my growing suspicion tight.
Hey, it *is* Ted! He flicks his white tie to spill a
spot of his usual charm and spray a blight

through Todd's Deep End: "Bud Light with a cherry,"
he warbles. Todd, bless him, doesn't even blink.
This night, he sees, will make the Mountain Nuns merry,
so they can save a flock of orphans from the brink.

The other three ask for root beer, no fruit.
Ted slips a covert photo from his jacket;
He slides it slick, just like on cop show poot.
"Psst. Know this guy?" His whisper sifts barroom racket.

Todd takes the photo. "Sure. That's Boss Moe.
He was in the paper. Made a big donation
to that Science Museum. Put on a show."
Ted squirms, as if on lunar rotation.

Now, Todd's not one given to giggles,
but watching Ted suck on that cherry
inspires his mind with several prank niggles.
To send this idiot hunting a dingleberry

flits utmost. But where? To a ski resort
to freeze? To Trinity's site to burn?
How about Roswell, where he could consort
with statewide loonies, each in turn?

Then Todd spies the entertainment rag.
That opera, not quite a week away!
He eyes the cover's pale beauty—no sag
in her pineapples—and that muscled black gay

singing, strutting, screwing, and strangling!
Perfecto! "Say, you know, that Boss Moe
lug came in here weeks ago, wrangling
with some suit from the lab. Don't know,

"but I feel certain they were both going
to fab a do at that swank sing-a-long
in Santa Fe. *Otello*? Lab rat kept showing
The Boss blue printouts. You think a wrong

"lies in the making?"

                    Ted's wide eyes abide
on the weekly rag. The prima's bosom makes him
blush. Still, duty first, he toughly decides.
Red lips, big tits—they won't shake him.

"Did either happen to mention a day?"
Todd smiles. That opera house will close
this very weekend. What a bang fine way
to put rich snoots and their fake music pose

into a great black hole: send these four be-tied
idiots about to roam. "Closing day, I think.
I mean, I'm sure I guess." Todd's smile gives ride.
The be-tied four waddle foot-to-foot, on the brink

of tumbling like clownish bowling pins, excited
and rumbling. "Well gosh, well gee, well golly."
Do Todd's ears hear truly? Benighted
fools, and look here comes one just as jolly,

a secretary who hangs around that charming
Carmen and her pal Lorrie. This gal gives
a wiggle to toss a flirt alarming
at where no woman who on this planet lives—

save this dweep's mother—has ever wandered.
"Your name's Ted, ain't it? My friend Carmen
says you're sugar sweet and keep that white tie laundered.
She also says a gal'd find no harm in

"you, that you're a sandstone in the rough.
Ain't that nice?"

                The gosh-gee-golly bells do ding.

For Todd, a straight face and smile come tough,
but he holds that pose to complete his sting.

Throughout the night, the Mountain Nun tip jar gives ring.

Chapter Forty-one:
The flight out to Albuqurq;
an unplanned meeting with a jerk;
Trixie clears, then makes more murk;
at Mystic Cactus Hotel, spice and joy both lurk

The way that Trixie's rubbing me
makes three stewardesses giggle.
And now she's moon-eying and loving me;
my hand gets squeezed so tight my fingers wriggle.

"That ring," she touches my old tiger's eye
gold camco. "It's the one Don Walker spotted.
A chance that Linda dear's the reason why
you wear it?"
                No use denying what's trotted:

"For my thirtieth birthday. One year later
we split."
            "And one year after that, guess who
into this world made skip? Joe, you're quite the satyr."
While wishing for explosive gel, I rub at my shoe.

Remember that guy who tried lighting his Keds
aboard a jet? No? Fame, as often pointed out,
is bleating. Fleeting too, but my meds
just now are kicking in, so an anointed shout

ain't likely, especially on a Southwestern flight
to Santa Fe at eight on Friday morning.
I take Lipitor—with Pixie's nuzzling, I might
needs swill blood pressure meds too. Fair warning.

"We'll spend tonight in Albuquerque.
I could have rented a car, but remembered
'Donna's with all them tits.' Joe, you turkey,
we'll see if UNM coeds dismember

"you as fast as nubile little Wildcats
can do. A hotel sits across the street
with the sappy name of Mystic Cactus.
We can practice tantric under a sheet.

"That is, if any lovely coeds get you stirred.
They should be lathering, school's just begun.
All tanned from summer, chirping, flitting birds.
I sure expect they'll make your member run."

I fume, "It takes a woman to get me hot."
I gaze out the window—I guess that *portal*
is the aeronautic name, like as not.
With Pixie spewing tantric I feel immortal,

like I'm Spinoza's aspect of God in flight,
just hovering the earth to calmly inspect.
Should I give frown and turn sad, or smile and be bright?
No. Keep sub-Godly emotions low; just detect.

Watch out, Bud, I tell myself: with that Higgs
boson weapon spouting all that purple,
even writers who think they're *au courant* big
could wind up as a crispy cinnamon durple.

One connecting flight later, we land at three
in Albuquerq. A taxi to Donna's—
Trixie stays true to her word: a sex spree
glows in the works. Cocaine is what I'm gonna

need. Damn if I don't spy Carmen's half-bro
at the bar grinding. Poor gal, Don Walker
is right: it's just her mom's good genes that helped her grow
into someone quite nice, and not a stalker.

I realize that Blue'd be just the gent to score
some cocaine from. My pocket is burning
with fistfuls of twenties and more.
Cocaine, would it really aid my yearning?

I nudge Pixie. "It's that Blue fellow. See
his tattoo?"
        "You never wrote about a
tattoo!" she yelps.
           "You know I can't be
supplying all the details without a

"mountain of paper and more gigabytes
than common home computers can handle.
The reader has to take her own flights
some time or other. The author can't dandle

each reader on his knee." For that I get
a glare, and Trixie—Pixie has just faded—
stands up and starts toward the bar. I set
a fearful glance out and grab her. "Don't be jaded.

"It's him. Besides, remember time-travel tales:
your interfering with the past can turn the now
awry, in fact, can send it straight to hell."
"This isn't the past, Joe. This ship's prow

"is cutting waves of New Mexico sand
in the here and in the now." She twists from me

and slinks up to Blue. "Blue, right? I understand
you have snow for sale." What a Holy Family

we three could make. Blue turns. Lord, his eyes snake
an ugly slate of gray. "This here's the desert.
Snow's only in the mountains, so take
your understanding away. I don't want to hurt

"a pretty old lady." Dixie submerges
her right hand in her red purse. Where the hell
is Hank when we need him? Two dirges
soon will play and I've yet to get one smell

of any UNM gal's rites of fall perfume.
"Uh . . ." I walk up to say, flinching at the creep's
gray eyes.
                T blurts, "Lay hand on me, and doom
will fall. That anchovy pizza still steeps

"up yon in Los Alamos cop lab.
You can yet serve hard time for stalking
sweet Carmen, your own damned half-sister, drab
sap!" This gets Blue's hands raised and him walking

to back outside the place. "Time machine be damned,"
Dixie spits. A blonde with pineapple tits
struts up behind the bar. "I've wanted to ram
that ass from here forever. He's the pits.

"First drink's on me. I'm Donna and I own
this joint. Say there, you got a sis up Santa Fe?"
Hot Trixie blushes as if innocence was sown
to waft about her face like new-mown hay.

"First cousin. Real estate, just like me."
"Her start came right down here. I bought this bar
through her."
                    "She's coming down tomorrow early
to carry us to Santa Fe in her pink car."

My head almost smashes hard wood on the bar.
"Whiskey," I manage, "double over ice."
How can this be? Trixie's cousin is not some far
off dream?
            "*Otello* tomorrow, tonight some spice,"

says you-know-who. If this had happ'ed on stage
the peeps would mock it as improbable fiction.
These Trixies are blooming like A-bombs a-rage
Wish Shakespeare could e-mail his depiction.

On second thought, maybe not. With all those
bodies he drops, what's a few multiplying
Pixies? At least they're lively, not comatose.
So there. With Willy I'm not vying:

let's not mind 'im. My Pixie's fingers are rubbing,
and in walk three tanned UNM lasses.
I'm old enough that my eyes start drubbing;
hope my mouth's smart enough to not make passes.

First drink goes down. We order one more when
back in again walks Blue. "What the hell you mean,
she's my half-sister? Who are you to spin
such trash at me?" Blue's showing heavy spleen

and snarls at me: "Say, what type of
wimp man lets a woman pick his fights?" *Damn,*

I was just thinking that when Blue pipes up
and says it. "Wimp!?" But I then clam.

That skull tattoo and those grey eyes look mean.
"Uh," I start, but Dixie cuts right on in,
"Your sister, dork. Ask your dad to come clean
about the Mexican wife he hid in a bin.

"And look at your lower lip, his, then hers.
You know, poor Bud, a little self-inspection
might could arrange you, leave life with fewer blurs."
Blue studies the bar's mirror. A connection

gets clearly made. "Get down! So I can ball
my own damn sis! Won't that just be the rave!"
His pouty lower lip, no more nearing a fall,
curls up, perverted spit to slurp and save.

"Thanks, cunt. You gived me a grand juicy plan.
Do wish I had some coke to sell to you and fag.
It wouldn't help. He's a foppy poet, no man."
I ball my fists. "I don't have that much jet lag!"

But Blue's gone, humping space and playing air-prick,
not –guitar. "That didn't work out too well,"
Pixie admits. "But Carmen carries a big stick
in that Mex purse of hers. She'll blow him all to hell."

"She," I disclose, "and the other three all take
karate lessons in a dojo that's swell."
"You never wrote on that! Joe, a deep lake
of murk—trust me as a realtor—is hard to sell.

"You ever thought of graphic novels?"
"Comics, you mean? Are we men and women,

or orphans swirling dust in hovels?
Don't answer. Brains in this land are slimmin'.

"Please understand: describing that dojo
would have slowed plot, made it grovel.
I want matters to progress with mojo.
I'm slamming down a power-chord novel."

I spot a lithesome toothsome sweet young blonde
whose tan flows deep, a mineral spring.
Her cute flipped nose turns up to send me beyond.
Two bracelets jingle, the right amount of bling.

Her sandals whisper soft leather and gold;
they give her pearl toenails room to sing.
The skin about her knees has turned just old
enough to crinkle a smile that would fling

all worries from any man left so lucky
to lie in her arms and feast on her lips,
both upper and nether, if he made plucky
enough to descend and go plip, plip.

Her breasts! Oh la, have I time to describe
'em? Imprisoned by bright pink so bold,
they push up taut, though to imbibe
'em would certainly render one rolled

in heaven's cotton. Bared tan shoulders so
firm and round, arms so lithe and model-thin,
the fingers of a pianist, pearl nails that glow
to match her lovely toes. It'd be bad sin

if I did not again mention her lips un-cruel,
responsive enough to kiss or give grip.

Their gloss alone has surely made many a fool
endure the pains of love's sweet whip.

She's Venus herself, descended on earth to rule
in Albuquerque town where hearts do skip!
My buttocks tighten hard against the stool
as her eyes—those heaven-bound air ship

portals!—briefly transmit cobalt blue beams
to mine. I fancy myself a miner
riding a bumpy track down her love seams.
Be she a screamer, be she a whiner,

whate'er, my moans will ascend to above,
while answering her clenched soft nubile thighs
and we commerce in pure, altruistic love.
E'en now methinks I hear our blending sighs . . .

Pixie gives sudden yank to my magic wand
"I knew coming here would be the thing
to shove the plot beyond any beyond.
While that blonde bimbo put you in sling,

"Donna and I've been wondering about your
dojo. Is it the one on Bluebird Way?"
Donna pipes in, "That's a fine one, for sure."
I clear my throat before making my say:

"Describing the dojo would delay the plot,
as I have told you."
          Trixie gives my wong a mash,
and blessed Prima Donna pours me a shot.
"Joe, you're a gas. While you were ogling that brash

"young lass, Donna laid gossip, I drank gin.
How many times did your eyeballs give scan?
You could've described ten dojos by then."
I shoot the shot, cough, and stall for a plan.

"While you gathered clouds, I gleaned clues to your plot."
I study her eyes: the usual shifting hazel.
I lean to hear, but Donna spews this rot:
"First, pay her in spice, one hotter than basil."

The two give titter. I swear the coed joins in.
But I won't complain. We debark for Mystic Cactus
Hotel, where Pixie and I will engroin in
until midnight, tantric sex to practice.

Sweet Goddess Love, how she hath whacked us.

Chapter Forty-two:
Trixie shows her wrath;
both your author and philosophy
get in her path

A Trixie yelp awoke Our Beloved Writer.
"Ee-ee!" would make a fair transcription.
It conjured flight-or-fight after their all-nighter,
until Trixie's laughter threatened mare conniption.

"Joe, just listen: my cousin can't make it,
and guess out why: MM, her lover-pal, doth lie
a-bed with priapism: he can't shake it;
she claims it's reaching toward the sky.

"She says some ancient witch gave him a potion
to make it grow and extend toward rafters.
Oh my. When your Miz W gets a notion
people really do forget hereafters."

Our Beloved Writer took the China black
T proffered. Sipping it, he felt his own sore sword.
Through all last night his Pixie'd coaxed it back.
Omne animal, she sternly had ignored,

proclaiming that old saw'd been shoved aside
by Wiccan magic and New Age tantric.
"Sad after sex?" she'd yelped on their first ride.
"No way! Be glad! Keep our humping antic!"

And now she turned, in clear Trixie style:
"I rented us a car. We're going a-spa-ing."

Our Beloved Writer demurred; T scraped a file
—whose noise gave OBW no ha-ha-ing—

across her five nails, a trick entirely
unfair. "Remember how I said I'd picked up clues?"
OBW gave low nod. Too slick entirely,
these morning moves. And those red spiky shoes

already clicking the room's tan desert tiles!
"That Donna told she'd overheard two Boss Moe
minions singing bad Italian that gave her piles.
More later. But big Boss does always go

"to Sacred Saguaro Sanctity Spa—"
"To *where*?" Our Beloved Writer stared
at China black tea. If he shouted hurrah,
would sense derive from what his Trixie just flared?

"You heard aright. What name would you expect
from folks who video all day, then read
their graphic novels, whose morals lie suspect,
do drugs and wallow in some fake Native-Am creed?

"At any rate, before each opera, there's
the place our good Boss goes. So now a car I've got
on rent and there's where we shall follow. Don't be scarce
or sketchy like you were on the dojo. A lot

of lithe masseuses will no doubt be roaming,
so your colt's tooth will clench and give bite
at one or so. But Joe, do strive for homing
in on Big Boss and plot. For once, live right."

"You finished?" OBW half-said, half-asked.
He clanked his cup of tea. Did he get away

with his blurred slur? For one smug second he basked,
but hurled car keys grazed on his ear, so no blest way.

They banged against the door so very hard
a roaming maid stopped and asked, "You two okay?"
"Oh hon, just trying to light this tub of lard,"
replied Trixie. The maid grinned and went on her way.

Outside, into the rental they climbed. A Mustang!
Whoa! Our Beloved Writer drifted back
to youth when he spun out the fastest thang
in L-town. At least till that cop gave whack

to lift his license for 90 days.
Soon Trixie tugged her GPS. "We're only eight
miles from that New Age spa whose fool name sways
inglorious." OBW pressed his pate.

"Is something wrong?" T inquired; "I didn't throw
those keys that damned hard." Our Beloved did rub
his not inconsiderable snout. "A No-show.
Your cousin, I mean. Could other characters flub

"up too? This Boss, Hank, Dave, C and Laura?"
"Lorrie, Joe! Talk about a Freudian slop,
that's you! You're harboring a real deep horror
that truth will chomp down hard enough to plop

fair you in Daddyland. Don't worry, no
damn way she'll hit you up for child support."
OBW banged the steering wheel to show
his manly frustration. "Let's abort

this argument," he hissed.
                                        "You won't wish

that word when you see how noble your daughter
has turned. A charming lovely dish
who could lead any guy she chose to slaughter."

"Pineapples. Linda had 'em too."
                                        T'd been
glommed on cacti, something never seen in KY,
but at that she chirped, an angry wren,
"Miss 'em, do you? Joe, did you sigh a huge glad sigh

"whene'er they drooped on your great bulbous snout?
You know what the boys say, darling Joe:
'Don't look for more than can fill up your mouth.' "
OBW tried to not roll his eyes, hard go,

though he did okay. "So you think we're really—"
Two HumVees and one Maserati zipped by,
fast enough to leave any state trooper silly
with tickets he could have slipped by

in traffic court.
                            "Unless they flip and wreck,
there speed a group of your star actors.
No! Don't try to catch 'em; I highly expect
barrages of bullets would greet us. The factors

"I like the best are us. Just meeting Blue gave test
enough." At T's advice, OBW eased from
the gas, agreeing, "Yes, let's give druggies a rest."
"That's fine, we've got oodles of time." Released from

those worries, they counted cacti until the
state prison sign advised to not pick up
hitchhikers. "Refusing might really drill the
plot if we passed a stranded Lorrie. I'll stick up

"for not believing all that you read."
"Not good practice for a fiction writer,"
OBW replied.

   "Say, Joe, how do you plead?
What's more real? Our recent all-nighter,

"or this or any such tale you indite?"
OBW squirmed: his butt clenched, his willie
churned, his Kantian Pure Will took flight.
"Oh stop the car! There Lorrie stands! Really!"

OBW gave the brakes a fine hard test.
They passed, thank goodness, or this very book
you hold would have sunk to its final rest,
trash-tossed, and globally ignored, o'erlooked.

"Where?" OBW gave query. Trixie grinned
and pointed to a cactus that had a green blouse
around it wrapped, by joke or by wind.
"Just thought I'd let your Kantian Pure Will delouse

"itself. I Just know it would've rolled out a
white lie and claimed that life took precedence
far over all that you write, that life folds out a
fine royal carpet, that art confers decadence.

"Still Joe, I'll ask: Do people really think
that Kant guy lived so pure? I think he sold
a line."

   "You're wrong. At his last earthly slink
on death bed's brink, to all around he told,

" 'I die a virgin proud.' " OBW heard
a cackle cram the sport-blue Mustang.

"Joe, Plato diddled little boys, that turd.
Well, evens I say. Philosophy's a real wang

"dang doodle, ain't it?" T's GPS gave a ding.
"We turn left in three miles. Let me drive.
"Your muse can bide, describe the spa, and sing
as loudly as it did for that bimbo whose lithe

perfumed bod set your wong on wing."

                      But the fine mind
of OBW took flight. From Kant to Greek lads
to Linda's pineapples to what he might find
tonight when he at last met L. Some sads? Some glads?

Could Trixie be right? Could L be his child?
"Joe, Joe! Slow down or you'll miss our turn.
You really should let me drive. You're way too wild."
So that's what they did, so his mind could churn.

Both they and we, Sweet Reader, have highway to burn.

Chapter Forty-three:
An unscheduled hot spa relaxation,
wherein the plot doth thicken;
a checkered, stumbling conversation,
whose sentiment all caring pulses will quicken
P.S. Can yours truly still deny parental incubation?

A brick drive stretched one-half a mile. The expense,
the labor, the intent pressed full, extravagant.
Our writer thought, *Yes, population growth will wrench*
us worse than some damned Plantagent

wrenched ye grand old England. Cream now gloats
upon assorted soured milk and whey, curd,
and Limburg's cheese. Impressive moats
now separate one-half percent from the loath herd.

Our loving one-half percent! Don't tax 'em!
Our loving one-half percent! Please let 'em know
how we adore 'em! Don't let anyone ax 'em!
Our loving one-half percent! They put on a show!

Their smiles bestowed from righteous gods
of bullion's commerce! Their each dictum
not just a tweet, but glorious lightning rods!
Our loving one-half percent! Great Fate picked 'em!

. . . OBW's lofty scorn thus flowed as T drove
into Sacred Saguaro Sanctity Spa,
whose bumpy red bricks jiggled his brain-trove:
Paypal, they niggled. *You're a real shitty-ha*

for issuing your moral discernments
while holding bucks from Carol's poor sap Tim
in escrow with interest-raising internment
You stand as ready as the next to trap skim,

so clamp your moral white lily pen.
OBW slumped so shamed he overlooked
the poor mixed metaphor delivered then
by conscience or whaddyacallit. It cooked

his high proud stance to thought's digestive
confines—at least till lunch when a *tres cher*
broccoli puree with "hints of cumin restive"
would be served by a sexy *au pair*

in fishnet blouse and apron.
                              "Earth calling!"
Dixie squawked, giving OBW an elbow
that caused the Mustang to go trawling
toward the bumper of a black HumVee. "Whoa!"

both shouted. Two drugged and angry black beards
gave stare. "Thank great god Heisenberg
you missed," OBW praised. Still, he feared
retribution. Why hadn't they done Gatlinburg?

Why couldn't T's cousin have shown, and Boss
Moe been taken down with priapism?
Alas, time's crankings slowly slough sad loss
to human intent. Bucket loads of spilt jism

faux-hatch the glum and final picture. "Think it's safe
to get out?" Pixie whispered, looking at four
arms folded under two black beards whose state
lay anywhere but friendly. "That spa door

"sits fifty yards off. My high heels, I can't—
say, Joe, what type of truck does sexpot Dave
have?"

      "Dave rides a Harley to make girls pant—"
"He's got a truck, too—"

            "No."

                "Joe, can you save

"one plotline morsel in your damn thick head?
It's gold, remember? His dad and Chelsea
parked it on that lane where that poor dead
UCLA wannabe—"

          "Traci Rosa."

               "See,

"you did take your ginkgo. We'll need
some lavender soon—"

          OBW exclaimed:
"Shit! Those two goons with their bad seed
are coming!"

      A gold truck, owner yet unnamed,

slid in to park before the two. A beauty
with chesty pineapples got out and grinned.
If they'd remembered, the goons forgot their duty
and bowed. And you can bet: within their skulls they sinned.

Melodious Spanish trash-talk drifted
the air from them, to truck, to Mustang.
"We're saved, evidently." Trixie sighed. She lifted
her purse's flap revealing mace. "Donna rang

"it on our bill, when she learned who we
just might be meeting." But T was speaking

to a passenger seat. OBW knew he
must fast confront this fine younger tweaking

of his ex wife. "Linda?" he squeaked. His hand
it shook, his teeth they clicked and ground. And when L turned,
her pineapples, her hair, her eyes made demand
on his glandular titration, for though he spurned

tears in those who wear a penis, salt gave threat.
"That ring," lone Lorrie pointed. "Its two emeralds,
its tiger-eye cameo. My mom had one set
for her sole husband, who proved ephemeral

"and gone."
        "Gong?"
                "Gone. Run down by a dump truck."
"Linda!—your mom—how could she tell you that!?"
"Don't know. She said the guy never had no luck."

"A double negative, that fits Linda, all right."
"You knew my mom?"
                "I—"
            "She—"
                "You?"
                    "Yes."
                        "She?"
                            "We—"
"It was the last—"
        "Past?"
            "Done."
              "My mom?"
                  "—the last night."

"So that ring—"

        "Birthday—"

                "Yours?"

                        "Yes."

                                "She?"

                                      "To me."

"Then you—"

        "I might—"

                "But how—?"

                        "She never—"

                                    "—told?"

"That's right."

        "The last—"

                "night."

                        "Where?"

                                "Her mother's farm."

"Granny?"

        "Loretta. We—"

                    "You—"

                        "Yes."

                                "And Mom?"

                                          "Rolled—"

"Oh gosh!"

        "Oh golly!"

                "So you two—"

                        "—in love's last charm."

"Green."

        "Yes?"

                "My eyes."

                    "Yes?"

                        "Yours too."

                                "I guess."

"My nose—"

    "Mine too."

        "A hill."

           "That's sure correct."

"Donald Duck."

    "Quack."

        "Johnnie Walker Black?"

           "The best."

"Menthol cigarettes."

    "No way."

        "Nor me. Just a check."

"That Spring—"

    "May?"

        "Cardinals chirped—"

           "*May?*"

              "Bees buzzed."

"*May?*"

    "*Yes.* Marigolds."

        "February."

           "No, May."

              "No, I was born."

"In Feb?—"

    "Yes. Nine months from—"

        "When peaches fuzzed."

"Granny."

    "Loretta."

        "Me?"

        "Her."

          "Linda."

            "Mom?"

             "Forlorn."

"By you—?"

      "Yes."

          "Then you—"

               "That's my guess."

                    "On G's farm . . .

". . . the barn?"

      "Attic."

          "My mom?—"

               "I thought no harm

"would—"

      "Come?"

          "Yes."

             "And did you—"

                    "I . . ."

                        "You . . ."

                           "Like barm."

"And she?"

      "Cried."

          "Mom?"

               "Yes."

                  "You?"

                    "It felt like pure Dharm—"

a nearby spa masseuse swooned, taken by charm.
The two black-bearded goons coughed, in male alarm.
Poor Trixie grabbed Dave's scrawny but muscled arm:
"Make them stop, please? Before we wallow in smarm."

Brave Dave inhaled hot air to say: "I got a joke."
All heads then turned toward his salvation.
One goon, still sniffling, rolled then lit a smoke.
The masseuse moved back, forbidden inhalation.

"These two Navajo meet an anthropologist . . ."
Though all from the West had heard it thrice
they listened as if Dave were an oncologist
doling out diagnosis and advice.

OBW filed jokes with taking pictures:
like black holes, they skewed the flow of time.
Still, he listened and emitted no strictures,
thinking how young Dave would serve sublime

as hubby to this daughter. When Dave's joke ended
the roar of laughs came stunning. *One more*?
Dave pondered. But the masseuse fended
encores with these words so bright: "*Discoveries Galore!*

"That's just the right two-couple therapy—
er, I suppose we could make it three . . ,"
She glanced to the goons, but ere a plea
could be stated, that non-grammatical he,

Less Ugs walked out. "The Boss is get the Sacred Stone
Massage. So here come I to light a stogie—
say, do you I know?" His eyes made roam
to L's pineapples like they formed a hoagie.

"I—"
       "You—"
               "We—"
                       "Dear God, please!" Trixie exclaimed.
"No more tic-tac-toe. Time runs, like the sun!"
Less Ugs had already gotten Lorrie framed
as *la chica* whose friend pointed a gun.

He shook a finger at her and spoke:
"And your *amiga con la pistola*?

She comes also this day, I give much hope?"
L eyed the man with his poor face like granola.

Should she tell the truth? Should she lie?
Before she could decide, one goon spoke:
"*Es su padre*. This make their first ever see-eye."
He pointed to OBW. Not broke

like his tongue, his finger meaning conveyed.
Less Ugly had been raised without his dad.
He'd felt outcast and thrown to drugs, betrayed.
He'd felt mad, sad, as if he'd been had

by Fate. So he gave snarl at Our Beloved:
"Only a low, rotting, *pendejo*, thievin'
would his *hija* desert in this rugged—"
He gripped his Walther, the worst believin'.

"He didn't know!"
                    "I didn't know!"
                                "*Su madre*?"
L fast affirmed her mom had caused the severance.
"*Amigo*, you make up? Be a *bueno padre*?"
OBW nodded with reverence.

"*¡Vino!*" shouted Less Ugly. "To make a cheer!"
The masseuse countered, "Great Discoveries!"
Less Ugly glanced at her in joyless leer,
but made a turnabout recovery

on reading *Rosa* on her nameplate of gold.
"*Mexicano*?"
                "*Sí, mi madre. Mi papa
son de* New York." When Less Ugly's eyes rolled
a maddened way, she let her voice drop a

low sultry note to add, "They live in Tucson,
where I was raised."

           "*Bueno.*" Less Ugly
smiled, glad at least one dad kept his shoes on
and stayed. The masseuse became snuggly

and grabbed his arm to say, "Our Great Discoveries
has wine served as a complement to El-
emental Massage. Great recoveries
have occurred." Despite his thick red scars, one could tell

Less Ugs was dropping *muchos* emo thoughts.
He waved his sub-goons off and said,
"This Great Discoveries I will now boughts
for señorita and her new *bueno* dad."

He looked at Rosa then to add, "I will return."
With corn cob pipe and five-star hat
he might have been a *jefé*. Rosa's thoughts did burn.
And that, to make things flat, was almost that.

But under many a five-star hat lurks a rat.

Chapter Forty-four:
A hot spa interlude
wherein indeed the plot doth thicken—
your author owes great gratitude
to T for listening at Donna's whilst he did quicken
to granite in his bimbo attitude

Describe, T had insisted. Our Beloved
took her command with high seriosity.
He did not covet pearl nails unglovèd
by their masseuse so lithe. No curiosity

expended on her luscious pear-like rear.
The name of *Rosa* set no Mozartian
fine cadences to ring, enticing and clear.
Instead he heard a fountain imparting an

immense "Aqua Discovery Journey,"
then climbed a pleasant winding stairway,
where, near a heaven-bound masseuse's gurney,
some fool stood turning hall into fairway,

by practicing golf club swings. Our Beloved's soul—
he became almost convinced he had one—
ignored the fool since copper mirrors, whole
body in length, gave tingles. He felt he might run

a marathon or two. The door to their room,
adobe-fake, without the least small whisper,
released, dispelling all anguish and gloom.
Inside, more mirrors, golden now, did glister.

Less Ugly, true to his word, had bought a deal,
escorting them upward. He gave a snort
at the faux golf swinger, saying, "The Boss, for real,
might that sad swinging *tonto's* life cut short.

"The Boss, he hate the little white ball game."
Was true enough. Eight private clubs had denied
The Boss a membership. An angry flame
had to The Boss since then stayed hot and tied.

"Well, here I you must leave, *hija* and lost papa.
Take your cares good and *vaya con dio*."
"So sweet," T said as Less Ugs left. "Not a droppa
unkind, despite his face that looks like the Rio

has gulley-washed it for lots of eons."
Rosa craned her neck as Less Ugs strolled away.
A sigh escaped her lips. Quite clearly, she on
his him her heart had set. But no time now for play

She led the four into the suite, to point out
its lush amenities. The boys she sent to change
in one room grand, the gals another. Just about
that time, a racket outside the suite gave range,

but Rosa blithely shrugged. The rich one-half percent!
Who ever knows what diddles they might put on?
It's they who spiral our moral descent.
Yet they perceive poor folks as if soot on

them will spore some vile contamination.
Chihuahua! she cursed. Ignoring the clatter,
her heart recalled *el hombre*, in inflammation:
Less Ugs had flung her mind to Cupid's matter.

The guys, unbent by any outside racket,
emerged, and Rosa gave examination.
This pair, she judged, could heartily hack it
And lend the two sweet ladies ramification.

The fresh floor tiles, imitating sand—
surely New Mexico's choice décor—
did render their terrycloth robes so grand
that even Dave appeared a virgin, or

at most, as if his wick had only once been dipped.
Then Pixie stepped out—not quite like an angel,
but in some spritely plane whereon she skipped.
OBW? His very teeth did mangle

each other champing love's sweet bit.
The room's gold mirrors glowed me-ism enough
to make a media star give blush and hide her tit.
Well, maybe not. That task presents one rough

and craggy tor, since Endemic Media Disease
roams all this land—not in amble, but in run.
But best for last: A sweet fulsome breeze
did quiver the golden mirrors and stun

all waiting in the Great Discoveries Room
when Lorrie strolled on in. Her eyes,
sharp emerald now, dispelled all earthly gloom.
Her feet, impressing heated tiles, gave rise

to this hallowed image: A virgin conquering snake.
Her pineapples with La Leche League did side;
the mirrors on each wall gave quake,
as she, in glory from the boudoir did stride.

"Daughter," sighed OBW. Was a flick
from Trixie to his left ear that provoked
his lengthy discourse. Soon Rosa did her shtick.
Still secretly craving Less Ugly she invoked

her usual oration plus invitation
in broken Spanish, not her dad's New York-
ese. *El's* and *la's* littered her recitation.
Was all quite charming really, not dork

like you might think. She then instructed
both males in massaging *la planta*, the sole,
and soon the willing guys conducted
their gals to bliss, so they might leave this hole

called Planet Earth, which sails the same ellipse
ad near *infinitum*. A "nosy" red was quaffed,
and Our Beloved made a sappy toast with lisp
to "time reclaimed, my writer's cap doffed

"to that unbending beauty who reserved
our airplane tickets so that fate's pink fingers—"
with that, his Dixie's patience shred unnerved
to snatch his second glass. "Too much drink lingers

"from last night's fun. Remember *Otello*."
"Wild beans!" Dave exclaimed. "We're hitting that movie
too."
        At that, L delivered a swat. "Hello!
it's an opera and onstage, goof."
                                "Groovy!"

Dave had just talked with Chelsea about his pop,
who lay sick from downing too many tamales:

was why her sixties slang messed his craw. He'd stop.
Besides, as penis owner, the recent follies

of sentiment made him sway, so with a gag
of lowest sort he made to save the day
for testosterone. You think that male word gave sag
to meter? Please consider how it bends the play

of life: graft, theft, wars, rapes, Higgs boson guns,
Boss Moes, Less Uglies—no, let judgment hold
on the last. Judge no man till his life hath run,
said some Greek of old. You'd think we'd make bold

and move past 'em. Well we have: Snoop Dog Snoop,
J Lo, Dog Whisperer, Justin Bieber,
Dennis Rodman—they all dish the real poop;
they all contort us into true believers.

Alas, too soon Great Discoveries was done.
The hallway with its mirrors so copper
did tingle—but what! The faux golfer sprawled mum,
a steel golf club protruding improper

from his bare butt. That view Rosa blocked with a shrug,
for sexual peccadilloes here came quite frequent.
All five of them gave thought, Just who are we to judge?
Lives fretting other's kink are lives misspent.

The winding stairway down, sure enough wound;
the Fountain gurgled its great Aqua
Discovery; and lo! the lobby did abound
with friends a-gaggle, enough to rock a

petroglyph. Miss W with her bags of cookies,
Don Walker with his sack of stones,

Sweet Carmen, Hank, and four-white be-tied rookies
With no bless'd clue, on lookout for telltale bones.

Of course, the au courant top crime list
involved one steel golf club and Higgs boson durples.
But yet, this group created a pop clime mist
of patriots and majestic mountains purple—

the only thing that lacked was some spirit-creature
to swoop and shed his grace on them and thee.
My promise! So no spooky double feature.
Instead, I fear what swooped would make lone children pee.

Adobe doors, before so silent, gave clatter;
the winding stairway, it shook and rocked;
the aqua fountain did ice and shatter;
every eye down in that lobby upward locked.

The Boss. He shed a clinging masseuse to wag
his trigger finger at the group below.
His frown spread down enough to cause jet lag
in nearby guests, stop *Otello*, or any show.

Two lawyers, then two goons ran down to pay his bill;
three goons swept the room before, two took aft;
the Maserati curbed itself with pure free will;
those standing in this wake went nearly daft.

My dear freethinker . . . thus expectations
of saviors often stumble and founder:
instead of imbibing, come expectorations;
instead of a guru, up shows some rounder.

But dark hours sometime send out a glimmer:
Less Ugs approached OBW and Lorrie

to advise that just paired-up familial shimmer,
"When at *Otello*, don't keep there the whole story.

"At halftime go-leave, make-take some starshine stroll.
An awful thing will shake out a zapping,
will unexpected bad make on a toll."
He said no more, a goon was rapping

the chamber door. Sweet Reader, we must get flapping.

Chapter Forty-five: Otello near Santa Fe;
I don't think Shakespeare (or Verdi) wrote it this way

Act 1: Cookies, gems, and guns in hand;
for some, fine wine enough before
    to elevate a snore;
for others, espresso enlivens a gland
    or two . . . or more

For the spa visit and the vicarious
drive over blood-red bricks to elicit
joy, this ignore: Those bricks held multifarious
bone dust and gristle derived from illicit

doings done—in vicarious mode of course!—
and diddled too, through outsourcing, raiding
retirement funds, and grinding workers down to horse
grub for fine French poodles. In essence parading

99.5 percent on cross, screw, or rack.
While life's morals drizzle far into the red,
Its bank accounts flow obsidian black.
Spa? Psha! This opera's much more swanky. Enough said.

An outdoor venue: behold its spires!
Approaching boldly, our separate crews
envisioned angelic (or satanic) choirs,
themselves and friends enthroned with those disparate few.

Behold the roseate New Mexico sky!
The Boss's entourage parked feloniously
nearby, but our good guys parked aright. The shy,
Beatitudes claim, walk ceremoniously.

These shy righteously plodded through the parking lot,
when screams gave sound nearby. All eight looked.
The fab four's white ties hung sparkling a lot,
beside a stand where sushi got cooked.

What? Cooked? If the communion tie four had their way
the stand would so stand. Raw seeped unclean, bedazzled.
FDA peeps should investigate, have their say
before venereal disease left all frazzled.

"Those shrimp appear vulgar and suspicious.
Almost, I swear, I saw that one wriggle."
"Oh no, kind sir, they are delicious."
"Penile."
    Sushi Suzi suppressed a giggle.

Her stifled laugh, a sign of scorn or fear, or both?
Was hard to say. Ted, moreover, packed a knack
for finding blueblood daughters who made loath
to meet his cummerbund come-ons, which sorely lacked.

Just then one walked by, diamonds a-dangle.
I do swear! I recognized her from Calumet!
These horsey people—always ready to wrangle.
"Excuse me, filly, but haven't we met?"

Was not my said, but Ted's.
     Near, Carmen shook her head:
"They should hire out to work a comic quartet
and not four spies maintaining America's thread.
They could use snares and sizzles and a bass drum set.

"Oh well, one more conundrum for the gipper!
. . . Say, Dad! You wanna 'dopt me too as your daughter?"

C winked at Our Beloved, who checked his zipper.
How Trixie howled! "Joe, these girls will make you fodder!"

Presenting tickets Our Beloved gave
no grimace seeing the extra for Don
Walker—they entered. A nasty wave
emitted from The Boss's wineglass, so eight bon-

nets hastened to stop, look, and listen.
C opened her purse, fingered her Walther.
Don Walker checked his gems as they gave glisten.
And even Dave from Lorrie-land love did falter.

So maybe espresso, and not fine wine—
How often does one line but *Oh shit*
enjoy such hard acclaim? That coffee line
did tingle all the eight Through luck's inspiring flit?

Just common sense? Whichever, Our Beloved
ordered and paid for espressos eight.
A second glare from Boss. His rugged
face, scarred like metal, confirmed the worst: its weight

convinced the sober crew that no *juguete*
no silly skit, was likely to take place.
"Otello kills someone at this play's end, yes?"
"Afraid so, Son," Our Beloved had the grace

to answer Dave's solemn, whispered query.
As if confirming, The Boss's spumy face
of pocks and grime and oil enough to worry
Mother Teresa, twitched with a hell-worm's grace.

Our Beloved—you'd think that notes he'd be writing,
but no, he licked his lips and kept on looking

from hills to sky to sunset, not inditing.
No thought gave he to how this plot was cooking;

no thought gave he to whether his daughter would live;
nor whether his loving Pixie would breathe
and sling her hips to make him cry, "I give!"
By dark night's end, would all involved have grief?

No thought gave he. The wonderland of desert air
bestrewed his worries over Boss Moe's perversion.
A star—Venus of course, though beware,
it's Lucifer too—like that conversion?—

peeped out to shaft him further in his daze.
As Love's star shone brightly, he could barely count
the many buxom opera-goers who raised
his wishes for Viagra so he might mount . . .

Let's leave him mired, ignoring fear for lust.
Sweet Reader, we have work enough! Our shoulders
to the wheel, put heartily now we must
and inspect the venue, study distant boulders.

As told, the seating lay outdoors, covered and
ex-quis. Ol' Sol was tossing streaks of pink;
a peace did nearly settle, though it hovered and
absconded, fast belying joy's brief brink.

A distant dust devil gave roll—
Our Beloved could never make this scene up—
to shimmy—oh not like some dancer on a pole,
but like a sidewinder ready to stream up

your leg and venom your precious middle.
Out West, they're usually tan, tall, and skinny—

dust devils, not dancers or snakes. They don't fiddle,
besides to make stray cowpokes and horses whinny.

Out West, those skinny whirling devils
are filled with sand and last no longer than a whiz.
But this sky's black one hung to make loud revels
to show it meant a serious bit of biz.

A clap of thunder followed heat lightning.
Misnomer? You couldn't convince our eight.
The roof above them glowed a frightening
blue manner. "*El batador* has found a mate,"

said Carmen.
             "Do what?" A puzzled Hank inquired.
"The outrider—" but when her slim finger pointed,
the dust devil had left, as if its dance had gyred
its single nature into one triple-jointed,

fast trying to convey bad omens by skewed lines.
The eight located their balcony seats.
Their front row held the four old wheezer's spines;
the row behind, young pricks and teats.

The sky now gave roseate bleat, just as before.
While life *shows* boring, its chaos brings stores
of mishaps and catastrophes galore.
So don't dare snore. Beware life's shoals; beware its shores.

Beware its this, beware its that.
Beware it clothed, beware it nude.
Beware when it dons, or when it doffs a hat.
Just beware it, sweet friend, for life can grow so rude.

Miz Walburn and the Don knew all this and
some more. Indeed, that's why Our Beloved picked
'em, trying his best to secure bliss and
one happy end, despite bad guys who might inflict

their spins so devilish.
                              Just so, Miz Walburn grabbed
Don's arm, already taut as his jaw from grinding.
He feared relaxing, feared they'd be jabbed, nabbed, or stabbed.
"Look, Don, look who's down there minding

"the store on stage far right." There stood one Hanson, and
behind him, Son Blue.
                              "Now look at stage left."
They both would have given one ransom and
more for this to not be true, but bereft

of luck, they spied, on stick-legs, Strickland shifting grim.
Both older men held oblong boxes of . . . lilies?
Of course not. "The G-gun's about that thin,"
C leaned to note.
                              "Don't yet get scared chillys,"

insisted Trixie. "Not one thing will happen
until 'The Willow Song.' "
                              "The what?" six asked.
OBW stayed silent, his mind was flappin'.
You likely can make guess just where it basked.

With angry grunt, his Trixie twitched her
right hand at him, for those pink opera glasses
were silently focusing on—Trixie snitched her
new pink glasses back. "Show some class as

"we sit before your daughter," she hissed.
Of course OBW was focusing on
a fine thin neck and ringlets—the rest he missed.
" 'Willow,' " said T, "precedes the hocusing on

"Desdemona. The Boss, I learned from my sure source,
always sheds tears at that song." T was turning back
to explain. "Tears embarrass him of course,
so mostly he leaves, though twice a sack

"went over his head."
                              "He's seen this more than once?"
"His favorite show."
                              "How'd you hash all this out?"
"Oh, Joe. At Donna's. You were . . . I had a hunch
and Donna filled it—straight from the horse's mouth."

I switched to D, explored the coming bad scene,
which wouldn't occur until the fat lady
made ready to sing. "It's gonna be lean
and fast, so no room for any maybe.

"Let's take account of weapons we've got."
Miz Walburn held up cookies, two bags.
"One makes your balance and vision rot;
the other gives your bowels instant jags."

But little did she know that she'd need neither,
for one small item she almost forgot:
the potion that extended MM's peter
and rendered him hotter than hot.

For his show, Don Walker shook a satchel of gems.
"Got one that blinds, one could change stones to stark mad,

a sulfur crystal and a spider trapped within."
He swung a turquoise locket. "We'd all be sad

"if this talisman left. The sulfur crystal
takes just one half an hour to do its work;
whoever holds it then turns two-dollar pistol,
no sense at all; goes flat out berserk."

Dixie showed her mace. No one held doubts that
virago's aim would stream hard true, not fizzle.
They looked to Our Beloved. He had sent pouts that
upwelled since pink glasses stopped tickling his pizzle.

Now huffing bravely, Our Beloved insisted,
"The sword . . . is oft' . . . outdone by . . . pen."
When they awaited, he hemmed, he resisted,
said he'd purchase a Bic at intermission. When

Trixie hissed, "Lame," kind Lorrie took pity
and pulled an emerald-green pen from her purse.
"Here, Dad. My gift. Wish it was more big city."
Then *she* inhaled to toss her breasts. "They'll nurse

"some sap into distraction—don't be jealous,
Dave. Necessity's the mother of distension.
These boobs of mine intend to get zealous,
distracting badsters from their evil intention."

Dave mocked a snarl and curled his biceps.
"Been lifting weights and taking karate.
Who locks on your breasts better make high steps."
Our Carmen, meanwhile, looked as if she'd gone potty.

She opened her purse the tiniest crack
and showed the barrel of her Walther.

Some knew; two were flat thrown aback.
A weapon of mini-destruction, a daughter

of Eve?! Didn't those doubters watch *Monster*?
Or read? Indira Gandhi? Iron Lady?
Golda Meir? All threw down mean as mobsters.
Hilary Clinton? Not exactly the *Grady*

Bunch. And tonight C bought an extra clip,
just on hunch. Hank's turn. His reveal came last,
and he glowed cocky. His weapon was a trip!
Like L, he breathed in—*his* result blew not so vast—

and gave a boy-smirk. "This weapon will work
or my true name ain't Gunga Din Din Din!"
he blurted loudly, just like a dockside clerk.
Fourteen eyes waited as he spent his grin.

Then from his fancy jacket from Mr. Thrift,
he went to pull—
        BA BA BAM BOOM!
The opera, it started. A prop boat sailed adrift.
A chorus happily sang, but shifted to doom.

"The universe is torn apart, a spectral
North wind crushes through, titanic trumpets—"
La! Italian rings so much more clarion. Pectoral
is what that language is. Even dago strumpets

hum come-ons tingly. Hot spaghett and olive oil
slip-slide their wares. And don't forget that wine.
The musk from Chianti turns plebe glands royal.
But now, on stage, in real people time,

a prop mast cracked, to smash a large prop wall.
No harm or death, but hey, was that dust devil
out roaming yet? Did it not care at all?
Society high tones sat here holding revel.

The chorus sang on! The show, let it go on!
"Her mainsail's torn away!" This from motiveless
Iago. One more crack left actors' faces froze on.
Damn show and boats would row much better if less

onstage constructs fell mashed. Otello came on.
"Rejoice!" he warbled.

"Gosh he's really black,"

someone exclaimed.

Before you get a flame on,

remember, New Mexico has three races track

the census: gringo, injun, wetback.
Last count, only nineteen blacks stayed in-
state. So this show of surprise should not set back
opinion of the eight. Not weighed in

that same defense are Trixie and Our Beloved,
from KY. No slur from them, for they were counting
their toesies in amour. One bare foot shovéd
another. Skin! Skin! Skin! It keeps on mounting.

". . . the dark kisses of that swollen-lipped savage—"
What? Oh yes, the opera doth go on.
Good, it reminds us how love's pips ravage:
"He who hath tasted Bacchus' fine draught . . ." and so on.

Wait, look! Onstage now Cassio doth draw sword.
Who wrote this dread? Its damn first act shows blood, not fun?

Alas, our human blight can ne'er be ignored.
Wait! Now Otello plays the honey-bun

with Desdemona on the ramparts, which sway.
In fright, they scurry down; to act, they share a kiss.
The show, the show, the show, must make its way.
That's why all actors take a pre-play piss.

"... *I see your end. Your evil genius drives you on.*"
Has Iago stepped out of this opera to survey
what's happening in Los Alamos? The shoe is on,
it fits, if so. But no, he meant to purvey

Otello's hate with his own "*primeval slime.*"
Oh say, The Boss, who sat in front-most row,
was giggling and tapping his fingers in time,
inspired by hatred building in this show.

"*Beware my lord, of jealousy, a dark hydra . . .*"
Trixie-Dixie-Pixie gave Our Belov'd Writer
an elbow right then, "Take love's side or a
so-tony lad will take it for you."

$\qquad\qquad\qquad\qquad$ "Spider!"

While they once more rippled toesies,
onstage bad Iago snatched the handkerchief
from Bianca. A side thought though, a posy:
as many times as this so sad riff

plays out onstage, do counter-melodies
get sung in life? The differences blur.
Life: a rhyming novel chanting out threnodies,
all written by an idiot, whose low rhymes occur

in syncope, to mimic life's sad whir.

Chapter Forty-six: Otello near Santa Fe;
I KNOW Shakespeare (or Verdi) didn't write this,
this way

Intermission

About the time when Iago sang his so-sad news
concerning Lady Des's handkerchief
and warbled out his dream with its green envy views,
two further props, one more wall went down, ker-spiff.

Just who to blame, all eight gave wonder
on leaving seats to softly tread down stairs.
Was it gross Fate, a poor set crew, or thunder
from that meddlesome wind still raising hairs?

The P. A. relayed intermission would take
some fifteen mins extra. "See? It's always human
fault," Hank declared. Miz Walburn gave good shake
of head. "Hank, you're too young to be spumin'

"so bitter," she said. "Besides, we have work
to do."
        "Yes! Engines! Man your stations! Fire in
the hole!" Ms. Dixie commanded. Therein did lurk
—somehow!—meaning enough to inspire them.

No maps to cognize, no watches to synchronize,
they spread about, on missions intent.
One black helicopter, and they'd squiggle like spies,
or maybe like somber clerics in Lent.

Miz Walburn craftily made search for Boss Moe.
She knew that he'd recall her porno story

from Todd's. On finding him, her reaching went slow:
five women, one gaggle, surrounded his glory.

But wait! One of the five was flavored transvestite!
Miz Walburn recognized him/her from years before.
She gave a wink and whisper, "Hold on tight,"
then handed him the sex-potion that its galore

had worked on MM. "Don't be greedy,
just take one nibble." She gave his/her cheek
a buss. The Boss, catching this, made speedy
to recognize the oldster from Todd's, the freak

who talked about men's strombolis and jism.
Bruja, he thought. He opened his arms and
sent out a grin, resulting in cataclysm.
As mentioned before, his breath was barm and

its brewing yeast not FDA inspected.
A quick path cleared; Miz Walburn approached
his open arms to brave his breath infected.
Surprised that such an old hag had encroached

their space, the drug groupies gave collective sniffle;
The Boss's eyes gave gleam as Miz Walburn's hand
went teasing his root. "Never again a piffle,"
she foretold. "Pink Potion Five will make you so rand-

"y stallions will gaze thereon amazed."
He reached, but she pulled back. "Don't be greedy,"
she warned, her lips caressing his ear. She'd raised,
she knew, that selfsame vice, so furious-needy

grew evil in this man. "One nibble shakes a good
and hardy night. More is not advised. Discretion

gives high ride to the sexual plane." Her eyes did hood,
her smile did bide. Boss Moe gave out impression

of royalty receiving trifling peasants.
"¡Soy un hombre vigoroso!" He gave
his chest one thump, expelling breathy un-pleasance.
With three proud chomps he ate the bar; the groupies raved.

Miz Walburn's eyes went wide. Even MM
had not been so entirely marred. She backed away,
her job completed.
                              Elsewhere, to blend in
played last on Lorrie's mind. Her breasts did sway

as she searched hard for Blue. She gave one button
a tear, to let it dangle there, on thread.
Within two seconds Blue, sacrificial mutton,
spotted button, breast, and thread. Straight for them he sped.

Five steps behind, Dave's righteous rage gave flare
as he spun through six karate katas.
Blue's eyes sought to fill, Dave's fists sought to bare.
A Boss Moe goon nearby had forgot a

drug message for Blue. On spotting Dave's ill intent
he tried to intervene. Biff, whoppo, blap,
boom, oof, and splat. Time enough was spent
that L stayed free to whisper this pineapple zap:

"Blue, I'm up in the balcony, seat B-2-2.
Watch there throughout the show; I'll slip a nipple,
large, rosy, wet, and dedicated to you."
All out of synch, Blue's eyes did ripple,

since whatsoever three drugs he'd taken,
despite Dad's warning, were now jagging and quaking.
From breasts and drugs he swayed so shaken
that he missed catching the terrific raking

Boss Moe's emissary was taking.
Two rent-a-cops had stopped, but seeing Boss's goon,
they turned away, for trouble in making
lay more abundant somewhere else. Each balloon

prepared to celebrate this season's end
had been set loose too soon by four dumb goofs
immaculately tied. It seemed one could depend
on idiocy and gas to raise the highest roofs.

Five thousand had been filled, four set them free.
So many never owed liberty to so few.
The Battle for Britain, Pass at Thermopylae—
and Jonestown, should your mind let slip a screw.

Now, to *Otello* nineteen kids had been dragged,
their mouths gave twist, their shoulders gave scrunch.
But when these airborne balloons turned adults all fagged,
they pranced about like a surprise school lunch

of sodas, chili dogs, pineapples, and fries
got served.
                    The opera's director stood weeping.
What else can spiral wrong? Her mouth spent sighs.
Oh dear, my dear, to question fate, always leaping

from some far mountain, runs foolish. Keep mum, sweet chum.
Chum-ess? Regardless of sex, mum's your key.
Fate angered, hath over rougher obstacles clumb.
Don't bless it, don't curse it. Just let it be.

Indeed, let us tiptoe away.
$\qquad\qquad$ So far, L, Dave,
and Miz Walburn have their assignments completed.
When at the spa, Our Beloved slyly gave
a wink to Rosa, penned her number. Defeated,

he claimed, by Spanish idiom, he'd call to consult
on this and any novel he might ever write.
Her lips had given subtle start—the real result
had been a twist to OBW's ear in spite,

as Dixie grimly chortled. And now she held out
her palm. "Give Rosa's number. To stop damnation,
we have a soul to save. 'Language consult'? You spout
such fool come-ons, Joe."
$\qquad\qquad$ With self-incrimination,

he handed over Rosa's number e'en as they
went strolling through the opera's attendees.
"You see," he mumbled, "Pens do hold more sway
than—"
$\qquad\qquad$ "Lover, quiet. Let's just find Less Ugly, please."

They watched small tots and tall adults grow giddy
from slapstick falling props and flying balloons.
The Fat Lady—who wasn't fat but slim-pretty—
would need some real fine wail to bushwhack this cartoon.

"There!" Dixie pointed. Less Ugly was blowing
a black cigar's gray smoke and munching pretzels.
D shifted her pink bra, for moment showing
the milk of kindness. "Nice man so special!"

she exclaimed, giving Less Ugly's elbow a rub.
"Rosa asked me to bestow her number;

she said you'd left your thing. I think she has a lub-
light lit for you, big guy. It's hardly a wonder.

"She's here, you know, with her young sis. Tickets
aplenty went for free this late season show."
At these hard words, Our Beloved swallowed. Ricketts?
Not yet. Just anger superheated to glow.

Last ticket fees lay heavy in his craw.
He watched as Less Ugly bit a Henry Clay
then twisted it with his great brown paw.
Does everyone but me ride in the golden way?

"*¿Aquí?*" Less Ugly licked his thick cigar,
believing it his social pretzel. Dear Freud,
our lives are wont to stray in fields afar.
How each of your slips, like a swollen adenoid,

betrays our slop subliminal.
                                    Just so. Now done
with task, the cooing pair from Kentuck, their mission
completed. Less Ugly beamed like he had won
four queens. He flipped his cell to dial his vision.

"Ah Rosa, Rosa, *tu es aqui, mi amor!*"
Pleased, Trixie gave OBW a swat:
"Now ain't that grand? Ain't that what love is for?"
Smart enough to nod, he safely spun more plot.

Don Walker, elsewhere, spun his entrappéd spider
for Hanson, his almost-daughter's worthless father,
the man who'd wronged his easy rider.
Don spotted Blue, who did not bother

to hide the five illegal pills he was popping.
No fruit falls far from a rotting tree,
Don thought. And soon enough, he spied Hanson mopping
his brow. *¿Caliente? Just wait. You've offended three,*

and now your turn has come. Don bumped into
the boxed G-string gun, which sent Hanson thrashing.
Don found it easy to shuffle and blend to
an aged vendor, clumsy and smashing.

In this disguise he slipped the sulfur-y spider
inside Hanson's natty jacket pocket.
Your punishment for screwing my easy rider,
Don thought, dangling the talisman turquoise locket.

"Son of a bitch!" Thin Hanson snarled and spat
as Don fast walked away. *May not even take*
half an hour to hit, with an attitude like that.
Assured that he had driven a cedar stake

deep in this creep's foul heart, Don felt released;
he now could throw the mescal by his bed away.
Though Carmen watched Don's work, she was not appeased;
she too desired to give dad Hanson's skin a flay.

¡Hola! she thought, *I don't need a gun.*
She pulled out her badge, the one that slipped her
by the naïve M.P. She danced and spun
that badge aloft. Before, when she'd stripped her

tit, his own daughter he couldn't see. But this badge?
Oh yes, she knew, his no-count eyes would take
it in. Always on hustle, ready to cadge
what all he could: an underage girl or flake

of uranium, a gluon, or muon—
anything his thin slime could steal and sell,
he would, to catch chiquitas to chew on,
if they purred soft enough and young. *Well, well,*

we'll see, Carmen thought, dancing around him
thrice. Badge and spider, spider and badge,
badge and spider—that dance did surround him,
and C thought right: her thug dad did imag-

ine law's long sticky arm stretching out.
This fear, combined with the sulfur spider curse,
incensed canine snarls, left his mind in rout.
C danced away, recalling Bible verse.

An eye for eye? To punish his many torts?
She pictured the blue shoed Mexican girl
and Traci the L. A. lass, their lives cut short.
No more handsome, Hanson. Away she did whirl

as sad Dad's hatred gave delirium tremens
a meaning new. He trembled, he quaked,
his mouth went puckery, as though filled with lemons.
Hot spittle drooled, to never be slaked.

Our last on mission, Hank, in his thrift store
sport suit kept a hidden paper, upon it
displayed complete guidelines to life and more.
Strickland's second hateful G-string caper, on it

was now exactly where Hank placed his bets.
A slather of Super Glue on paper . . .
"What in hell you—policing cigarettes?
Counting ticket stubs? Moonlighting makes you taper.

"I could report—"

                    "I'm here to see the play."

"Opera, you mean. It's French, so surely you can't

comprehend. Loading dock to here roams astray."

Confiding, Hank said, "You say right, it's all blue rant."

He slapped his guidelines on box's bottom.

With that, the eight their good tasks completed.

Above, balloons cascaded like flotsam.

Below, a crash did sound. Chaos: undefeated.

The warning bell went ding. Onward, all bleated.

Chapter Forty-seven: Otello near Santa Fe;
I don't think Shakespeare (or Verdi) wrote it this way

Act 2: Great God Hydrogen! Otello weeps, Iago stings, Desdemona strives hard to sing

It happened this way; it happened that.
From wobbling tower, Desdemona saw it best.
Now, Desdemona's stage name was Toni La Platte.
Once she waited tables, but gave that a rest

after karaoke singing in KY
where Nashville agents had chanced to be.
She wailed "Coal Miner's Daughter" with such a sigh
those agents knew that Toni would sail fame's true sea.

In this eve's staging, while Otello, Iago,
and Cassio with hankie did fiddle,
D perched atop that tower, not as virago,
but sighted seer unwinding a riddle.

As she gazed out, purportedly toward the sea,
she spied four women by a sushi stand—
no wait, she made out five: one danced in glee
whilst four made whirls about the hugest male glans

Ms. Toni La Platte ever did see, a cactus
in size. All four climbed astride to ride while the
fifth conducted daintily, his too exact fuss
belying his real sexual side. Toni filed the

lewd scene away: onstage, the time occurred
to moan and beg with Otello her lord

for Cassio. Still, she went wet and was spurred
to speed the tempo, buy some sushi, go get gored.

Four screams of ecstasy did ring. *The show,*
Toni reflected, *on must go.* That cactus prick
sure caught her fancy, though. She watched it grow
and grow and grow and grow and grow and get so thick

that Secretariat would stumble in shame.
She felt a nudge. *What? Oh, the show must go*
"On my knees . . . in the livid—" This was fame?
Soon back to tower, where her music would flow

in Willow Song. While climbing steps sturdy and neat—
praise Dan'l Boone the stage hands got 'em fit to go—
she saw, down in front row, a bare head keeping beat.
He flipped a thin box—*my roses après le show*?

An expert reader of lips—she worked by prompts—
T made out, *Jabberwock?* He jerked as from a blow.
T raised her chest as great purple romps
of light the dome gave rip. *Oh no, the show must go*

on. Two more rips, bright, angry, and purple.
Toni's proud breasts still rose, claiming, *Horseshit,*
on with the show. As she sang *"Willow,"* a durple
glowed stage right, two stage left. *". . . show your pit-*

"y. Pray for those who bow their heads." And get
this wretched night gone without me being dead!
Otello, snarling grandly, menaced his knife bit.
A piece of roof, T supposed, hit his head.

One balloon, another, her wig gave knock. The set
was crumbling. A wonder the cast hadn't fled.

She hoped not fleeing wasn't something to regret.
Great Colonel Sanders! Three in row one looked dead!

Her solo ended and she gazed about.
One old Indian, one young Tex-Mex lady stood
and left. *That's right*, Ms La Platte wanted to shout,
get, while the dome's structure still holds good.

Time passed. O stuck his knife. She gave the Colonel
of Chicken thanks. Her nerves were blanks. One power
song left—but three shots rang, then one light infernal,
then two more shots. From her vantage on the tower,

dead Desdemona, aka Toni La Platte,
looked to the source of that last noise
as over her, Emilia and O sang their spat.
When young, all Toni's cousins were boys,

so she stayed sure those last two shots came from
disparate pistols. She let out a gasp:
The cactus prick had grown. Would it never cum?
A woman wriggled, fast atop its grasp.

No bullet *her* life had taken, Toni
concluded, as over her Iago swore
to silence, then off did run. Otello, stony,
stabbed himself and fell, full gore-bore

on both her tits. The oaf could *never* get that fall
down right! "Look there," she whispered, nodding toward the prick.
As they both watched, the woman writhed and gave her all.
"Sushi Suzi?"
              "Think so."
                          "She'll die atop that dick,

"my God."

      "Indeed. After the cast party, let's ball."

"A woman of words succinct."

                "A man with a stick."

"After singing, it's my foremost call,

though I admit: it could never get *that* thick."

The clapping came on quick, whilst Suzi humped the prick.

Chapter Forty-eight: Evens

OBW surveyed the scene. *Evens,*
he thought, remembering poor Linda in the roots,
Lorrie's mom who caused so many grievin's.
Whene'er OBW kissed one cheek she'd hoot

and bid him kiss the other. Whiffing
a suckle on one nipple would never do,
his lips must spend an equal time on spliffing
its mate. This sudden forage into private goo

gave him a wince. He guessed the three dead rogues
compressed as durples sent him all this pause,
held him captive here thinking things not so vogue.
The three had killed each other off, in anger's claws.

And near the sushi stand, hooked in the likewise craw
of death, there lay four women plus a Boss Moe thug.
Someone gave shout and pointed. All saw
astride a huge pink cactus, one perverted fug,

up there wailing. Would one more body join the group?
Nearby, C's Walther had left a thug kaput
just when Don Walker's flashing crystal gave swoop
to send his shots astray. Hello? Above, a foot

fast jiggled. Even as they fetched a ladder
to pull this frenzied woman down, the cactus spent
pink energy growing. "Wow! Was that rad or
what?" So Sushi Suzi's gasping words went.

She gazed upward. The cactus, now twelve feet high,
spewed jism. "Oh me, oh my. I'll never—"

The rest was left to guess. She died, so blithe
she couldn't finish, unable to sever . . .

"Don't be sad," Miz Walburn directed.
"All got just what they wished. Did you, by the way,
espy a blonde guy—in a dress?" she corrected.
"The thug was shooting at him. His shots went astray.

"My almost-dad's crystal blinded thug eyes.
The blonde, he danced away, in that direction."
Life, OBW realized, had tossed a surprise
among so many flaws. He halted inspection

and gave ol' Linda credit for her insistent
demands. In honor of her, he made plans
for evens. Happy and resistant
to scars emergent from this planet's glans—

what else to name the filthy source of, Lo
so many evil, thoughtless mutations—
he would amend this mule into a horse of, Lo
fine soaring wings, a Pegasus in rotation—

a noteworthy thrum, a muse's invocation.

Chapter Forty-nine:
EVENS, Or, Wedding Bells chime,
while Schrödinger's cat lives sublime,
but Rosie Rabbit dies—metaphorically, so it's fine

The British stay strict in their narratives,
be they from Scotland or Wales-o.
But never any showed such flare as this,
concerning our six jaunty fellows.

As once we dropped two bombs on a Rising Sun,
here now we drop one more on fathers dear.
And mothers, too! Remember those hard-working ones!
Thus Yanks refute both Newton and old Shakespeare.

What I mean is, the cactus death of Boss Moe
emerges ironic as the grand demise
of Hamlet, say, or Lear, that poppa slow.
And surely it leaves us, say, as wise

as that beamish boy in "Jabberwocky"
who ne'er again will stray a tulgey wood,
or roam in outlandish flabbermock'ry
toward something as fully no good

as Messrs. Groves and Oppy's WMD.
It was that very poem which Hank affixed
to Strickland's oblong box with scheming glee.
And said fine poem's words indeed left Strickland nixed:

his brain could lovingly enfold equations,
but poems—funny or sad—made it screech.

Facing L Carroll's rhymes, Strickdick's deviations
became so harsh, his energy and aim got leached.

Rejoice! Sans his evil we might roam wise and free.
Yes WE—and now I speak not only for Yanks
but for all this round globe that spins so golly gee—
will SEE our errors. Each and every gave stanks!

Thus might we leave Devins, McGuire—and son!—
to search a cure . . . for cancers, hunger,
or mayhap just make video games more fun!
No pineapples will drop, give lunge or

in other manner impart a hindrance.
This I ascertain like Bishop Berkeley,
who danced his grand metaphysical dance,
which Johnson kicked about inartfully:

Let our world—hooray!—flow both ideal and real!
Let gravity act through loving attraction!
Let hate and war lie in a casket sealed,
so deep that their sole reaction be inaction!

Forget Tiananmen Square! Forget
the woes of Turkey! Forget Syria,
for Great God Hydrogen's sake yes! Don't let
any such worries infect like bacteria.

Evolution means to improve, not weary ya . . .

❀ ❀ ❀

I have always desired to outdo Mozart,
whose date of birth I share. Just so, this fine tune

will leave—with Blake's excess!—not only its art,
its rhyme, its thoughts that spoon the moon in June,

but loving nuptials too. O frabjous day!
Dear Carmen and Hank were first to tie the knot—
Gordian as it may prove—but say,
with that next May there came a whole great lot

of weddings, rings, and bridal bouquets.
Count 'em: Mike and DC, MM and Trixie,
Less Ugs and Rosa, all made their marital says.
Dave and Loretta, even me and Pixie,

Dave's pop and Chelsea, all exchanged bright rings.
Miz W and Don attended each wedding
to hand out cookies and New Age bling.
So close to that long night were they heading

they played it sharp to live in wanton sin.
"Go out defiant," they both cajoled.
Thus I conclude: go dare to make a spin
against Fortune's wan wheel. We're all enrolled!

P. S. Someone got prego! Care to bet who?
PayPal is calling, odds on the big board are up.
Just Google my number, they'll surely let you!
Toss in Otello and Ms. La Platte, more stars up.

They turn odds tough, but not too far up.
Get out and vote—I mean make a bet.
Use your computer, needn't start your car up.
Come on, be rad, be hep, get set.

Come dance with chance! You won't regret . . . I guess.

Retraction

Good 'nough for Chaucer, good 'nough for me:
I hereby retract this and all my work,
'cept *Joe and Pixie Find Virginity*,
in case there is a God, in case He is a Jerk.

Poetae Personae,

OR, Characters, somewhat in order of appearance:

ROBERT OPPENHEIMER, yes, the man with the sad mushroom plan

BETTY OPP, Betty Oppenheimer, aspiring botanist stuck with said
    mushroom and ten happy toes

GENERAL GROVES, who could ever know about his fat toes?

DAVE MCDOWELL, aka D, a lank guy just trying out his Harley

HANK RISER, aka H, a lank guy just trying out his BMW bike

LORETTA TAYLOR, aka Lorrie, aka L, could she be related to someone?

. CARMEN BROWN, aka C, spy extraordinaire, could *she* be related to
    someone?

HANSON, a creep, father to a nice gal (see above) and another creep (see
    below)

BLUE, son of Hanson, and half-bro to C

DEVINS & MCGUIRE, co-inventors of the gravity ray or G-String Gun

TODD, barkeep, glad owner of Todd's Deep End

JOE TAYLOR, aka Our Beloved Writer, aka OBW, our sometime narrator

TRIXIE, Pixie, Dixie, muse, consort, first and last resort to the above

DON WALKER, a cantankerous, ornery, damned injun—excuse me! Native
    Am!— mystic

MR. MCDOWELL, father of Dave and tamale aficionado

TED, a member of the Four Communion Tie Brotherhood, all co-spies
    with Carmen

CHELSEA, a hippie nymph and sometime tamale chef

STRICKLAND, aka Strictprick etc., co-inventor of the gravity ray and
    conspirator

Don Juan José Carlos Castaneda, aka Boss Moe, aka The Boss, a Mexican
    drug dealer

Less Ugly, right hand man to The Boss, so named since he's not as ugly

Juanita Doe, first victim of the G-String Gun

Morguemeister, aka MM, Santa Fe mortician in need of Viagra or better

Trixie, again? Please, please, please calm this woman—these
    women?—down

Toni, aka Tony, a real estate agent, SPCA volunteer, sometime
    ball-crusher

Mike, MM's assistant, a gay, ex U of Colorado football player

The DC Doc, aka DC, visiting CSI, with a crush on Mike

Miz Walburn, dispenser of magical cookies, righter of wrongs

Carol & Tim, so sad, so soon gone gonged

Rosa Traci Johns, aka L. A. chick, an aspiring physicist, in the wrong
    place and time

Rosa, a masseuse with an eye for inner beauty

Toni La Platte, an opera singer with mystic vision

Sushi Suzi, what a climax!

Joe Taylor has had two previous novels, both with mouthfuls for titles: *Oldcat & Ms. Puss: A Book of Days for You and Me,* plus *Let There Be Lite, OR, How I Came To Know and Love Godel's Incompleteness Proof.* So *Pineapple* presents vast streamlining. He's also published three story collections, edited several anthologies, and directed Livingston Press at the University of West Alabama for nearly 25 years. He walks the woods in lovely and rural Coatopa, Alabama, Native American for "wounded panther"—often enough apropos of his emotional state.

Photo by Angela Brown